LEE BROOK

The Cross Flatts Snatcher

MIDDLETON
PARK PRESS

First published by Middleton Park Press 2022

First edition

This book was professionally typeset on Reedsy.
Find out more at reedsy.com

For you, Son—

You are the best son a father could ever hope for. You make me proud every day. I love you.

Contents

Chapter One

The snatcher had already been there for a couple of hours and watched as the fierce morning sun glinted off blond curls. A gentle, cool breeze provided a slight relief against the blistering heat. The undergrowth the person hid in was an ever-changing mosaic of light and shade as the summer winds moved the deepening foliage.

The young blond boy laughed as he kicked the football to his older friend, those golden curls bouncing and glinting. His laugh echoed around the deserted park. Usually, a shriek of delight like that would not carry—lost in the noises of countless other children playing cricket or football, running around the playground, or bolting down the paths of Cross Flatts Park on scooters and bikes. But it was Sunday and far too early.

The older boy, the brunette, was a menace. But not the young blond. He was so young. So sweet. So innocent. Especially wearing his blue superhero pyjamas and a detachable red cape.

The older boy kicked the ball towards the foliage where their watcher was hidden, waiting for their chance. But, instead, the young blond dashed toward the football, his legs pumping as he ran, catching the ball before it landed in the undergrowth.

"Hey!" the young boy shouted. "If it goes in there, I'll lose my ball!"

"Soz, mate," the brunette said with a grin. He looked about eleven or twelve, too old to play with the young lad.

The watcher eyed the boys and waited as the two boys kicked the ball between themselves, waiting and hoping for the brunette to launch it straight into the undergrowth on the park's east side.

In their bubble, the boys were oblivious to the world and unaware of the watcher tucked away in the overgrown bushes.

Then the brunette boy relaunched the ball, another grin on his face.

The ball landed directly to the watcher's left with a dull thud. *Perfect.* A mix of courage and fear elevated their heart rate. It was the opportunity they wanted, the one they desperately needed. They'd waited far too long for that moment.

The young blond moved closer and attempted to peer through the mosaic of shadows and light, not seeing his ball.

"Archie!" the blond screamed. But all Archie did was laugh. He didn't attempt to help his young friend.

It was the moment the watcher needed. First, a rush of adrenalin thundered through them. Then, silently, he reached his hand towards the young boy, holding their breath. But the boy didn't enter the bushes. Instead, he turned back to his friend.

"Archie! You idiot!" the young blond said.

Archie shrugged. "It's your ball, mate. Not mine. You go get it!"

"But you kicked it in the bushes, Archie. And you're bigger than me. Please?"

"It's your ball, mate. You get it." Then, as if to finish the argument, Archie turned his back on the blond, took out his phone and refused to look up from it as Benjamin continued his protests.

He was so young. So sweet. So innocent. He was the perfect little boy.

"Please, Archie?" Benjamin said, continuing his protests. "It's dark in there. I'm scared."

"Get it yourself, Ben; otherwise, I'm going home."

With careful steps, Benjamin walked through the bushes and was soon surrounded by the heavy swell of summer vegetation. Finally, it was the chance the watcher had been waiting for. The watcher reached out and engulfed the blond boy.

Then, suddenly, Archie noticed the protests had stopped.

"Ben?"

Nothing.

"Ben!" Archie shouted. "Where are you?"

Nothing again.

He looked around the field and saw nobody. He checked the foliage at the edges, but still, Benjamin wasn't there. He couldn't see the ball, either. *Maybe he's gone back home?* He questioned. *Yeah. That must be it.* Archie breathed a sigh of relief and placed his hands in his pockets. With his head down, he headed back to his house on Back Cross Flatts Avenue.

* * *

Chantelle noticed the lack of warmth and the cramping in her legs from lying on the sofa. Chantelle's head throbbed, and her eyes stung as she looked around the room. Where was Mitchell?

She was sure she had shared the sofa with Mitchell. Positive.

So where was he? She trained her ear towards the kitchen but heard nothing. There was also no noise coming from above. What time was it?

As she slowly straightened out her legs, Chantelle groaned. When she sat up, her head shrieked in protest. She was braless. Why? After standing up, she clutched a white vest and pink cheque skirt, which she found heaped on the floor along with her dirty plimsolls.

Bollocks, she thought as she pulled on her clothes. It was Father's Day, and she'd promised Benjamin's dad he could have him for the day. She couldn't deal with Henry without a coffee, especially if he saw the state of her. Chantelle still didn't know the time and hoped she'd have enough time to have at least a shower and put on fresh clothes. In a way, she still loved Henry. Yet Mitchell was everything that had been missing in their relationship: the danger and the fire. And the drugs.

Chantelle padded barefoot towards the kitchen. A large dog jumped up at her after she pushed open the kitchen door, its claws catching the fabric of the skirt as it furiously wagged its tail.

"Down, boy!" she commanded. The kitchen stunk of shit and piss, shit that Chantelle nearly stood in as she headed towards the back door. "Get out!" she said, giving the dog a little kick before shutting the door. She couldn't be arsed to adult today, never mind look after an animal.

As she waited for the kettle to boil, she wondered how much they had drunk last night or how much they had smoked. She had no idea. Not really. But her head was banging, and her eyes hurt. And she hadn't washed the dishes last night. She cursed as she dug around in the pile of used cups and plates in the sink for her favourite coffee mug before rinsing it under the tap. An image of her having sex with Mitchell on the sofa last night flashed across her mind. A third person was there, watching and filming. But who? She let it retreat into the fog of her hangover and spooned coffee granules into her mug.

The bitter liquid took away the dry taste in her mouth—she'd forgotten to buy sugar and had run out of milk.

As she headed towards the living room to find her cigs, she noticed the front door was open. *Had it always been open? Was that why it was so fucking cold? Where the fuck is Mitchell?* she wondered as she closed the door with her free hand and shouted up to Benjamin.

He didn't answer, but she wasn't concerned. He'd be on his tablet, with his headphones on. That, or his PlayStation 4. She groaned in frustration as she pushed aside empty beer glasses and cider cans before slamming her mug down in the space she'd created. She found her cigs, popped one in her mouth, lit up and drew in a lungful of smoke. Her head buzzed from the nicotine rush.

The house was quiet, too quiet. Chantelle reached for her mobile phone and was about to hit contacts when she saw the time on the screen. "Shit! It's after eleven." Henry said he'd pick Benjamin up between half-eleven and twelve.

She sniffed her pits and winced. *Fuck!* She didn't want Henry to see her like this. He'd already shared his concerns that she wasn't coping well with Benjamin's diagnosis. He'd recently been diagnosed with ASD, Autism Spectrum Disorder. She hated the label and everything that came with it. She wished Henry had never gone to the doctor about Benjamin, especially as it had been behind her back. *For fuck's sake! You should've set your alarm, you silly bitch.*

She needed to ensure Benjamin was ready to go to his dad's. He'd made Henry a card at school—which was lucky, as she couldn't afford to buy one—and would spend the entire day with him. She'd have the house to herself and wouldn't have to adult for the whole day. The thought cheered her as she headed upstairs to Benjamin's room.

The door to Benjamin's room was open, and as Chantelle approached, she could see it was empty.

"Benjamin?" Chantelle approached the wardrobe. He liked to hide in there and jump out at her and scare her, the little shit.

But he wasn't in there.

"Benjamin!" Chantelle got down on her hands and knees and searched under the bed's wooden frame. Nothing. Panicking, she got to her feet and searched the bedroom again, then the bathroom, before heading into her room.

Nothing. Benjamin wasn't there.

"Benjamin, where are you? Come on; your dad will be here soon." Anxiety increased her heart rate and prickled at her skin as she jogged downstairs into the living room to find Mitchell sitting on the sofa with a cig in his mouth.

"Where the fuck have you been?"

"Out." He raised his brow. "Why?" His tone was threatening, just daring her to challenge him.

"It's Benjamin. He's gone, Mitchell. He's not here."

"You what?" Mitchell was sitting on the sofa wearing only his jeans, with ash from his cig falling on his bare chest. He wiped it away, a look of confusion on his face.

"He's not in his room. He's not upstairs." Her voice was shaky and raspier than usual.

"And?" He took another drag and closed his eyes.

"What do you mean, *and*? My boy is fucking missing, you prick! Get up off your lazy arse and look for him!" Chantelle shrieked at Mitchell.

Mitchell stared at her with tired eyes, not comprehending the seriousness of the situation.

Then she remembered. "The front door was open. Did you leave it open when you left earlier?" Mitchell shrugged. She took a deep breath. "He'll be outside. Probably playing with Archie, or one of the neighbour's kids."

Chantelle hurried to the door and pulled it open so hard that it hit her on the arm with a thud before she stepped outside. *Another bruise to add to the others,* she thought. She ignored the heat from the paves on her bare feet and ran through the open gate onto the pavement. Her heart hammered in her chest as she looked both left and right.

He wasn't there.

"Benjamin!" she screamed as she ran towards an entrance to Cross Flatts Park, her eyes darting in every direction, hoping to see him. Then she had a thought, a terrible thought. A thought a mother should never have, and a cold fear wrapped around her chest. *What if he had gone the other way, towards the main roads?*

Benjamin, being run over by a reckless driver speeding through the warrens of Beeston, flashed through her mind. She tried to breathe, but the crushing weight on her chest, and the perceived lack of oxygen in the air, made her fall to the ground. Chantelle could feel the darkness threatening to take over as her vision blurred and her head spun. She sobbed before she forced away the panic and took off through the gate and onto the gravel path, the tiny stones stabbing her feet. The pain held the darkness at bay.

Chantelle entered the park and looked around. Trees lined the park's east edge and were full of summer greenery, blocking out the light. Hardly anybody was about. She ran onto the field of green, calling out, but all was silent. *I need some help; she* thought as she turned and ran back to the house, looking up and down Back Cross Flatts Avenue. She thought that someone would've seen him and brought him back home if he'd come this way.

When she returned, her next-door neighbour, Andy, was standing at his gate.

"Everything all right, Chantelle?"

"No." Chantelle bent down as pain tore through her chest. "Benjamin is missing."

"Missing?" She noticed a look of fear spread across his face. "Do you want me to help you look for him?"

Chantelle shook her head and went back into her house without a word. She could hear Mitchell calling out as he searched the house.

"He's not here," Mitchell called out from the stairs. "I've checked all the wardrobes and cupboards. Everywhere."

"I'm calling the police, Mitch."

Nausea rolled in her stomach, and she felt the bile rise up her throat as she picked up her phone from the table.

"Wait a minute, babe," Mitchell said as he pounded down the stairs. "Don't call the pigs yet. You know I can't be here if they come. So wait whilst I get my shit together and then call them when I've left." He sprinted up the steps, and she could hear him rummaging around in her bedroom.

After five minutes, Mitchell appeared at the living room door. "Right, babe, I'm out of here. Text me to let me know what's going on, yeah?" He pulled on a pair of filthy trainers and left without a goodbye.

Chantelle sank to the floor, and tears spilt from her eyes. The house was unnaturally silent, and as she wiped away the tears with the back of her hand, she realised she had never felt so alone in her entire life. Then, with hands that were trembling, she dialled triple nine.

Chapter Two

While Chantelle Coates frantically searched her house for her son, Benjamin, Detective Inspector George Beaumont was taking advantage of a rare Sunday morning lie-in. With his eyes still closed, George fought against the nausea caused by the hellish hangover which had made itself at home inside his throbbing head. His eyes throbbed, and there was a ringing in his ears. Shakily, he pulled at the duvet and forced himself upward.

George opened his eyes, and before taking in the everyday objects of his bedroom—his bed, his wardrobe, his bedside table—he saw a man with bloodshot eyes and wild blond hair staring back at him from the rectangle mirror on his wardrobe.

Why had he let his old mentor Luke Mason talk him into the shots when all he'd agreed to was a 'quick pint' to celebrate?

Yesterday, George received a call from the ecstatic family members of Anna Hill to thank him for bringing her murderer to justice. Earlier that year, Boris Jarman, a person of interest in the Bone Saw Ripper case, admitted to killing her. There was now the hope that, with Boris being sentenced for her murder, Tony Shaw, another person of interest during that case, would also be convicted for her murder, too.

George twisted his body and draped his legs over the side of the bed before he stood up.

Then he suddenly sat back down again with a thud. George rubbed his head as he muttered, "Shouldn't have done that." He breathed out stale air.

After a minute or two, he was ready to try again. But, before he could try, the bedroom door swung open and brought the most beautiful woman he'd ever seen. Isabella Wood stood in the doorway and regarded him with a mixture of both pity and amusement. She set a pint glass of water on the bedside table beside two paracetamol.

"Did you enjoy your night?"

With legs as wobbly as Bambi's, George stood up and chuckled. "Did I enjoy it?" He thought back to the continuous flow of Jägermeister DS Mason kept providing and blew out more stale air. Then he laughed. "I don't know. I really don't. But I need that water."

Isabella grinned as she watched George stagger around the bed while he clutched his sore head. Whilst this wasn't the first time she had seen George in this state, she was glad that he'd been out and enjoyed himself instead of staying home and drinking himself to sleep. Moreover, she was happy that he was enjoying other parts of his life again.

"It's Father's Day, and you promised Jack you'd pick him up at noon." Isabella smiled.

George winced. He loved his son more than anything in the world and wished he hadn't drunk the shots last night.

"What time is it?"

"It's half-eleven—"

"Shit!" he said with a croaky voice before gulping down the pint of water. He needed a shower and a shave. *Shit!*

"I was going to wake you earlier, but you looked so peaceful."

Smelling faintly like a brewery, he staggered towards her. Even red-eyed and worse for wear, she thought it was remarkable how handsome George looked. She watched him run a hand through his thick, blond hair that stuck out at interesting angles. And rather than looking unkempt, the layer of stubble on his jaw gave him a more rugged look. But, then, those bright, emerald-coloured eyes gave her butterflies every time they met. *Damn, how did I ever get so lucky?* she thought.

He refocused and took her in. A gorgeous woman with dark features, Isabella was stunning. He desperately wanted to drag her onto the bed and make love to her, yet he knew that would make him late. As much as he loved Isabella, he couldn't let his son down.

"Give us a snog," he said with a smile.

Isabella pulled a face and tapped at her wrist. "You could use a shower first." She sniffed at the air, then winked.

"That's an excellent idea," he said with a smile as he edged her backwards, out of the bedroom and towards the bathroom. "Why don't you join me?"

* * *

As the other senior detectives of the Homicide and Major Enquiry Team were busy looking into the usual occurrences of GBH and manslaughter following the inevitable drunken brawls that had occurred over the weekend, the Control Room of the West Yorkshire Police dictated that George and Isabella had to disregard their allocated day off, cancel their Father's Day plans, and drive—separately—into Beeston to coordinate the search for a young boy named Benjamin Davidson who had been reported missing at quarter to twelve.

Their relationship was still a secret, and neither wanted it to be common knowledge—there was too much at stake.

The drive towards Beeston wouldn't take long, but George knew he needed all the information he could get before getting to the scene. So he called the station and was put through to DS Yolanda Williams.

"Morning, sir," Yolanda said. "A young boy named Benjamin Davidson, five years old, vanished from Cross Flatts Park this morning. The mother, Chantelle Coates, called it in after a search of the area, with no trace of the boy. DC Scott and DC Blackburn are over there already. DS Wood is on her way. I've sent DS Cathy Hoskins since she's the best FLO we have."

Cathy Hoskins, a vigorous, kind woman with a compassionate nature and a calming voice, was precisely the woman you wanted beside you during a missing child situation.

"Detective Superintendent Smith was keen to start house to house and has sent as many uniforms as Uniform can spare," Yolanda added. "I thought that was enough until we know what we're dealing with. You're Senior Investigating Officer, sir."

It was the kind of case that every officer dreaded, especially after the cock-up of the Shannon Matthews case. George felt the adrenalin kick his hungover body into action, and various scenarios began running through his head. "Great job, Yolanda. Anything else?"

"We don't have pictures yet, but he's Caucasian, about four-foot tall, short blond hair that falls in curls, and hazel eyes."

"What was Benjamin wearing?" His anger at missing his first Father's Day slowly ebbed as he pictured the missing lad.

"The mother doesn't know. There's something off about her, sir. I've advised Cathy to keep her eyes and ears open. There have been zero sightings so far, which worries me as whilst it's a busy area, it's quite small. He should have been found by now."

"What's the working theory, Yolanda?" George wasn't far away and had just passed the KFC on Dewsbury Road.

"He was playing football with one of his neighbours in the park this morning. A young lad named Archie Morris, sir. Archie told Tashan that he kicked the football into the bushes, and Benjamin went in after it. Archie played on his phone whilst he waited for Benjamin to come back. When Benjamin didn't, Archie went home."

"Okay, thanks, Yolanda. Get maps of the area printed, and as a precaution, contact search and rescue and put them on standby. Also, get DS Fry to check and see if any known sex offenders have moved into the area. They should be registered with us. Is DS Brewer back yet?"

"No, sir."

Elaine Brewer had told George of her desire to become an FLO—Family Liaison Officer—so he had asked DSU Smith to second her to a different team for a couple of months to give her training and experience. She was a good detective and would be missed during this case.

"Hopefully, the young lad has just wandered off, or there's a father who has taken custody issues into his own hands. Once DS Mason is in, get him to see what he can find out about the family."

"He's already in, sir."

George smiled. The guy was ten years George's senior, yet he could drink him under the table. "Good. Get him to send me that information as soon as he has it."

The streets around Cross Flatts Park were a labyrinth of roads lined with red brick terraced houses. He noticed a few of them had scaffolding up where Leeds City Council was updating their properties. As he drove up Cross Flatts Avenue, some gardens were well kept, while others were overgrown with weeds. George drove towards the top of the road and turned right to where Chantelle Coates lived.

DC Jason Scott greeted him as he got out of the car. "Plenty of undesirables live around here, sir." George raised his brow but said nothing. "Honestly. It's home to druggies and ex-cons."

"Where's your compassion and understanding, Jay?" George said. "There are a lot of elderly folks who live around here, as well as young families trying to make a go of things. It's cheaper to live here than in other areas of Leeds. Nothing wrong with that."

"I guess not, sir," Jason said. "It all looks so... scruffy?"

"Who're you to judge, DC Scott?"

"Come off it, sir. Half the estate is full of dealers," Jay said.

George knew that to be accurate but said nothing for a moment. "Come on, DC Scott, let's see what we've got."

* * *

DC Scott followed DI Beaumont into the park, where DS Wood and DC Blackburn were already waiting. The park was a hive of activity, with police and civilians wandering everywhere. George had expected a police cordon yet was presented with chaos. Finally, a PCSO, with a sudden look of relief on her face, came over to greet him.

George introduced himself and then got straight to the point. "Why do we have civilians roaming around a crime scene?"

"They're locals, sir. There are so many park entrances we don't have the numbers to stop people from coming in."

George knew she was telling the truth. There were two entrances to the park from Back Cross Flatts Avenue alone, never mind all the other streets that formed the labyrinth around the park. "Right. Thanks—"

"Alison."

"Thanks, Alison. We'll handle it from here." Unfortunately, well-meaning members of the public were a hindrance in missing children's cases. He knew they were trying to be both helpful and kind, yet they would often end up obstructing, becoming less useful than they intended.

"Lindsey's not going to be happy, is she?" DS Wood said from behind him. She was walking next to DS Joshua Fry.

"You're right about that, Wood." He took in the chaos once more. "She's gonna have a bloody field day over this." George liked the Crime Scene Co-ordinator, Dr Lindsey Yardley, but she had a certain way about her. She was terse but efficient, with a reputation to match.

He needed to stop the locals as quickly as he could. It was bad enough that they had to find a missing boy who had vanished from a popular park. But unfortunately, the locals searching would destroy any shred of evidence before Yardley and her team even got started.

"Right," George said, his voice sharper than he felt, as he turned to his team and started delegating. "I don't care what you have to do, but enforce the cordon and get these people out of the park now. Benjamin isn't here; otherwise, they would have found him by now. We don't want the locals destroying any evidence the SOCOs may find. Take their shoe makes and sizes, names, and addresses. Josh, you're in charge whilst DS Wood and I interview the mother."

"Yes, sir," Josh said with a nod.

Chapter Three

On the way back to Chantelle Coates' house, George barked sharply at any locals to leave the park immediately because it was now an active crime scene.

Most were respectful, but others dithered, and George had to get tough, threatening to arrest them for obstructing a police investigation.

As the pair walked through the park gate and passed an old rusting fridge, he could see police officers knocking at doors a little further up the street. A Police Constable George knew, called Sally Fletcher, opened the door of Chantelle Coates' house as they approached.

"How're you, Sally?" George asked the policewoman.

She shrugged and smiled. "The mother is in the kitchen with Cathy." She stood aside for them to enter. He asked her to join in with the house-to-house, and she nodded before walking off.

George crossed the threshold into the kitchen, and his nostrils were immediately assaulted by the suffocating odour of piss, shit, and cigarette smoke. Luckily, the window was open.

The family liaison officer, Cathy, greeted them with a nod

before continuing to wash dishes in the sink. A mixture of dirty plates, empty cups, and ashtrays on the kitchen counters filled to the brim. The oven was dirty with food encrusted onto the ceramic hob, and a pile of dirty clothes were heaped in front of a grimy washing machine. George felt his shoes sticking to the grubby tiles and had to step over a piece of wet newspaper, already knowing from the smell what was underneath.

A woman with caramel-coloured hair sat hunched at a round wooden table, her face in her hands. When she looked up and stared at George, with her pale skin, sunken eyes, and a cig in her gob, he estimated her age to be early or mid-thirties, but it was difficult to tell.

"Chantelle, this is DI Beaumont and DS Wood." Cathy indicated to the two detectives, then turned back to the task of washing up.

With a voice that was barely a whisper, Chantelle said, "Have you found Benjamin yet?"

"No, I'm sorry, but there's no news yet. We need to ask you some questions," George said.

"But I already told the other female officer everything," Chantelle said and sniffed before wiping her nose with the back of her hand. "Why are you here? Shouldn't you be out looking for him?"

"We are, Chantelle. There are officers out looking for Ben."

"Benjamin," she corrected.

"Benjamin," he smiled. "They're also talking to your neighbours to see if they've seen anything. But, it would be beneficial if you could give us as much information as possible. Starting from the beginning." George gave an encouraging smile.

As Chantelle was about to speak, DC Scott entered the house

and breathed out in disgust. He wasn't the most tactful detective, and George winced.

It didn't seem as if she'd noticed, though, because George saw Chantelle glance at Jay and, despite the grim situation, she grinned seductively at him. George had noticed similar looks from young women back at the station. DC Jason Scott was eye candy that never failed to get noticed. He wondered what Isabella thought, then shut the thought down immediately.

Chantelle stood up, wiped her hands on her pink skirt, and then offered her hand to Jay. "I'm Chantelle Coates." He grinned and told her his name but didn't take it, looking at George with a nervous look on his face that said, 'help me'.

She was still grinning when DS Wood said, "Come with me, Chantelle. How about we go into the living room and have a chat? You look exhausted. Perhaps Cathy can bring you a hot drink." Isabella looked at Cathy, who nodded.

The pungent smell of cigarette smoke and a sweet, cloying smell lingered in the air as George followed Chantelle and Wood into the living room. Jay hesitated before following them. George scanned the room. An overflowing bin stood in the corner, and the coffee table was covered in empty beer glasses and cider cans. There was a large flat-screen TV on the wall and a box of toys to the right. The once cream carpet was stained and dirty, the walls stained by nicotine. He noticed there were no pictures of Benjamin.

Chantelle slumped down on the sofa, leaving two armchairs free, which George and Wood sat down on. Jay perched next to Chantelle on the edge of the sofa and took out his notebook. The sweet smell was overbearing, and he couldn't quite work out what it was.

"I understand Benjamin is five years old," George said.

Chantelle nodded.

"Do you mind telling me how old you are?"

"Twenty-three."

George looked down to hide the surprise that inevitably showed on his face. She looked haggard and more than a decade older than she was.

"Do we need to be aware of Benjamin's medical conditions?" Jay asked, much to George's surprise. It was a good question, a question he was getting to.

"No, not really. Benjamin has an inhaler as he has asthma, but the nurse recently reduced the daily dose he takes. He has ASD—Autism Spectrum Disorder, but that's not... Well, that's just Benjamin." George noticed the look on her face. Was it a look of shame and embarrassment?

"Asthma and ASD," Jay said, making notes. "Thanks. Can you talk us through what happened this morning?"

Chantelle took another cigarette from her packet. "I went to get Benjamin up because his dad was coming over to take him for Father's Day, but he wasn't there. So I went to search for him and didn't find him."

George noticed the tremor in her hands as Chantelle attempted to light her cigarette.

"You called the station at eleven forty-five. Did you see Benjamin earlier in the morning?" Wood asked.

"No," Chantelle said, fidgeting in her seat. The tremor was becoming uncontrollable. "I—I slept in."

"There you go, hun," Cathy said as she walked into the room and handed a mug to Chantelle. She waved for Cathy to place it on the coffee table, which George thought was rude. "Can I get you three anything?" Then, she turned to the detectives. They shook their heads and thanked Cathy before she left the room.

"What time did you sleep in until?" George asked, continuing the interview.

"Quarter past eleven." She continued to stare at Jay.

"Was anyone else in the house when you woke up this morning?" George continued.

Chantelle hesitated before she said, "No." George caught it, as did Wood and Jay. They all shared a quick, knowing glance.

"What time did Benjamin's father arrive?" George asked.

"He hasn't yet. The prick said he'd be here between half-eleven and twelve," Chantelle said with a scowl.

George checked his watch. It was well after noon. So where was the kid's father? "Does he have regular contact with Benjamin?"

"Yeah, he has Benjamin every weekend. Picks him up from school on Friday and brings him back on Sunday afternoon."

DS Wood immediately got stuck in. "Then why hasn't he had Benjamin this weekend?"

"And what's his name?" Jay cut in.

"Henry Davidson. He had him this weekend, but he dropped Benjamin off last night because he had a work meeting he had to attend. He didn't want to miss Father's Day, so he asked if he could pick him up today."

"Have you spoken with Henry today?" George asked.

"No, why would I?" Chantelle said.

George looked perplexed. "To let him know his son is missing," he said with his hands held out, palms up.

"Oh, shit. I—I didn't think of that. I was—I was preoccupied trying to find Benjamin."

"We understand," Jay said. "Please provide Henry's phone number and address."

"Yeah, okay."

Henry lived in Hull, just under an hour and a half away by car. Jay wrote the details down, and George turned to him. "Give DS Fry a call, Jay, and ask him to check out the father. See where he is."

As Jay left the room to call Josh, Chantelle's eyes followed, her eyes burning a hole in his rear. Then she turned to face George. She said, "Do you think Henry has Benjamin?"

It was the only theory that made sense, especially considering Archie Morris' statement. Had Benjamin's father picked him up without telling Chantelle? George leaned forward in the chair and raised his brow. "Is there a reason Henry would do that?"

Chantelle shrugged and puffed on the cigarette that was being held by yellowing fingers.

"Are the family courts involved in your agreement with Henry, or is it private between you?" DS Wood asked.

"Private. I have Benjamin from Sunday night to Friday morning, so he has to take Benjamin some time. It's only fair. Right?"

"Do you work, Chantelle?" George asked.

"Yeah, at Asda on Old Lane. Ten 'til two Monday to Thursday."

"So, things between you two are amicable?" Wood asked.

Chantelle looked at her blankly.

Jay returned to the room and said, "Henry doesn't have Benjamin. He slept in and was headed here. I've asked him to head directly to Elland Road." George nodded at the young DC, who didn't resume his position on the sofa but stood next to George.

"You're on good terms and not falling out? That kind of

thing," George explained.

"I guess."

"And was he happy with the arrangement?" George continued.

Chantelle shrugged.

That's a no, then. "What time did Henry bring Benjamin back yesterday?" George asked.

"It was about five. Henry seemed as if he couldn't wait to hand Benjamin back."

"Did he come in?"

"Into the house?" George nodded. "No. I go outside when he comes."

The back door crashed open, and a woman entered the room through the kitchen. She was dressed in a black dress and heels. She rushed over to Chantelle.

"Have you found Benjamin yet?"

Chantelle's lip quivered. "Not yet," she said, and tears flooded her eyes.

"And you are?" Jay asked. He had a bright smile on his face. George had seen that beam before—he was interested in the attractive woman. She rubbed her chin with her left hand before answering, and Jay must have seen what George had seen on her ring finger as Jay looked disappointed.

"I'm Chantelle's older sister, Claire Murray." She sat beside her sister on the sofa and put her arm around Chantelle's shoulder. "I'm sure he'll be found soon."

"Henry says he hasn't taken him," Chantelle said to her sister. "But I think he's lying—"

Claire frowned. "Of course, he hasn't. Why would Henry do that?"

He thought about what Jay had just told him—that Henry

was on his way to Elland Road. "We've no reason to believe that Henry has taken him, Chantelle, but we have to rule out every possibility," George said by way of explanation.

Claire pulled a disgusted face and shook her head. "Well, I don't think he'd pull a stunt like this." She paused for a moment. "No. He wouldn't do this."

"Of course, you wouldn't," Chantelle snapped. "You think you know Henry, but you don't. The sun doesn't shine out of his arse! You've no idea what he's like."

Claire looked furious but said nothing. The tension was palpable.

"Henry is on the way to the station and an officer from my team will speak with him. But, for now, we have to explore other possibilities," George explained.

"Other possibilities? Like?" Chantelle's teary eyes widened.

"Chantelle, can you talk me through what happened the last time you saw Benjamin?" Wood asked.

"What happened?" she said, not comprehending. "Nothing happened. What are you trying to say?" Chantelle folded her arms across her chest.

"I simply meant, what time did you put Benjamin to bed?"

"About half seven."

"And did he fall asleep right away?"

She shrugged. "Benjamin didn't make any noise."

"Then what did you do?"

"Had a drink, and—" Another hesitation. "A smoke. The usual."

George raised his brow whilst Jay continued to document the interview. "Alone?" he asked.

"Yes."

George caught the look that Claire had shot Chantelle. Of

course, Chantelle was lying to them—they didn't need Claire to tell them that.

"Oh yeah, Andy came over for a little while. Sorry, I forgot." Chantelle began tapping her knee frantically.

"Andy?" Jay asked.

"My next-door neighbour," Chantelle said.

"Why was your next-door neighbour here?"

Chantelle looked embarrassed. "I'm a single parent, so he checks in on me sometimes. He makes sure we're all okay. I fell asleep on the sofa and woke up. That's it."

She told them the house number, and Jay scribbled it in his notebook. Then Jay looked at his boss, who nodded and said, "You said you woke up, and Benjamin was gone. Do you keep the doors locked whilst you sleep?"

"Have you seen where I live? Of course, I keep them locked." Chantelle sobbed and looked down at her hands. "The—the front door was open this morning."

"You mean you left it unlocked?" Jay asked.

"No. It was wide open."

"You what!" Claire stood up and turned to face her cowering sister. "Why the hell was the front door wide open? He could've walked out all by himself. He doesn't know what danger is. His ASD... What the hell, Chantelle?"

"I didn't leave the door open, Claire." Chantelle continued to sob.

The last thing George would do was put his son at risk by leaving a door unlocked. He was furious inside but needed her to answer his questions. "Can Benjamin open doors?" She nodded and sobbed harder. "Okay, does he know how to unlock the door?"

"No, he can't. It's too hard on his wrists. He has hypermobility and has pain in his wrists."

"So if you left it unlocked, which it looks like you did, then he could be anywhere right now," Claire said as she sobbed before retaking her seat.

George couldn't help but think Claire was right as he looked at the two sisters. They had the same caramel-coloured hair and were about the same height, but that was it as far as similarities went. Despite being older, Claire looked a decade younger than Chantelle and sat with her right leg crossed over her other knee, running a manicured hand through perfect curls. Chantelle sat with her legs open and shoulders hunched, her hair straggly.

"Is there anything else you can tell us, Chantelle?" George asked.

Chantelle shook her head, but Claire interrupted and said, "I called in last night around ten because I had some clean washing to drop off."

George looked at Claire, wondering why she was doing Chantelle's washing and dropping it off so late.

"Oh yeah, she came 'round. Sorry, I forgot," Chantelle said.

"More like you were too—"

"Enough, Claire," Chantelle said. "Stop judging me, all right? Saturday is normally my night without Benjamin."

"Yeah, but you had him at home last night, you idiot!" Claire snapped back. "You're so lucky you can have children, you know. A lot of women out there would kill for what you have."

George observed the growing tension between the sisters and tried to disperse it. "Did you see Benjamin when you called Claire?" George asked.

"Yes, he was asleep in his bed when I put the washing in his room."

"Anyone else call 'round?" George turned his attention to Chantelle.

"No."

Claire cast her younger sister another dirty look, and George decided not to push the question but to talk to Claire later in private to find out what Chantelle wasn't telling him.

"Did you leave the house last night?"

"No."

"Going back to last night," George said. "Claire came and went, and you went to bed at what time?"

"About midnight," Chantelle said and plucked another cigarette from its packet.

"Did you check in on Benjamin?"

"No, I—I didn't want to disturb him." Chantelle stood up and put her hands on her hips. "Look, can you lot just stop wasting time and get on with finding him?"

"Fine, but we need to look at Benjamin's room first." George stood and gestured for Chantelle to lead the way.

Claire stood up, too, but for forensic preservation, he said, "Just Chantelle, please." It was doubtful Benjamin had been abducted from his bedroom, but they couldn't be too careful.

Chantelle lit her cigarette and led the way upstairs. They entered a tiny box room and, after noticing the bedroom window was closed, George looked down at the bed. The duvet was on the floor, exposing the sheet-less dirty mattress covered in stains. The only other piece of furniture in the room was a shabby wardrobe, and the floor was a mess. It was a shame that the only beacon of hope in the room was a basket of neatly folded clothes that Claire had placed in the room's corner.

George desperately wanted to reach out to her and reassure

her parent to parent, but he didn't. He couldn't. "We'll do everything we can to find Benjamin," he said, not promising anything.

"What was Benjamin wearing when you put him to bed last night?" DS Wood asked.

"His superhero pyjamas," she said. "They're blue and red and have a big S on the front." She looked around the room and sobbed once more. "His cape isn't here."

"Cape?" Wood asked.

"Yeah, the pyjamas came with a detachable red cape. Henry got him them last Christmas. Benjamin loves them. Claire bought an extra set because he has to wear them every night for bed."

George nodded his head. He knew about ASD and how it affected people in different ways. For example, some had obsessions and liked to constantly wear the same clothes. "Is anything else missing from the room?"

Chantelle stepped further in and looked around before shaking her head.

"Okay, Chantelle," George said. "Thank you for that. I understand how difficult this must be." He wasn't lying. He knew how hopeless and powerless it felt to not be in control of your precious child's life. His son Jack had been held hostage by the Blonde Delilah and never wanted to feel that way again.

After they had walked down the stairs and into the living room, George told the two sisters that Cathy would stay with Chantelle and keep her informed of all the progress relating to the case. He also asked for an up-to-date photo of Benjamin."

Chantelle looked around the room, and a look of desolation and sorrow settled on her face. She realised for the first time that she didn't have a single photo of her precious child in her house. She sobbed once more but took out her phone. "I only have pictures on my phone," she eventually said.

"Can I have a look, please?" Jay asked.

Chantelle unlocked her phone, found her recent images of Benjamin, and handed it to Jay. He asked permission to send copies of different photos to the station, to which she agreed, before handing back the phone.

"Thanks for your time," George said and stood up. "We may need to come back to ask you some more questions. In the meantime, Cathy is here to help you if you have questions. We'll see ourselves out."

Outside, George inhaled the fresh air. He didn't think he'd ever be able to get the smell of shit and piss out of his nose. He was about to complain to DS Wood when the sound of a Jack Russell terrier alerted him to the presence of Chantelle's next-door neighbour, standing at his gate.

George knew he needed to speak to the man as his son was the last person to see Benjamin, but he had other tasks to complete first.

"What do you think?" George said to DS Wood as they walked back to the park.

"A druggie with wandering eyes," Jay said with a grin.

"I wasn't asking you, but all right?"

"I'm not joking, sir. I need a shower after that. I've no idea how DS Hoskins copes," Jay said with a grimace. "Place was bloody filthy."

"We don't discriminate, DC Scott. Chantelle may lack domestic skills, but as far as we're concerned, it's irrelevant. Her child is missing, and we need to find him. Okay?"

"Yeah, okay, sir. Sorry. But I still stand by my judgement. She looks like a user."

"The place did have a distinct odour."

"Eau de dog shit," Jay said, "mixed with Eau de weed."

"Candid as usual, Jay," George said with a laugh. "She was hungover. You could smell the alcohol. And you're right about the shit."

"I'm worried about the working theory," DS Wood said.

The two men turned to look at her, confused looks on their faces. "Why?" George asked.

"Yeah, why? Despite what he told me on the phone, it seems most likely it's the father who took him," Jay said.

"Just because Archie Morris didn't see Benjamin go home doesn't mean he didn't. Or didn't attempt to."

"Yeah, exactly. Benjamin's dad could have scooped him right from the street. Nobody would have batted an eyelid," Jay said.

"Chantelle is suspicious, that's all," Wood added. "I think there's the possibility that she is involved."

"Do you think? I think she seemed genuinely upset," Jay said.

"She could be faking it," Wood said. "She wouldn't be the first mother to snap, and she won't be the last. Chantelle's not coping that well—that's clear from the state of the house. Regardless, time is against us, and we must find that boy as soon as possible. News will soon spread on social media, and if Benjamin was abducted, whoever did it will be pressured to make the next move. Let's hope it's letting Benjamin go."

She let that thought hang in the air as they headed into the park to meet Lindsey Yardley and the rest of DI Beaumont's team, the responsibility for finding the child already crushing down on them.

Chapter Four

"Detective?" At the entrance to the park, Chantelle's next-door neighbour—the man with the Jack Russell terrier, George recalled—stood watching. "Any sign of Benjamin yet?"

"I'm sorry," George said, "but I can't comment on an active investigation." DC Tashan Blackburn nodded his head at George from beyond the park gate. "Tashan, did you get all the details?" It allowed him to move on and ignore the nosey neighbour. He nodded goodbye.

"Of course, sir," Tashan replied. "Names, telephone numbers, and email addresses. And all their bloody life stories. Practically filled an entire notebook."

George laughed. "Yeah, people like telling their own stories. Any word on CSI?"

"No, sir. I called DS Williams, and she said they'd be here soon. The dog squad will be here soon, too."

Despite being dismissed, the nosey neighbour did not leave. George glanced more closely at the man. He was tall and athletic, tidy and clean-shaven with a fresh trim, broad shoulders, a thin waist, and a firm jawline. He didn't look like the usual type he saw around the area. The man wore a pair of jean shorts and a black vest and looked unassuming—it was a hot day. George wasn't getting warning signs from him, neither visual nor gut instinct. "Can we help you, Mr—"

"Mr Andrew Morris. Andy. I'm Archie's dad."

Of course, it all made sense. No wonder he wanted to know whether Benjamin had been found. Guilt.

"We heard all the commotion this morning and wondered what was happening. We're a tight community, and everyone knows everyone—when I heard Chantelle shouting—" He glanced at Chantelle's house, and his face fell further. "I asked her if she needed help right away."

"You mentioned 'we' heard the ruckus?"

"I was in the back garden working out. My other neighbours, the Pickerings, were weeding their garden; I chatted with them on and off."

"Did you see anybody leave Chantelle's this morning?"

"Other than Chantelle?" Andy asked. George nodded. "No. I think it was Chantelle, anyway. She had her denim jacket on. The one with the skulls on the back."

"What time was that?"

"Half ten. Yeah, Archie hadn't come back from the park yet."

That didn't match what Chantelle had told them. "Okay, Mr Morris," George said, handing him his card. "We may need to speak to Archie again. Get in touch if you hear anything else, yeah?"

Andy narrowed his eyes at the second dismissal. "Yeah, sure."

George moved towards the cordon in the empty park, noticing that CSI was now on site, sweeping for evidence. However, he didn't want to bother Lindsey Yardley just yet, and so asked DC Blackburn and DC Scott to stay in the park whilst George followed his gut.

Andy Morris seemed unassuming at first, but the way he hovered around and ignored George's instructions bothered him. He took DS Wood with him back onto Back Cross Flatts Avenue. George had to consider that the boy had been taken by someone who knew him, or perhaps even his mother was involved, like DS Wood said, even if it sounded insensitive. It was the most common result. But the law stated that people were innocent until proven guilty, but George's mantra was that everyone was a suspect until proven otherwise.

They ignored Chantelle's and Andy Morris' houses and went straight to Morris' neighbours. He saw several officers in their fluorescent jackets who had already started house-to-house searches higher up the street. As Andy had told them, an older couple were out in the garden, watching.

George flashed his warrant card at them. "Detective Inspector George Beaumont. If you don't mind, I'd like to ask you a few questions?"

"Sure, no problem," the man said with a Glaswegian accent. "We've heard the news about the missing bairn. How can we help?"

"Terrible, isn't it?" said his wife as she shook her head. "I hope you find him."

"Can we take your names, please?" DS Wood asked.

"Maurice and Thora Pickering," the man answered, offering his hand. DS Wood smiled, and George nodded his head.

"May we record this conversation?" George asked.

"Of course," Mrs Pickering said. "We have nothing to hide."

"Whereabouts were you both this morning between ten and noon?" Maurice didn't look offended when he pulled his unshaken hand back but didn't like the question.

"Where we always are. Here. We were sorting out this mess of a garden like we are now." Maurice jabbed a thumb at the weeds.

"And then what?"

"We briefly went inside. For a drink. Came out again to finish what we started, but we heard the commotion soon after and got distracted." George could see half the floor was freshly weeded. A black bucket stood by a set of gardening gloves and a kneeling pad.

"Have you seen or heard anything that might help us find Benjamin Davidson?"

"No, I'm sorry," Maurice said. "We know Benjamin and would have noticed him coming past. We would have taken him back home. He has *special needs*, you see."

George frowned. Some people were old-fashioned with health conditions, especially those they didn't understand.

"Do you know much about the family that lives there?" DS Wood asked, pointing at the Morris' house.

"Andy's family?" Thora asked. "Andy and his family are lovely. The family who lives in the house at the end is a nightmare, you know? They're always partying and playing loud music. Benjamin's mother is just as bad. But at least she'll turn down the music if you ask. But Andy and his family are very considerate."

"So, you know the family well, then?" George asked, steering her back on track.

"Well enough. They've lived here for ten years or so—"

"Was he out here this morning?" George asked, cutting Thora up. He didn't need to know all the details, but he soon might. The man lived right next to the park where Benjamin had vanished, and from what Chantelle told them, Andy was trying to help them. Those factors in George's eyes made Andy a man of interest and more likely a suspect, no matter how lovely he appeared.

"Yes, Andy was working out in the garden this morning," Maurice explained.

"What time did you see him working out?"

Maurice pondered before he answered. "The same time we were. Well, a little later than us, I wasn't watching him the entire time. But he was out here since at least half past ten."

"I was watching him," prompted Thora. "Do you remember? When we returned after a drink, he was leaning by the gate, resting."

"What time was that, Mrs Pickering?"

"Oh Christ, I'm not sure. About quarter past eleven?"

George nodded. What they gave him was not enough to put Andy out of the question but not enough to put him in it, either. But they had partially verified his alibi. "Right, okay. Thank you both. I'll try next door—"

"Oh, they're not in. They're on holiday," Thora said quickly. "They went abroad for the week."

"Lucky them," said George, wishing he'd taken some time off to get away. "Thanks again, Mr and Mrs Pickering."

"We hope you find little Benjamin," Thora called after him as he left.

Chapter Five

Incident Room Four was crammed full. Detective Superintendent Smith had called in everyone who could make it to assist in the growing hunt for the missing boy, cancelling all leave.

"I've put Henry Davidson in an interview room," DS Luke Mason said as he joined the team in the room. Then, he turned to DC Jay Scott. "Can you get him a cuppa?"

"Get anything from him?" George asked.

"No, he didn't say much, but he seemed genuinely shocked at the news; I gave him a pretty good grilling. He says he dropped Benjamin off last night, went to a meeting at work, and then was supposed to pick him up this morning but got up late. The 'meeting'," Luke said using air quotes, "was a piss-up by the looks of it."

George imagined Henry Davidson being dragged into an interview and faced with Luke Mason, and he instantly felt sorry for the guy, especially as he may be innocent.

Still, he had a lot of respect for how Luke got the job done.

"Did he give you any reason to think he's involved?"

"No, not at all. If Henry had snatched the kid, he'd be well away by now."

"Makes sense, but we can't rule him out just yet. I'll talk to him again after the briefing."

Everybody took their seats, and even the Super stood at the back. "Okay, so for those who don't know, this is Benjamin Davidson." George pointed to the photograph of the smiling blond child DS Wood had pinned up, one Jay had taken from Chantelle's phone. He was a picture of innocence that George knew would pull at the heartstrings of every officer in the room. Yet, all George could see was Jack. How would he react if Jack ever went missing? He dismissed the thought immediately, not wanting to tempt fate.

"He is five years old and went missing from his local park in Beeston early this morning." He informed his colleagues of the information they had collected from Chantelle earlier, then paused to let the information sink in as DS Wood continued to update the board.

"Chantelle is a single parent of one and, to be frank, doesn't seem to cope well with keeping a home, looking after a young child, and working part-time. She *is* or *was* once a drug user, judging by her appearance. There was a strong smell of alcohol, and she certainly appeared to be hungover when we talked to her. DS Mason has already spoken to Benjamin's father, Henry Davidson, who suggests he slept in this morning, which needs checking out. Henry's downstairs, and we'll talk to him again later. We must assume that he hasn't taken him for now."

"At the moment, we are looking at three possibilities. One—someone took Benjamin from the park. Two—Benjamin headed home after retrieving his ball and was abducted. Or three—somebody close to Benjamin is responsible for his disappearance."

"So you're not ruling out the parents or the family members?" Mason asked.

"No, and I'm not ruling out the neighbours, either. Did you check if there are any registered sex offenders in the area, DS Fry?"

"Yeah, I have a list from a twenty-mile radius. There are many names, and I've already started to check them all out." Josh fiddled with his glasses.

George nodded at him. It was a lot of work but appreciated. "If there's any reason to suspect someone from the register is involved, then get Uniform to bring them in."

"If Chantelle is responsible for Benjamin's disappearance, that would mean getting out of the house unseen, taking Benjamin somewhere, dropping him off and then getting back in again without being noticed," Josh Fry said.

"True, but I'd argue that even if she didn't abduct her child, she might have had help. There's something about her I don't trust," Wood said.

"I guess, but what's her motive?" Josh said with a shrug.

"There's more than one reason why someone would abduct a child," George said, his attempt to diffuse the tension that was building. He knew what Wood was getting at: money. "But, from the interview, I get the impression Chantelle is genuine. Yes, she has no money, but I think we can rule out kidnapping for money."

DC Scott sneered.

"Something funny, Jay?" George challenged.

"No, sir." Jason looked down at his tablet.

George thought about the morning and what he needed to share with his team that they didn't already know.

The search of Cross Flatts Park had provided nothing. The park was an enormous expanse of land without CCTV and the local area, a labyrinth of streets, was similarly lacking in anything helpful.

He'd left the Morris' house alone for the time being because the Pickering's description of Andy's activities checked out. The neighbour's house was also vacant, as they had suggested.

George explained that though there were still plenty of households to check, the house-to-house searches had come up with nothing—there had been no witnesses regarding the disappearance or sightings of Benjamin. Lindsey Yardley and her team of SOCOs complained that the entire crime scene was a disaster. The park had many exits, bushes, paths, playing fields, and play areas, but they found no evidence.

"What a shit show!" a frustrated DI Beaumont said through gritted teeth as he stood in front of the board. "Does anybody else have anything to add?"

To a sea of hopeful nods, DS Williams said, "Poor boy's probably had some kind of accident—"

"I've checked the hospitals—Jimmy's, LGI, and Pinderfields. No one matching Benjamin's description has come in. Same for the local GPs within a two-mile radius, either," offered DS Fry.

"Great. Thanks, Josh. Chantelle's sister, Claire, told Jay that Benjamin doesn't like busy roads. The sounds of the cars terrify him, so he likely didn't wander off. But if he did, the roads are busy, so he would have been seen."

The room broke into a murmured agreement, and George held a silencing hand. "There's only one logical conclusion—Benjamin was abducted." It was all they were left with that somehow, in a popular park, the boy had been snatched.

Silence. Abducted. The word hung in the air. It was their worst fear. George could see the downcast eyes and shaking heads.

"Anything else?"

Silence.

"No? Good. In the meantime, I want background checks on every man and his dog. The mother, father, family members, and friends—anyone connected to that child." George continued, "We need to search through mobile records, financial records and anything irregular or suspicious." The detectives in the room were instead typing notes on their tablets or furiously writing in their notebooks. "Is that clear?"

He looked around to nodding heads.

"Let's hope it's not a hoax again," Luke Mason said, referring to hoax kidnappings. Hoax kidnappings were an attempt to claim huge reward money for finding the victim fraudulently.

George knew some of them would remember the 2008 infamous case of Shannon Matthews. It was a major missing person police operation compared to Madeleine McCann's disappearance and one of the most extensive searches in police history. Eventually, West Yorkshire Police found out she had been under their noses all along.

DSU Jim Smith and DCS Mohammed Sadiq would end George's career for a screw-up like that. So they needed to do everything they could and leave no stone unturned.

George looked at DSU Smith and said, "Have you got anything to add, sir?" George felt a keen sense of urgency and wanted to end the briefing. They needed to be out there, trying to find the boy, not stuck in here talking about it.

DSU Smith's Geordie baritone boomed from the back as he said, "Benjamin Davidson is officially a misper until we know otherwise, and I think it would be wise to activate the CRA, given Benjamin's age and medical conditions."

The CRA, or Child Rescue Alert, came about following the abduction and murder of Sarah Payne. The CRA intends to alert members of the public to abductions or disappearances quickly and to provide a system so that the police can receive and prioritise critical information. It can mean the difference between life and death for the victim.

Smith came to stand in front of the group. "We need as many people as possible out looking for Benjamin, and that means the support of the public. As you alluded to earlier, trafficking is on the increase, and if it's not already too late, we need to make sure that Benjamin is not moved out of the country." As he turned to George, a grim expression was plastered over Smith's face. "Benjamin's image is already in circulation nationwide, and I will arrange a press conference and appeal. Juliette Thompson has advised me that all the local TV and radio stations have agreed to broadcast it in their news, and it's going in all the papers too. If required, we can pull in resources from other stations. Keep me updated."

George nodded at his boss. "Will do, sir."

Chapter Six

George left his team to their tasks and headed to the interview room with DS Wood. When they entered, George saw the cup of tea standing untouched on the table, and Henry Davidson was pacing around the room. *So he's rather distressed about his son's disappearance,* George thought. *That or an excellent actor.*

DS Wood pulled up a chair, sat at the table, and George followed her. "Sorry about the wait, Mr Davidson," George said, turning on the DIR, and quickly made the introductions.

"I shouldn't be shut up in here. I should be out there looking for my son," Henry complained.

George agreed with the man, but they needed to follow protocol. "Take a seat, Henry. I understand your frustration, and believe me when I say I want to be out searching for Benjamin rather than being stuck here, but we need to ask you a few more questions. I assure you that we are doing everything we can to find your son."

Henry stared at the two detectives, then reluctantly took a seat opposite. George surveyed him. He was dressed casually in a pair of black cargo shorts and a white t-shirt, not quite what George imagined Chantelle's ex-boyfriend would look like. George fiddled with his collar, wanting to take off his tie. Unfortunately, the mercury had steadily risen, becoming unbearable.

DS Wood asked Henry to recount his movements from yesterday afternoon to this morning when he arrived at Elland Road station.

Henry told them nothing they didn't already know, other than that he had taken Benjamin into Cross Flatts Park last night before dropping him home and became increasingly frustrated at having to repeat everything he told DS Luke Mason.

"Can anyone corroborate your movements from last night and this morning?" Wood asked.

"Yeah, of course, they can. I went out drinking with my mates last night, so they'll confirm that." DS Wood slid her notebook across the table, and Henry provided their names, numbers, and addresses. "I live with my parents, and my mum stayed up. She saw me get in at 2 am and had to put me to bed." Henry's cheeks flushed. "She woke me up because she knew I wanted to spend Father's Day with Ben. I fell asleep and rushed over when I got the call from Detective Scott."

George nodded and nodded for DS Wood to continue questioning Henry whilst he messaged DS Joshua Fry to check Henry's alibi.

"How much did you talk to Chantelle yesterday?" Wood asked.

"Not much. Same as usual. We only speak if there's an issue or if Chantelle wants more money. I rang her Saturday morning and asked her if I could bring Ben back and then pick him up on Sunday morning. In hindsight, I should have got my mum and dad to have him. Then we wouldn't be in this mess, would we?" Tears flowed freely from his eyes. *Was he distressed or an excellent actor?*

"I—I—I should have kept him, then he wouldn't have gone missing. But, please, detectives, you've got to promise me you'll find him."

George and Wood said nothing. The silence was deafening, and finally, Henry spoke. "Look, I need to be honest with you. I've been talking to a solicitor because I want custody of Ben. She thinks I have an excellent case." Henry put his head into his hands and sobbed again. The pair saw a man who appeared to be struggling to keep his emotions in check. But was it real?

"I appreciate you telling us. Is that because it gives you motive?"

"What? No, I—I. Yes. But I don't have a motive because my solicitor told me I had a solid case. I didn't take my son. I wouldn't do that."

"Tell us, why would you want to take custody of Benjamin?" Wood asked.

"Because he's my boy and the most precious person in my world. Chantelle can barely look after herself, let alone him. She never wanted him in the first place, and when she learned about his ASD, it was like she had given up entirely. As far as I'm concerned, if she were a good mum, then Ben wouldn't be missing, would he?"

DS Wood stopped writing and stared deeply into Henry's eyes. "What do you mean by that?" she asked.

"Detective Mason told me about Ben playing football with Archie." Henry took a calming breath, then went on a rant. "Why was he allowed out that early and without an adult? Ben doesn't know danger. He's an intelligent boy but doesn't use his intelligence in the real world. Everything is impulse. He can't cross a road without guidance. Ben can barely get up and down the stairs without guidance. So he should not have gone into that park without an adult. And the adult looking after him was his mum. She's let him down. Massively."

"It's difficult being a single parent," George said, thinking about his son's mother, Mia. But then, she wasn't exactly a single parent. She had a support network; Chantelle didn't.

"I do more than my bit and more than she does, anyway. I pay maintenance monthly, which I wouldn't expect from her if I got custody. Yes, she works part-time, but she often gets her sister Claire to pick Ben up from school because she can't be arsed. Does that sound like a competent mother to you?" Henry ground his teeth and clenched his fists.

"It sounds like you have a good reason to want to take Benjamin," DS Wood said.

"I get it, all right? But I told you, I haven't got him. I don't know where he is. I wish I did, and I'd love for Ben to live with me." Henry smacked the table with the bottom of an enclosed fist and then closed his eyes, attempting to control his breathing. "Sorry. I'm so sorry, but my son is out there. I swear to God, if that bastard Mitchell has done anything to him, then I'll fucking kill him!" He hammered his fist on the table again.

George ignored the outburst, more interested in a name they hadn't heard before. "Mitchell?"

"Chantelle's boyfriend." Henry bared his teeth. "Mitchell Cook."

The jealousy was obvious, but then George understood. He and Isabella had spoken about her relationship with Jack and how Mia would feel if she knew about it. It felt wrong to involve Isabella in Jack's life without his mother knowing, but it would do more harm than good to let Mia know. George also had nightmares about a man replacing George as Jack's father when the inevitable happens, and Mia moves on. He knew it was wrong, but he hoped Mia stayed single forever so that somebody else couldn't play daddy to his little boy. Perhaps Henry felt the same.

"Chantelle didn't mention a boyfriend," Wood said.

"Why would she? As you probably know, she's not allowed to see him."

The two detectives shared a confused look, and Henry must have noticed it as he elaborated. "There was a drugs raid on the house, and Mitchell was arrested. So you're not doing your job properly because if you were, you'd know all about this." Henry shook uncontrollably, and George could see him losing control of the interview. "You're fucking pathetic, the lot of you. Let me out of here. Now. And get your arses out there and find my boy!"

George gave Henry a moment to compose himself but didn't break the eye contact. He could see Wood texting from his peripheral. Henry had enough reason to take Benjamin, but that would blow any chance of getting custody. Mason didn't think Henry was involved, and George respected his opinion. George hoped the case was going to be open and shut and immediately felt disappointed.

"Is there anyone else you can think of who would take Benjamin?"

Henry shook his head. "No."

"We will talk to Mitchell, Henry," Wood added.

"Good. Can I go now?"

"No. When you and Chantelle were together, did she ever take drugs?"

Henry didn't answer, and George noticed his discomfort.

The problem was that George's patience was slipping. Finally, he took a deep breath and said, "I'm not interested in what you got up to when you were together, Henry. I'm trying to find your son, so I need to know everything you can tell me about when you and Chantelle were together."

"Fine. We smoked a bit of weed on the weekends. Chantelle likes to have a good time. She was so fucked off when she found out about the pregnancy and even threatened to have an abortion. I tried to get her to give the weed up and make a fresh start. I did because I wanted to be a good father."

"And Chantelle?"

"Yeah, she smokes weed a lot. We argue about it all the time."

"What about other drugs?"

He shrugged. "I'm not sure. Can I go now?" He got up from his chair.

"Yes, but for elimination purposes, please allow us to take your fingerprints and a DNA sample before you leave."

"Fine." Henry stood. "I've got nothing to hide."

"In the meantime, you need to stay away from Chantelle."

"You can't stop me looking for my boy."

"No, but we wouldn't want you contaminating any scenes or interfering with the search. So keep your head down because we may need to speak to you again. We can provide a Family Liaison Officer?"

Henry's face darkened. "No."

"Fine. As soon as we have any news, we'll contact you." George stood and handed Henry his card. "My mobile number, in case you need to contact me."

Henry stormed out, and George stopped the recording.

"Do you think he's telling the truth?" George asked Isabella.

"I don't know. I feel like Henry knows something we don't."

"What, like, who's taken, Benjamin?"

"I don't know, but I've got a bad feeling."

"I agree. We need to monitor Henry and check out his family and friends."

His team talked on telephones or furiously tapped away at their keyboards when the two senior detectives walked back in.

"Got anything for us, Josh?" George asked.

"Yes, I got the text from DS Wood and can confirm there was a raid on the house six months ago, resulting in one arrest."

"Mitchell Cook?" Wood asked.

Josh nodded his head. "Yeah. We found enough cannabis for intent to supply in the house. Chantelle and Mitchell claimed they'd had a party at the house and that it wasn't theirs. Mitchell has previous. He did eight months for possession and got out a year ago. He was also arrested for GBH. His girlfriend before Chantelle. She wouldn't testify, so it never went to court. So we informed social services."

"Poor lass was probably frightened of what would happen to her if he didn't get sentenced," Wood said.

"It's often the case, sadly," George agreed. "Anyway, he doesn't seem like the sort of man you want around your child. Call social services and ask for all the information on Chantelle. Tell them we'll be over in half an hour." Josh nodded, and George turned his attention to DCs Blackburn and Scott. "Anything on social media?"

"Chantelle's already put out a post on Facebook to inform everybody that Benjamin is missing, sir," Jason said. "Makes her out to be the model mother. Her profile is open, and she has a ton of pictures of Benjamin on there. Unlike in her house."

"Thanks, Jay. Any comment patterns?"

"She talks to her sister Claire a lot on there," Tashan added. "She has a fairly small circle of friends, so we've made a list and are looking into them, sir."

"Good work, you two. Keep me, or DS Wood updated."

Chapter Seven

Senior manager Bryn Hughes was waiting for DI Beaumont and DS Wood in the reception area of the social services offices when they arrived.

"I haven't had long to skim through them, but I've got the case files," Bryn said as he led them into his office. "Whilst I've been present at some of the meetings regarding the welfare of Benjamin Davidson, it's not one of my cases."

George took a chair, watched Bryn spread the files across the desk, and said, "Thank you for seeing us so quickly." There were dark circles under Bryn's eyes and a visible shake of his hand.

"My pleasure. I just hope you find Benjamin." He ran his hand through his black locks as he scanned the files.

Wood took a seat silently, her pen poised.

"Okay, so we were called in initially when Benjamin's parents split up. Chantelle was struggling, but we weren't concerned. Then we were called in again just before Benjamin turned four years old when Chantelle was believed to begin living with Mitchell Cook," Bryn began. "It was difficult to meet with Chantelle and Benjamin at first. The neighbours told us she was at work every time we called around. So finally, we wrote to her requesting a meeting, and in the meantime, we visited the school that Benjamin attended."

"What happened during the visit?" Wood asked.

"There were no concerns raised at the school regarding Benjamin's welfare. He appeared to be clean and, most importantly, thriving. Eventually, my colleague met with them and determined there were no major concerns, even if the house was a little untidy." He continued reading. "Benjamin was up to date with his vaccinations and boosters."

George wondered whether it was tidier back then than it was now.

"My colleague raised concerns over Chantelle's appearance, but Benjamin looked healthy. The notes state Chantelle had dark circles around her eyes and looked pale and drawn. She was also severely underweight and had cracked lips." He looked up from reading, a frown on his face. "Chantelle said she hadn't been sleeping and had a bout of flu."

"Who made the complaints?" George asked.

"The initial one was Henry. We thought it was because of break up, and after two further visits, the caseworker was satisfied that Benjamin was not at risk."

"And the recent one?"

"Her sister, Claire."

A look of shock spread across the detectives' faces.

"Yes. It says that Claire did not trust Mitchell Cook, and although she seemed genuine in her concern for Benjamin, the caseworker made another assessment. But, again, the caseworker was satisfied that Benjamin was not at risk. It also states Chantelle denied Mitchell was living with her."

"Is that it?" Wood asked.

"No. This past year, Benjamin has been to A&E twice. First, with a cut to his chin, which resulted from Benjamin falling onto the corner of a television cabinet. Then the second time Benjamin visited A&E was for a fractured left wrist. Chantelle claims he fell off a scooter she had got him for Christmas."

George thought back to the living room and couldn't remember a television cabinet. Perhaps she got rid after the accident? "They both sound dodgy. Were Mitchell or Chantelle suspected of intentionally harming Benjamin?" George asked.

"We investigated," Bryn said. "As before, there were no signs of neglect or abuse. Chantelle eventually admitted that Mitchell was her boyfriend but denied that he was living there. She was adamant Mitchell hadn't been in the house when Benjamin got hurt, and we had no evidence to the contrary."

"Did anyone interview Mitchell?" Wood asked.

"No, because the caseworker was satisfied that Benjamin was not at risk, particularly as he was at school every day and regularly saw Henry."

George thought about the man they had just interviewed. He had a short fuse and seemed to care about his son a lot. The shared parallels weren't lost on him as he said, "I guess Henry was furious about Benjamin's injuries?"

Bryn didn't need to look down at the files and said, "Yes. But, unfortunately, he turned up at the office and had to be escorted out by security."

"I can't say I blame him," George said. And he couldn't.

Bryn nodded. "No, I agree. We made further visits after the drug raid because we put the child protection register on Benjamin. I was involved in the meetings to discuss the CPP, the child protection plan. Chantelle claimed she had hosted a party but hadn't known that drugs had been brought into the house."

"Where was Benjamin during this party?" Wood asked.

"Benjamin was with Henry that weekend. Chantelle agreed that Mitchell would not visit the house or have any contact with Benjamin. Chantelle seemed to keep to the agreement when we made subsequent visits. From the notes, the house was in reasonable condition, and there was food in the cupboards. Benjamin also seemed to be well and, importantly, happy. The school made no complaints. We signposted Chantelle to places that offered support, such as parenting and money management classes. She said she found it difficult while working and only attended a few. Overall, my colleague notes she seemed to cope well."

"So, what's happened? When we visited today, the house was filthy; even Benjamin's mattress was stained. That sort of filth doesn't happen overnight," George said. He could still smell the stale air that permeated Chantelle's house.

"It was disgusting." Wood wrinkled her nose.

"Benjamin was diagnosed with ASD—Autism Spectrum Disorder. Chantelle already struggled to care for him. He was still wetting the bed at four and being disruptive during the night. Chantelle blamed the lack of sleep when her house was reported to be filthy, but then concerns were raised that Chantelle was taking drugs."

George thought about the young boy. If his father had taken him, then he'd taken him away from a struggling mother. But if so, then where had he hidden Benjamin? "Was it Henry?"

Bryn shook his head. "No, it was her sister, Claire. She called on another two separate occasions. Both times, Claire claimed Chantelle wasn't looking after Benjamin or herself and said she was concerned for both her sister's and her nephew's welfare. She was also concerned that Mitchell was living in the house. Claire even suggested that Benjamin would be better off living with his father."

That was news to George. Interesting news.

"Again, we made contact to see Chantelle and Benjamin. When we finally saw her, she denied Mitchell was living in the house. She explained that the constant caring for Benjamin and her work at Asda meant the housework didn't get done."

"Could she not get benefits to help her stop work?" Wood asked.

"Yes, we explained she should apply for Carer's Allowance and DLA for Benjamin. Leeds City Council helped her apply for DLA, but she refused to apply for Carer's Allowance as she didn't want to give up her job."

"That's weird. You'd think Chantelle would've put Benjamin first. And surely cause to remove Benjamin from Chantelle's care, especially after you received the complaints from Claire," George said.

"That's not how it works. The argument Chantelle made was that just because she wasn't bringing up Benjamin the way Claire thought she should, didn't mean she was a bad or a neglectful mother. We had no evidence that Mitchell was living at the house. You understand we can't do anything without evidence, yes?"

"Yes," Wood said. "So, basically, you took no action?"

Bryn ran a hand through his ebony curls. "You must understand that we already have more children in care than the system can cope with. We work with families to help them improve their situation so that it is best for the child because there's a short supply of foster carers. In Chantelle's case, Henry and Claire were there for support, and we had zero evidence to suggest Benjamin was suffering from abuse or neglect."

"I appreciate that, Bryn," George said. He knew professionals had to make tough decisions; no matter what decision was made, it was criticised. "In your opinion, do you think Chantelle is capable of harming Benjamin?"

"I'm not Chantelle's caseworker, DI Beaumont. All I can do is read the notes. But, as there were no signs of neglect or abuse, I don't think Benjamin is at risk from his mother."

"Yet now he's missing," Wood said.

"Yes, and I pray to God that we missed nothing on the visits that could have prevented this. But, unfortunately, Chantelle wouldn't be the first mother to snap."

George got déjà vu and an awful feeling in the pit of his stomach. "Thanks, Bryn. Let's hope nothing was missed. Anyway, I'm sure your colleagues did their best." George smiled. He had to because he knew that doing your best sometimes wasn't good enough.

* * *

"Where do you think we should go next?" George asked Isabella Wood as he fastened his seat belt.

"Chantelle's. I think we should have a chat about Mitchell, especially after what Henry said. He sounds like a right piece of work. Maybe we should just bring him in for questioning."

George shook his head as he pulled out onto the main road. "It's too early for that, especially if he has Benjamin. We only have one chance, and I want a good reason to bring him in. We need evidence that he was there this morning. That way, we can keep hold of him and push hard for a search warrant. If we contact him now, and he's involved, it'll give him a chance to cover his tracks."

"Chantelle must believe he has nothing to do with Benjamin's disappearance; otherwise, she would have said something. Right?"

"I don't know," George said with a sigh. "She could be afraid that social services would take Benjamin if they found out he was there."

"Or think back to his ex. Chantelle could be afraid of him."

"True, but you'd think it wouldn't matter. You'd think Chantelle's only priority would be finding Benjamin," George said.

"Unless she wanted to be rid of Benjamin. Maybe she was fed up and wanted out," Wood said.

"True, but then there's Henry," George said. "She could have given custody of Benjamin to him."

As they pulled outside Chantelle's house, DS Wood turned and said the words George was dreading. "Maybe she trafficked him?"

George didn't answer and instead climbed out of the car. He didn't know what to say. For a parent to sell their child was disgusting. But, he didn't want to think about it, so he headed towards Chantelle's house when he saw PC Sally Fletcher walking towards them.

"all right, Sally? Anything new?" George asked her.

"No, the neighbours don't see a lot of Chantelle. I've just got back from Hull. Henry's parents were happy to let us look around. They seem genuinely upset that their grandson is missing. We found nothing, and Mrs Davidson confirmed Henry's alibi."

The sound of a car pulling up behind them made them turn around. DS Luke Mason got out and hurried towards them.

"Boss, Lindsey Yardley and her team found this in Holbeck

Cemetery." He held up a clear plastic bag with a red cape. "Dr Yardley wants the mother to identify it. Still no sign of Benjamin."

George took the bag and held it up to inspect it. It was precisely how Chantelle described it earlier.

"Thanks, Luke. I'll take it in and check, but it looks like it's Benjamin's. Since when were they searching the cemetery?"

"When they were searching the north end of the park, the dogs locked onto something," Luke said and headed back to the car. "They crossed the road, and the search team found the cape. So they're moving north as we speak, towards Holbeck Park."

"It's possible Benjamin wandered that way," Wood said.

George thought about what he'd been told about Benjamin and how scared of roads he was. But, to the north of the park was a bustling road. "Yeah, it is. Or someone could have walked with him." George knocked on Chantelle's door but kept his eyes on the cape. "I'm not sure whether this is good or bad news, Isabella."

Chapter Eight

The FLO, Cathy, opened the door and welcomed them inside. "She's on the sofa, curled up asleep, which is probably the best thing for her at the minute, as I doubt she'll get much time to rest in the coming days. Dr Yardley and her team of SOCOs have been."

"Is Claire still here?" George asked.

"No, her husband needed her at home, so she left. She said that if she could, she would be back later."

"Any other visitors?" Cathy shook her head. "Phone calls?"

"No, but Chantelle has been on social media all day."

"Thanks, Cathy," George said as he walked into the living room. He noticed the coffee table had been cleared and, whilst he was surprised to see an effort had been made to tidy up, it did little to improve the appearance. And then there was the stale smell that still lingered.

Chantelle opened her eyes and looked up at George, her eyes pleading. She had begun to realise the gravity of the situation. "Any news?"

"No, not yet," George said and attempted a smile. "I'm sorry, but there's something I need you to look at." George handed Chantelle the cape.

Chantelle sat up and pulled her knees to her chin. She turned the bag over and over in her hands, looking for something. Then she burst into tears. She eventually managed to say, "It's Benjamin's cape. You can see his initials there, look." George nodded. "Where did you find it?"

George nodded to Wood, who took out her phone and left the room. She needed to let DS Luke Mason know.

"In Holbeck Cemetery."

George sat down in the armchair just as Wood walked back in. She reluctantly looked at the other vacant armchair but eventually perched on the edge with a frown.

"We still don't know whether Benjamin is lost or whether he was abducted. If so, whoever did it may have walked with Benjamin through the cemetery and then north into the woods, where there is less chance of being seen, to get away," George said. "In the meantime, Chantelle, we need to ask you some more questions."

Chantelle clutched the plastic bag to her chest and said, "Oh God, what was he doing there? I can't stay cooped up in here any more. I should be out there looking for him."

Cathy came into the room with a fresh cup of coffee and sat next to Chantelle. "Here, love. Drink it. It's hot." Chantelle smiled and said thank you.

"There's a team searching the area," Wood informed her, "and lots of people have turned out to help. If Benjamin's there, then they will find him. We know what we're doing. It's best if you stay here and provide us with as much information as possible. And think about when we find him. Would you rather be here or searching someplace you don't know?"

"Tell us about Mitchell Cook," George said.

"Mitchell?"

"Yes, Mitchell Cook, your boyfriend," DS Wood said.

She shook her head. "I don't have a boyfriend." Chantelle swung her legs off the sofa and reached for her packet of cigarettes. "I split up with Mitchell ages ago."

"We've been told different," George said, his voice firm, his eyes hard.

"Yeah, people make shit up, don't they?" Chantelle said and scowled as she lit the cigarette.

"Was Mitchell here last night?" George met her eyes.

"No. I told you we split up." Her cheeks flushed, and George was convinced Chantelle was lying.

"Chantelle," George said, shifting forward in his seat, "if you're afraid of Mitchell— "

Chantelle laughed. "Afraid of Mitchell? As if."

Wood said, "We know about the GBH— "

"I still don't know why you'd think I'm scared of him. Mitchell is a good friend. And anyway, that silly bitch made all that up and said if she couldn't have him, then nobody could." Chantelle glared at Wood. "She was a proper bitch, and he's better off without."

"Do you talk to him, Mitchell?" George asked.

"Yeah, of course. We call and text every day—we're friends. Nothing wrong with being friends, is there?"

"No, there isn't, Chantelle," George spat, "but I need you to start and be honest with me. If Mitchell was here last night, you need to tell us because your boy is missing, and we're trying to find him!"

Chantelle's nostrils flared. "I told you he wasn't!"

"Okay, so you and Mitchell are *just* friends. When did you see him last?"

"A week ago." Chantelle took a drag of her cigarette and breathed an impressive ring of smoke.

"How is Mitchell with Benjamin?" Wood asked.

"Fine."

"We've been told Benjamin struggles to sleep at night. That he keeps you up?" George asked.

"Yeah, and? What are you getting at?" Chantelle shook her head and ground her teeth.

"We have to ask these questions and look at everyone who has had contact with Benjamin. Did Mitchell ever get angry with your son for keeping him up?"

"Oh, I see. How ridiculous. Mitchell wouldn't hurt Benjamin, and he hasn't got him."

"How can you be so sure?" George retorted. "Mitchell could have picked him up from the park this morning. They have a good relationship, or so you say. So what's stopping Mitchell from walking off with Benjamin?"

"I just know," she said. "I know Mitch, and you don't. Leave him alone."

George felt a sudden rage boil up inside him and had a desperate urge to shake her. Her son was missing, yet she didn't seem to want to help. All it did was make him more suspicious. He moved the conversation along and said, "We are going to run an appeal on the ITV evening news. We would like you and Henry to read a brief statement."

Chantelle looked horrified. "I'm—I'm not sure I—I can," she stuttered.

"It's important, Chantelle. If someone has taken Benjamin, we need to appeal to them to hand him back safely because it's likely to be someone known to you."

"No," Chantelle said. "They wouldn't do that. Everybody loves Benjamin."

"The stats don't lie, Chantelle, which is why it's so important you tell us everything, no matter how insignificant it seems. Do you understand? Has anyone shown a recent interest in Benjamin?"

"Yeah."

"Good," George said. "So, was there anyone other than Claire who called at the house last night?"

"No." Chantelle lit another cigarette.

George stood and attempted a smile. "Right, that's it for now, Chantelle. Cathy will bring you to the station for the appeal later." Worry creased Chantelle's forehead. George wondered why? She should do everything in her power to get Benjamin back, yet she was being difficult at every opportunity.

Wood closed her notebook, stood, and said, "Don't worry, Chantelle, it'll be fine. Cathy will help you prepare a statement to read out."

"Okay." Chantelle nodded. "Fine."

"Good," George said, "we'll see you later. If you think of anything else, then let Cathy know."

* * *

George pointed to the maps DS Wood had pinned to the board in the Incident Room. "Okay, DS Mason called me on the way to the station to let me know the dogs have locked onto a scent in the woods around Holbeck Park. It is unlikely that Benjamin has made his way there alone, but if he has, he could be wandering around the woods."

"It's a perfect place to dump a body," DC Scott added from the back. Every head swivelled towards him, and red burst in his cheeks. "Look, I don't like it, but I'm only saying what everyone else thinks. No sightings of Benjamin have been reported yet—if he had wandered near the main road, which he would've had to have crossed by himself, then someone would have seen him."

"Unfortunately, Jay has a point," George said, his jaw firm. "DS Mason is coordinating a search already, with help from volunteers. There's a danger that the public could trample over a crime scene, but I don't think we'll be able to keep them away. Besides, we need all the help we can get. Considering Jay's point, there's the possibility that if he's right, then the culprit will probably turn up to monitor the search, which means Mason will be in an excellent position to keep an eye out. Meanwhile, we believe Chantelle is lying to us, and as such, we'll continue looking into the family background."

His team nodded their agreement.

"Good. Jay and Tashan, I want you to interview the neighbours again and see if anyone has been seen hanging about on the estate or asking questions. In the unlikely event that it is a stranger who abducted Benjamin, then they will have been scouting the area." Next, he turned to DS Yolanda Williams. "Yolanda, if she is taking drugs, then she's likely to be in contact with some known dealers. Find out who."

"Of course, sir. I know there are plenty on the estate," she said.

* * *

George drove towards Holbeck Park woods and parked on Noster Terrace, where an officer stood at the cordon, looking bored. To his right was the cemetery, and to the left was a long block of terraced housing, like the block Chantelle lived in. In front, George could see the expanse of woods.

He checked his watch and realised they didn't have long before the appeal.

"Mason looks like he's in his element issuing orders," DS Wood said.

George followed her gaze. Luke Mason was surrounded by a group of people who appeared to be listening attentively as he pointed in various directions and gave strict orders.

"Looks like he's doing a good job," she added as Mason approached them.

"How's it going, Luke?" George asked.

"Slow," Mason huffed. "We've split the woods into separate grids and assigned people to each grid. They'll work in lines. The dogs are no use in there. Too many scents." He pulled a face. "I'm worried that he's fallen from exhaustion because he's little. We must find him before the light fades because he could be lying in the bracken or caught in the brambles."

"Do we know how the cape got into the cemetery yet?" Wood asked.

Mason's face darkened. "No. I'm worried somebody has planted the cape to confuse us, to get us to waste time."

"On the way over, DSU Smith explained he's sending over a news crew, as he wants an interview and some shots of the woods," George said. "I'll let you handle the interview." George smiled. "I'm sure you enjoy keeping the media under control."

"You know me, son," Mason said with a wink.

"He's also sending Uniform over to do house-to-house, concentrating on Noster Terrace first, and then the other Noster streets. It's unlikely Benjamin was down on the Morleys, but we'll get to that after prioritising this area."

"We're going to speak to Chantelle's sister, Claire. Chantelle was known to social services, and it seems Claire put in various complaints, as did Benjamin's father, Henry. Chantelle's ex, Mitchell Cook, is a lad known to us."

"Oh, for fuck's sake, we need to find the poor kid," Mason said. "So Mitchell and Chantelle are suspects. Who else?"

"I'm not giving up hope, Luke, and we still have to monitor the father," George said.

"Henry? He's a nice guy. He's out with the search party now. I don't get any vibes from him at all."

"Yeah, I know what you mean. Anyway, mate, I'll let you get back to the search. I'll send someone to relieve you later."

Mason raised his brow and shook his head. "Piss off. If you think I'm leaving before we've found this kid, then you don't know me well enough," Mason snapped in jest.

George nodded and laughed before gripping his old mentor on the shoulder. Despite their roles being reversed, he still had the utmost respect for the man.

"I'm staying until we have combed every inch of this place, Beaumont." He winked at DS Wood, then turned and sauntered towards the waiting group.

"He's a good man, is Luke," Isabella said.

"I know he is, but he's going to wear himself out. And the problem is, I don't think Benjamin's in there."

Chapter Nine

George drove the Honda south towards Middleton, the sun high to his right. It wouldn't set for another four hours, but each second they spent driving, talking, or searching, meant the darker it got and the harder it got to find Benjamin.

Claire Murray lived with her husband in the Dunlin estate, and so George indicated left and onto Middleton Town Street.

"There's a chippy just up there," DS Wood said and pointed to her right. "Old Village. Best in Miggy. I'm starving. I don't think I've eaten anything all day."

George nodded and indicated right.

The smell of salt and vinegar tickled their taste buds as they got out of the Honda. George ordered sausage and chips, whilst Wood opted for fish bites and chips.

They ravenously ate the food, chatting about the case between mouthfuls. It was as close to a date as they'd managed the last couple of weeks. "I love you," George said with a smile, balling up the paper and throwing it on the back seat.

"I love you more." There was a twinkle in her eyes, but he didn't believe her words. She couldn't possibly love him more than he loved her.

"Right, we better see what Claire has to say. Chantelle's

hiding something, and it seemed obvious Claire didn't want to tell us what it was in front of her sister."

* * *

George parked the car outside Claire's semi-detached house.

"Nice place," Wood said.

"Yeah, looks like she's had a better run at life than her sister."

They made their way to the front door and rang the bell. When nobody answered, George, brayed on the door.

Claire answered the door with a mobile phone held to her ear. "I have to go. I'll call you later," she said and ended the call. "Nice to see you again. You'd better come in." Claire turned and led the way into the living room.

George's eyes scanned the room and couldn't believe the stark differences between this living room and Chantelle's. Where Chantelle's was a complete mess, hadn't been decorated, and lacked any photos, Claire's room was neat, decorated in pastel colours and had a large picture of Claire and her husband, clearly taken on their wedding day, above the fireplace.

"Do you mind if we talk in the kitchen?" Claire asked, without waiting for an answer. She led them in and shut the door.

Claire turned to the hobs atop the oven where an extractor fan was sucking steam from two pans. She adjusted the heat by the dial and turned to face the two detectives. "I don't mean to be rude, but what can I do for you? I need to feed my husband before I go to the station, as I want to be there to support Telle when she does the appeal." She checked her watch and cursed.

"I don't have a lot of time."

Claire's makeup had worn off, and George noticed the dark circles beneath her eyes. Her eyes looked swollen as if she had been crying. "We won't keep you long, Claire, but we need to ask you some questions. Then, we can talk as you cook tea if that's easier for you?" George smiled, and Claire nodded.

"When you were at Chantelle's last night, did you go into the living room?" DS Wood asked.

"Only to briefly explain that I'd dropped the clothes upstairs and that Benjamin was sound asleep. Why?"

"Can you describe what Chantelle was doing?"

"Getting stoned and drinking alcohol." Claire sighed. "It's what she usually does."

"Smoking cannabis?"

"Yeah, the place stank of the stuff. I'm surprised you didn't smell it whilst you were there."

"Who was in the room?"

"Telle..." Claire opened the oven door and peeked inside.

George stepped back from the heat of the oven and said, "Who else was there, Claire?"

Claire shut the door, adjusted the dial, and straightened up. "Mitchell Cook was with her."

"Why didn't you mention this to us earlier?" Wood asked.

"As I'm sure you already know, he's not supposed to be there. If I'd said anything earlier, Telle would have kicked off and denied it."

The kitchen door opened, and a man walked in, his steps short and shuffled. He was dressed in blue pyjamas. He looked from Claire to George and Wood. "Any news on Ben?" George noticed he slurred his words, spoke slowly, and had a tremor in his hands.

"Not yet," Claire said. "This is Detective Inspector Beaumont and Detective Sergeant Wood. They just came around to ask some questions." She turned to the two detectives and smiled. "This is my husband, Kyle."

Kyle shuffled forward, freezing for a brief moment on the spot, before slowly stepping towards the two detectives. He offered them a shaky hand, which they both took, and said, "Did you offer them a drink, Claire, love?"

Claire looked at her husband and said, "They're not staying long enough for one, and I need to get ready."

Ignoring his wife, Kyle said, "I think the living room will be more comfortable. Go on and take a seat," he said. "Claire will bring you some tea."

Claire helped her husband to his armchair in the living room and pushed a tray on wheels towards him. The food on the tray smelt delicious, and Kyle nodded as the two detectives took a seat.

"We understand Claire is busy," Wood said.

Kyle smiled. "Whilst that is true, what is also true is that I'm sure you both could do with a cuppa. I'm having one." He looked at his wife. "Thanks, love."

A couple of minutes later, Claire came back into the living room carrying a teapot and four cups on a tray, and she placed them on the coffee table. She poured a cup for Kyle and stirred in two sweeteners. The cup shook violently in Kyle's hands.

"Parkinson's," he explained.

"How long have you had it?" Wood asked.

"When I turned forty, I was diagnosed with young-onset Parkinson's," Kyle explained. That was nearly fifteen years ago, but it seems like forever."

"That can't be easy," George said, looking between the

couple. That meant Kyle was in his mid-fifties, yet Claire, George didn't think, had turned thirty.

"We manage," Claire replied. She looked exhausted, and now George understood the dark circles beneath her eyes. Claire had herself to look after, as well as her husband. But not only that, but she also did Chantelle and Benjamin's washing. What else did she do?

"You were telling us about Mitchell," George said, moving the conversation along. Kyle nodded his appreciation and continued eating, his hand violently shaking as he spooned food into his mouth.

"As I said, Mitchell is there most of the time, but Telle will deny it if you ask her."

"You don't approve of their relationship?"

She looked disgusted. "No. I don't. Mitchell's a druggy and not fit to be around children."

"Is that why you contacted social services?" Wood asked.

A look of shock crossed Claire's face. "Isn't that information supposed to be confidential?" Claire snapped.

George understood why she was annoyed, but social services were at liberty to tell them, given the situation. He explained that to Claire, who nodded.

"To be fair to Claire, she had little choice," Kyle said. "Chantelle wouldn't listen to her and kept on seeing Mitchell."

"Look, I'd appreciate it if Telle didn't find out I'd complained. Who's going to keep an eye on Benjamin if she stops me going around?" Claire bit her lip and furiously shook her head.

"We understand, don't we, Wood?" George said, picking up his cup of tea.

Wood nodded and smiled. "Do you think Mitchell is capable

of hurting Benjamin?" she asked.

Claire turned to look at her. "You know about Benjamin's fractured wrist?"

"Yes, Chantelle said Benjamin had fallen off his scooter outside."

"You believe her?" Claire asked.

George thought for a moment. He didn't believe her, but he couldn't tell Claire that. "You don't?" he said. Claire shook her head, a frown on her face. "You think Mitchell was responsible, and Chantelle protected him?" George asked.

"Exactly. You don't know what Mitchell's like. You don't know what Chantelle's like, either. She's the most selfish person I've ever met, and I've met Mitchell," Claire said.

"But do you think she would put Mitchell before her son?" Wood asked.

Claire shrugged her shoulders. "I spoke to the neighbours when Benjamin fractured his wrist. They told me they heard the noise from inside the house. I explained this to social services, but they could never get a statement from them. You've got to be strong to break someone's wrist. I think it was Mitchell, and he has some sort of hold on Telle. That hold is probably the drugs."

"Have you seen Chantelle take drugs?" Wood asked.

"To tell you the truth, I only saw Mitchell smoking weed last night, but you've seen the state of Chantelle. Her clothes hang from her shoulders. She's lost so much weight, and I swear she's out of it most of the time. She looks ten years older than she is, like one of those druggies you see on TV."

George thought back to what Jay said and realised Claire had a point.

"Have you asked her about her drug use?" Wood asked.

"Of course, but she denies it. The smell is evidence enough, but I even asked around to see if I could find out who her supplier was."

George drained his cup of tea and sat forward. "What did you find out?"

"Nothing," Claire said. "They don't talk to you unless you're one of them. And I'm not one of them." She flushed.

"When we went to see them, social services told us that Chantelle seemed to cope and that they had no major concerns regarding Benjamin's welfare," George said.

Claire laughed. "Well, they would, wouldn't they? They could never just show up and catch her. So instead, they made appointments, which gave her a chance to get Mitchell out of the way, clean up that shithole, and put on her 'mother of the year' personality."

"Have you ever seen Mitchell be violent towards Chantelle or Benjamin?" George asked.

Claire shook her head. "Not personally, no."

"Do you know anybody who has?" Wood asked.

Again, she shook her head.

"all right, so we've talked about Mitchell," George said and took a biscuit that Claire offered, gutted he'd drained his tea. "But what about Chantelle? Would she hurt Benjamin? It's clear you think she's an unfit mother."

Claire thought for a moment, sharing glances with her husband, who smiled and nodded. "No, I don't think she would physically hurt Benjamin, but remember what she told you earlier. She left the front door unlocked and probably open. Benjamin can't open that heavy door alone. To tell you the truth, I think she needs help. Telle's always skint yet works part-time and is on benefits. We've spoken to her about

Carer's Allowance and Disability Living Allowance, but it's like she doesn't want that responsibility. You'd think more money would make it easier to look after Benjamin. Maybe if Mitchell were gone, she would clear up her act."

"Are you saying Chantelle was doing all right before getting with Mitchell?" Wood asked.

Kyle laughed, and his spoon fell to the floor. Claire shot up from her chair and retrieved the spoon before heading into the kitchen. "She's always been a party girl, which is why she split up with Henry. He wanted to settle down and do what was right for Benjamin. She didn't." Claire's voice got increasingly muffled as she got further and further away. "If she had stayed with Henry, then maybe this wouldn't have happened," Claire said, handing her husband a new spoon and wiping the soup off the wooden floor.

"So, you'd be happier if Benjamin had been removed from Chantelle's care?" George asked.

"Without a doubt, yes. To be honest, Benjamin would have been better off with Henry. He told me about his visit to the solicitor, and I will support him. I think it'd be good for Telle to see Benjamin every other weekend, maybe. I hoped it would give her an incentive to clean up her act. At least Benjamin would've been safe with his dad. I really don't think this would have happened under Henry's watch. In fact, I'm certain."

The custody battle would give Chantelle another motive, George thought. "Does Chantelle know about Henry's intentions?"

"To take custody of Benjamin?" Claire asked. George nodded. "No, I don't think so."

"Maybe she's frightened of losing her child?" Wood said, picking up on George's point. "Would she try to hide Benjamin somewhere to stop Henry from getting custody?"

Claire scoffed. "Chantelle's not all there. She's not smart enough to plan it, let alone pull it off. And where would she hide him, anyway? As for the potential custody application, I'm certain she doesn't know; otherwise, she would've caused trouble for Henry. She's an excellent liar."

"Trouble?" Wood asked, her brow raised.

Claire smiled. "She's complained to me before that Henry wasn't paying child maintenance, and that's why she was always skint. Henry showed me statements from CSA. I'm sure she'd lie about something to stop Henry from getting custody. What annoys me is she doesn't want Benjamin; it's as if she's just being spiteful."

"Do you think Henry would take matters into his own hands, then?" Wood asked.

It was Kyle who spoke, and he said, "No. By kidnapping Benjamin, Henry loses out on everything. He has a strong case for custody and our support. He wouldn't risk that."

"Thank you, Mr and Mrs Murray." George smiled and stood. "Before we go, could you tell us where you both were last night and the early hours of this morning?"

Claire's nostrils flared, and she stood up, her hands balled into fists. "Are you being serious? You can't seriously think I would abduct my own nephew."

"They have to ask, love," Kyle said. "It's their job." George nodded at him and smiled.

"I told you already." Claire stood firm, seething. George understood, but he also needed to exclude her from the investigation. So he stayed silent, knowing she would crack before he did. It didn't take long. "Fine. I went to Telle's around ten, dropped the washing off, and came home. Then I went to bed. Happy?"

"And you, Mr Murray?" Wood asked.

"Claire helped me up to bed at nine," Kyle said. "I got up at five this morning, and Claire got up at seven."

"Then what?" George said.

"We spent the morning together until Claire left to see Chantelle. I believe you were there when she arrived?"

"Benjamin's not here," Claire said. "Check. Go ahead, but you can show yourself around."

DS Wood got up and smiled. "Go on, love," Kyle said and smiled. "You can check us off your list. I'd offer to show you 'round—"

"Thank you," Wood said with a shake of her head, "but it won't be necessary. I won't be long." Wood put her shoe covers and gloves on and disappeared from the living room.

"What was Chantelle like as a girl?" George asked.

"Difficult," Claire said, sipping her tea. "Our parents died when we were in our teens. Of course, they were elderly, and it was expected, but it hurts still, you know?"

George didn't. He had no idea whether his old man was alive or dead and didn't care either way. As for his mother, she'd recently moved back down to Leeds to be closer to Jack, but their relationship was still fractured.

"How did Chantelle react?"

"Telle wallowed in it. Started drinking, smoking, hanging around older boys, and blamed it all on the grief."

DS Wood returned to the living room, and George said, "Well, thank you both for your time."

* * *

"Claire and her husband seem genuine," Wood said as they walked to the car.

"Yeah, I agree. But Claire has a motive."

"You think she has something to do with it?"

"Claire's on Henry's side, and Chantelle probably knows that, so there will be friction between them."

"So you think she's taking it into her own hands?" Wood looked doubtful.

"I'm not sure, but if Claire genuinely thought Chantelle, or Mitchell, was involved, I don't think she would keep quiet."

"But Chantelle's saying she woke up and Benjamin was gone. And the neighbours would have noticed her leaving the house if she had anything to do with it."

"I'm just trying to think of all the scenarios, Isabella. She could have gone out the front door and walked through a different entrance."

"True," Wood admitted.

"Or she could even have got somebody else to abduct Benjamin. So just because she didn't take him doesn't mean she wasn't involved."

"So that leaves us with Mitchell Cook," Wood said. "He could have been the one who snatched him."

George nodded before checking his watch. They still had over an hour before the appeal started at 7 pm. "Yeah, let's go pay that little shit a visit."

Chapter Ten

"That's the one," Wood said and pointed to the mid-terraced house. The smell of salt and vinegar from the balled-up paper on the backseat made George's stomach rumble.

George pulled over and pointed to the old, battered Corsa. "How lucky. It looks like he's in."

An overweight woman opened the door in her fifties with a cigarette in her gob. She had red, straggly hair and a tanned complexion.

"Mrs Siobhan Cook?" George showed his warrant card and introduced himself and DS Wood.

"How can I help you?" she asked, peering at his ID.

George smiled. "We'd like to talk to Mitchell."

"He's not–"

"We know he's here," George said, cutting her off and jabbing a thumb at the Corsa. "Can we come in, or would he prefer to talk at the door?" George could see net curtains rustling all around.

"Yeah, you'd better come in," Siobhan huffed and shuffled down the hallway. "Mitchell, the police are here," she shouted as she entered the living room. "They want to talk to you."

George followed her in and saw Mitchell slumped on the

sofa. He had the same shade of hair as his mother, which was cropped close to the scalp.

He glared at George. "What do you want?"

"We've come to have a chat about Chantelle Coates." George plopped himself down in an armchair. "Are you happy with your mother sitting in, or would you prefer to do this alone?"

"Fuck off into the kitchen, Ma," Mitchell snapped. "They're not staying long."

Siobhan hovered nervously by the door to the kitchen, and Wood took a seat in the other armchair.

"As I'm sure you're aware, Chantelle's son is missing," George said.

"Yeah, and?" Mitchell stretched his arms behind his head, and George could see the stretch marks that indicated rapid muscle growth. He was a big guy and no doubt knew how to use his size. George was wary. "It's got nothing to do with me."

"You're Chantelle's boyfriend," Wood said, shaking her head in mock disgust, "so it has everything to do with you."

The two detectives agreed to play up on their suspect's relationship, hoping Mitchell would slip up.

"Boyfriend? Nah. Not me. Got the wrong guy."

"Let's not waste time, Mitchell. We know you're together," George said.

Mitchell sneered and shook his head. "We fucked for a while. Not any more. She was just a bit of fun."

"Until you were arrested for possession and intent to supply and told to stay away?" George offered.

"Not my drugs." Mitchell smirked. "Case got thrown out, so what does that tell you?"

That you're a slippery little shit.

"I'll tell you, shall I?" Mitchell scoffed. "That I was innocent."

"When was the last time you saw Chantelle?" Wood asked.

He shook his head. "Last week?"

"Last week?" Wood repeated. Mitchell nodded. "That's funny because we have witnesses who saw you at Chantelle's last night."

"Nah, not me. Guess Telle's shagging someone else. Someone who looks like me, yeah? It wouldn't surprise me." He leered at DS Wood, suddenly taking an interest.

"More than one person saw you, Mitchell," George explained. His blood was boiling, and his tone had sounded clipped. "Many people live on that street, and you'd be surprised by how many of them watch. We've been told who came and went and at what times."

Mitchell sat up and pulled a packet of cigarettes from his tracksuit bottoms. "Then you'll know I was only there for five minutes. I borrowed Telle a tenner. No crime in that."

George hated it when people got borrowed and lent mixed up but appreciated the lies Mitchell was spinning, hoping he'd eventually trap himself.

"Where did you go when you left Chantelle's?"

"Came back home." Mitchell lit the cigarette and blew out smoke rings. George had seen Chantelle do something similar. He wondered who taught who. "Ma, tell the detective where I was last night."

"He was with me all night. Here, in the living room. We watched a film together," Siobhan said. "I got up this morning at seven, but my boy didn't come down until one. all right?"

"And what film was that?" Wood asked.

"Can't remember. Something shit and boring that was on

the TV. Does it matter?" Mitchell continued to blow rings. "That all?"

"No." George felt his skin burning. "Describe your relationship with Benjamin?"

Mitchell blew out a plume of smoke. "What relationship? He's Telle's kid, not mine."

"But you were in a relationship with Chantelle at one point. Right?" George asked.

Mitchell's jaw clenched. "Right."

George couldn't imagine how anyone could leave a child in his care but asked him anyway. "Did you ever look after Benjamin?"

He shrugged. "Yeah, in the school holidays sometimes. It's not that 'ard."

Probably not if you're stoned and take no notice.

"Did you ever get angry with Benjamin?"

"No."

"Tell us about the time you put your last girlfriend in hospital."

Mitchell snickered and said, "Didn't lay a finger on that daft bitch. She dropped the charges because she made the whole thing up,"

"Then how did she get the injuries?" Wood asked.

"I don't fucking know. She probably did it to herself to get me in trouble? That bint was obsessed with me."

"Did Benjamin deliberately break his own wrist to get you in trouble?" George asked.

Mitchell glared at George with anger in his eyes. Then, with menace in his voice, he pointed at George and said, "I never laid a fucking finger on that kid!"

"My Mitchell is a good boy," Siobhan said. "He wouldn't

hurt anyone. He's been in trouble a few times, but that's what boys do."

"I've answered all your questions, so can you fuck off now?" Mitchell said.

"Sure, no problem," George said with a smile and stood. "But I'd appreciate a look around first." George put his shoe covers and gloves on.

Mitchell stood up off the sofa and stepped forward towards George. "You got a warrant?"

"Do I need one?" George challenged as he stepped forward. They were a similar height, but Mitchell had youth and muscle to his advantage.

"Every household we've questioned has allowed us to search, Mitchell," DS Wood said. "What are you hiding?"

Mitchell shrugged. "Nothing."

"So allow us to search," George said. "Or I could arrest you and search the house, anyway. It makes no difference to me."

"Piss off; you've got nothing on me." Mitchell stepped forward one more step.

"Try me." George held eye contact.

"Fine, look around, but you won't find anything."

"I hope I don't," George said as he left the room and headed up the stairs, Mitchell close at heel. He was uncomfortable having Mitchell so close to him in a confined space but figured Mitchell wouldn't want to give them any reason to arrest him.

George first noted the single towel hanging over the rail in the bathroom, as well as the bottles of shampoo lining the edge of the bathtub. Next, he looked at the various perfume bottles placed atop the sink. Finally, he closed the door and moved to the next room.

"That's my mother's bedroom," Mitchell said from behind.

"I don't think you'll find the kid in there," he sneered, "but you're welcome to look."

George ignored the remark and scanned the room. There was a sage-coloured duvet on the bed, which matched the curtains and the bathroom towel. The cream carpet was clean, and the furniture was neat and ordered. George opened the wardrobe to find it empty before stepping back and closing the door.

"And this is your room?" George asked as he opened the last door. The bed was made, and the carpet smelled as if it had been freshly hoovered. A TV and an Xbox sat on top of a chest of drawers. The room didn't look lived in. It was suspicious.

He turned to Mitchell, who smirked and said, "Seen enough?" He was sucking on a cigarette. Where was the ashtray in the room? There was no way Mitchell would sit and play video games without smoking.

"Yeah, I've seen enough," George said and turned to face him. "You don't seem very concerned that Benjamin is missing. Why is that?"

"Not my kid, is he?"

"But you were in a relationship with Chantelle and stayed friends. You've admitted to looking after Benjamin in the holidays. So you must've got to know the kid quite well."

"That's your reasoning, is it?" Mitchell scratched his head and whispered, "Look, I've been around Beeston and Holbeck with my mates to help look for Ben, so don't sit up there on your fucking high horse and lecture me, all right? I've done my bit, and now it's your turn. You should be looking for him and not wasting your time hassling me."

"We are looking, but we're looking at everyone connected to Benjamin. That's the only way we will find him." George nudged Mitchell out of the way and walked down the stairs. "You're the only one who has given us trouble," he said as he took a quick look in the kitchen. When he returned to the living room, Mitchell followed him and plonked himself on the sofa.

"That's it for now, Mitchell, but I expect we'll need to speak to you again."

George turned to leave, but Mitchell said, "Whatever, dick-head. Don't let the door hit you on the way out."

George turned to Wood as soon as they were outside and said, "He's not living there. He's either living with Chantelle or has his own place."

Chapter Eleven

While DI Beaumont and DS Wood were speaking with Mitchell Cook, Chantelle Coates was at home, thinking about her son. She hadn't moved from the sofa since DI Beaumont had left and was still huddled on the sofa with a blanket draped around her. Her body ached, and despite the weather outside, she was cold.

Cathy was making herself busy in the kitchen, sorting out Chantelle's mess of a food cupboard. Chantelle didn't like the woman and wished she would go away. Her anxiety was through the roof already, but having a stranger in her house, one that felt like she was watching her every move, was highly unsettling. She longed for a joint to calm her down. The day had seemed endless, and her stomach was hollow from the lack of food. She coughed up phlegm and swallowed it, her chest hurting from the chain-smoking. She wondered whether Mitchell had left some of his stash upstairs.

"Are you okay, hun?" Cathy asked as she placed a plate with a sandwich cut in half on the coffee table. Then she held out a steaming mug to Chantelle.

Chantelle took the mug and snuggled back into the sofa but didn't answer.

Cathy smiled. "We need to leave in an hour. Eat."

Chantelle looked at the plate and felt her stomach turn. "I'm not hungry. But thanks."

"You need your strength, hun," Cathy said. "It will make you feel better. Trust me."

Chantelle didn't trust Cathy but picked up a half and took a bite. It was tasteless, but she chewed slowly, forcing herself to swallow as she watched Cathy settle in an armchair. She hated how nice the stranger was pretending to be.

"I can't—I can't eat any more," Chantelle said, pushing the plate away. "I feel like I'm going to be sick."

"That'll be the nerves. Why don't you go relax in the bath?"

Chantelle felt a jolt of anger in her stomach. "What are you suggesting?"

"Nothing, hun," Cathy said with a smile, "but getting a bath might help you feel more relaxed. The appeal will be difficult, especially sitting in front of the cameras. I'll be there, and so will Claire, but freshening yourself up will help you feel better. It'll help you focus, too."

Chantelle stood, picked up her packet of cigs, and headed upstairs. She locked the bathroom door and checked the panelling, hoping to find Mitchell's stash. Bingo. She rolled a joint as the bath ran. As she stripped, the room soon filled with steam. Despite being hot outside, she still felt cold, so she quickly lowered herself into the hot water.

She inhaled deeply after lighting the joint and let her head rest against the back of the bath. Her muscles relaxed, and her stomach unclenched after a couple of drags. It was exactly what she needed. She touched the hot tap with her toe and winced from the pain, but her eyes were drawn to the water ripple caused by the tap's drip. The warmth spread through her body as Chantelle watched the ripples. She felt her eyelids droop, and then she was asleep.

Fragments of memories from this morning drifted across her mind. Where had Mitchell been, and why had he refused to tell her?

"Chantelle, you've been quite a long time in there. Are you okay?"

Chantelle snapped her eyes open as Cathy's voice woke her up. How long had she been asleep? "Yeah, sorry. I'll be out in a minute."

When Chantelle came downstairs dressed in a clean blouse and pair of jeans, Cathy was in the kitchen. She blow-dried her hair and ran a brush through it. She looked around at Cathy's handiwork, hardly recognising the place. The dogs lay sleeping on the kitchen floor, a fresh bowl of water in the corner.

"Do you need any shopping?" Cathy asked.

Chantelle shrugged. "I need some more cigs." She suddenly felt ravenous, so she opened the fridge and took out a bar of chocolate. The fridge barely had any food in it. "Are those two detectives going to be at the appeal?" She bit into the chocolate bar.

"DI Beaumont and DS Wood?" Chantelle nodded. "Yes, I expect they will be there."

Cathy was still talking, but her voice drifted away as Chantelle thought about the two detectives. She didn't like them or trust them at all. They were nosey and wanted to know every detail of her life. The chocolate suddenly lost its taste and felt thick and heavy in her mouth. She tried to swallow the melted chocolate, but it stuck in her throat, and she coughed abruptly.

"Are you okay, Chantelle?" Cathy said and stepped closer.

Chantelle nodded and gulped the dregs of the coffee Cathy had made earlier, forcing the chocolate down her throat. "Nothing tastes right," she said as tears stung her eyes, and she threw the rest of the bar in the bin.

"It's okay, hun." A knock came on the front door as Cathy put a reassuring hand on Chantelle's shoulder. "Looks like it's time for us to go. Have you got a jacket or a coat?"

"Yeah." Chantelle looked around the hallway, but her jacket wasn't in its usual place. She quickly looked around the living room and went upstairs to her bedroom. She shouted down, "I can't find it!"

"What does it look like?" Cathy shouted up and started searching the kitchen.

"It's a denim jacket with skulls on the back," Chantelle said. "You can't miss it."

Feeling frustrated, they looked all around the house but found nothing, so Chantelle pulled on a jumper before leaving the house.

* * *

The short journey to Elland Road station made Chantelle feel nauseous, and whilst she longed for it to end, she dreaded arriving at the police station. She peered out the window when they got near the stadium to quell the panic, but her eyes found the woods on top of the hill. Her heart hammered in her chest as the panic set in, and all Chantelle could think about was the opinions of everybody who would be there. She knew they were going to blame her for Benjamin's disappearance.

Cathy swivelled around in her seat as they entered the station car park and said, "all right, Telle?"

Chantelle shrugged but didn't answer and attempted to open the door as soon as the car stopped. It wouldn't open, and the panic descended once again. "I need to get out!" she said.

"Okay, hun. Give me a minute."

"No, Cathy," she screamed. "I need to get out. Now!"

The driver got out immediately and pulled open the door. Chantelle jumped out, panting, her entire body trembling and sweat dripping from her forehead. "I need a cig, Cathy. I can't go in just yet."

"That's all right, love," Cathy said, placing a reassuring hand on her elbow.

"Will there be many people at the appeal?" Chantelle asked, sucking on a cigarette. She looked around the car park and imagined a room full of people staring at her, the terrible mother who allowed her son to be abducted.

"Yes, but that's a good thing. It means more coverage for the case."

"Fine. Let's just get this over with." Chantelle chucked the cigarette on the floor and ground it into the concrete with her trainer.

Cathy Hoskins steered Chantelle through the corridors and into a room where she saw a familiar face. Relief flooded through her, and she threw her arms around her big sister. "Thank you for coming, sis."

"You couldn't keep me away from this, Telle," Claire said. "Are you sure you're up to this?"

She sobbed and said, "No, but for Benjamin's sake, I have to try."

The door opened, and a tall, broad man in a suit walked in. He was dark-haired and greying at the temples, with intense blue eyes. The air of authority he oozed made Chantelle feel uncomfortable. She pulled her arms tightly across her chest and looked down.

"Hello, Chantelle, I'm Detective Superintendent Smith," the man said, his voice deep and booming. He offered Chantelle his hand, which she shook lightly, and pulled up a chair. "We've set up a room for the press conference, and Juliette Thompson, our press liaison officer, has prepared a statement for you." He handed Chantelle a sheet of paper. "Take a look and see if there's anything you'd like to add."

Chantelle read the first chapter but couldn't read the rest as the words seemed to dance around the page. Focus, you silly bitch, she thought. Focus. No matter what she did, the words wouldn't sink in, so she gave up and handed it over to Claire.

"Read that. Tell me if it's okay," Chantelle said.

After reading, Claire said, "I think it's fine," and handed it back to her younger sister.

"Great." Smith nodded his head. "Do you have any questions before we go in?"

"Are there many people in there?" Chantelle stared at a tiny black spot on the floor.

"Yes, but the more coverage we get, the—"

"Will I be on my own?"

"No, Claire will be with you. And Henry. He has his own statement to read. I will answer any questions from the journalists, so don't worry about that. I could get Cathy—"

"No. Don't." Smith narrowed his brows. It wasn't unusual for families to distrust FLOs, but Cathy was the best they had. He'd never had a single complaint about her. Chantelle felt her stomach tighten. "You're sure I won't have to answer any questions?"

"Not if you don't want to."

"I don't."

"That's fine." Smith stood and gestured to a door. "After you."

"What, now?" Somehow, her stomach tightened more.

"Overthinking it makes it worse. It'll be over quickly."

They walked through the door and down a corridor, and Chantelle spotted Henry talking to the young male detective who had been at the house. The fit one. He patted Henry on the shoulder before turning away. Irritation crawled at her skin. Why was he receiving all the attention when it was she who had lost Benjamin?

Henry turned, noticed her, and then gave Chantelle a tired smile.

Chantelle turned her head away from him and looked down at the floor.

"How are you, Henry?" Claire asked.

"Holding up. Just. Are you two okay?" When she didn't answer, he said, "Telle?"

"How do you think I am?" Chantelle snapped, wishing Mitchell was here.

Smith made a beeline for the two of them and said, "You need to show a united front, so it would be good if you two sat next to each other."

"Not a problem," Henry said.

"Fine," Chantelle said. She could hear the commotion from behind the door and imagined the feeling of a thousand eyes upon her.

Smith got up suddenly and opened the door. The commotion stopped instantly, and Chantelle kept her eyes down as she walked inside. The loud clicks and blinding flashes of the cameras made Chantelle want to throw up, and she hesitated.

Claire and Henry took their seats, but Chantelle couldn't move. Sweat poured from her head and down into her eyes. It stung, and all she wanted to do was cry.

FLO Cathy Hoskins took her by the elbow and gently steered her towards her chair. She remained behind Chantelle with a reassuring hand on her shoulder. But it only made Chantelle more nervous, especially when she noticed the microphones in front of everyone.

Smith stood in the centre, and the noise in the room gradually died. He talked through the day's events and then announced that Chantelle would read a brief statement.

She looked down at the sheet of paper but was aware of the eyes boring into her. She opened her mouth, but no words came out. Her tongue felt heavy, and her mouth felt dry. It was as if her tongue was swollen, and she couldn't breathe. Claire took hold of her hand and squeezed. Chantelle took a deep breath that hurt her lungs and tried again.

"If—if you have Benjamin, then you need to give him back. He will be missing me, his mum." Her voice sounded unnatural inside her head, and she didn't like it. Why couldn't she do something as simple as this, especially for her child? Because she was pathetic, that's why. It's all Mitchell ever told her. Chantelle felt her heart pounding against her ribs, and blood pounded through her head. The people in the room looked hazy, and she felt nauseous again. Thoughts of waking up alone, with the front door wide open, and wondering where Mitchell was, filled her mind.

"Somebody knows what happened to my Bennie. And others watching may know something helpful and may not even realise it," Henry said, his voice cutting through Chantelle's thoughts. Her entire body was shaking, and it took all her might to turn and face Henry, who sat rigidly and stared into the camera as he spoke.

"We know Benjamin was playing football in Cross Flatts Park early on Sunday morning. Benjamin was distinctively dressed in his superhero pyjamas and red cape. Did you see Benjamin? Do you think you *might* have seen Benjamin? Please, please, please call the appeal line with anything that might just help us bring Benjamin home because he needs his mummy and daddy, and we both love him very, very much." Henry's voice broke.

"If you have seen Benjamin Davidson, please call the appeal hotline." Smith's words cascaded over Chantelle, and she felt Claire's arm around her shoulder. Then there was a sudden rise in noise as the press shouted questions, and the cameras' loud clicks and blinding flashes resumed.

Chantelle allowed herself to be steered out of the room, and a cup of coffee was placed in her hands as she was guided to a seat.

"That was great," Claire said. "That must have been difficult, so well done."

"No, it wasn't. I looked like a right idiot."

The door opened, and DI Beaumont and DC Scott walked in. "How do you feel after that, Chantelle?" George pulled out a chair and plopped down his arse.

She didn't want to tell them how she felt, so she lied. "I'm all right."

"It's tough doing an appeal, Chantelle, so you should be proud of yourself for what you achieved. And you got the message out, which is the most important thing. Lots of volunteers have turned up to help search Holbeck Park woods, and after they've watched the appeal, many more will be looking for him. Now, I need to be honest and tell you it's looking doubtful that he wandered across the main road and into the woods alone. If that were the case, we would've found him by now."

"So you're convinced somebody took him?" Chantelle said. Her mind wandered back to the fragmented memories of that morning. Where was Mitchell, and why was the front door open?

"We've spoken to Mitchell," George said. "He told us he was at your house last night. We just need you to confirm what time he left."

"Erm, around eleven." She caught the smile on DC Scott's face. *Oh shit,* she thought. *Did he tell them a different time?*

"Why didn't you tell us before that Mitchell was at your house last night? It would have saved us a lot of time," George asked.

"Because of the idiots who keep telling me he's not allowed to stay over. All anyone ever does is interfere in my life."

"Do you mean social services?" Jay said.

Chantelle felt the heat rise up her neck and into her cheeks. "It's not fair. They weren't Mitchell's drugs."

"You said you didn't leave the house until after eleven, but you were seen leaving your house this morning before then."

Chantelle looked away from George's intense gaze. He was wrong; she didn't wake up until after eleven. She remembered nothing from before then.

"Chantelle?"

"No, you're wrong. I woke up on the sofa after eleven."

"You were seen leaving around half past ten this morning wearing a denim jacket with skulls on the back. You have a denim jacket with skulls on the back, right?"

"I do, but I can't find it. Ask Cathy; she'll tell you!" Pain stabbed at her temples, and anxiety gnawed at her stomach. "Maybe someone came in and took it."

"The same person who left the front door wide open?" DC Scott asked.

"Exactly." Chantelle felt her throat constrict.

"You were seen leaving using your back door," George added.

"Then I don't know." She put her hands to her head and massaged her throbbing temples.

"Is this necessary, detectives? I think she's been through enough today," Claire said.

"We need to know who was in the house and whether they were still there when Benjamin went missing." George stood. "I'll let Cathy take you home now, Chantelle, but I need you to think hard about what happened last night and this morning. If we're to find Benjamin, you need to tell us everything."

With tears in her eyes, Chantelle nodded her head.

Chapter Twelve

"All the background checks have come back," Wood said, then yawned and leaned back in her chair. "All Henry's family, friends, and work colleagues. Nothing."

George turned to the incident board and looked at the list of suspects. "Josh, did you find anything on the neighbour, Andy Morris?"

"Nothing. He's a teacher who's never had a parking ticket."

DS Yolanda Williams walked into the Incident Room and plonked herself down on a chair.

"Good response to the appeal?" George asked.

"Yeah, just taking a quick break. The phone hasn't stopped ringing." Yolanda sipped from a steaming mug.

"Anything solid?"

"The usual stuff. Lots of sightings. You know what it's like. The public thinks they're being helpful when in fact, their false leads are obtrusive. We've had a few people say they saw a kid that looks like Benjamin in the Asda near the park. A few people say they saw him in the park on his own. One claimed that Chantelle was renting her caravan in Withernsea over the weekend. She even had a little boy with her."

"Bloody hell, Withernsea?" Jay laughed. "They think

they're helping, but all they do is obstruct us." His phone beeped, and he checked it. "Oh shit, sir! Do you know about this?"

"What?"

"Paige McGuiness up to her usual tricks. They have an article out already, but not the one DSU Smith asked for."

DS Wood pulled the article up on her computer, and George read it. "Fucking hell! It says here we have an unregistered sex offender living in Beeston."

DS Wood read the article—titled The Cross Flatts Snatcher. "Convicted paedophile and child snatcher Kevin Hancock was spotted this morning in the area where Benjamin Davidson was last seen just before his disappearance. The convicted child killer was recently released, taking on a new identity in Leeds to avoid detection. Local vigilantes have identified the criminal in an attempt to save Benjamin from harm. Should this dangerous man ever have been released? Should he have been allowed to change his name? Has he already abused another young child? Has he killed again?"

"How the bloody hell did we not know Kevin Hancock was out of prison and living in Beeston?"

DS Wood finished clacking away and said, "He's not registered in our area, nor has he approached us to register. Our records show since leaving prison; he was living in Lincolnshire."

"This means he's breached the terms of the Sex Offenders Register. Fucking hell!" George slammed his fist on the table. "Find me everything you can about this guy! How did McGuiness even get hold of this? Even we didn't know, and he's living in our area!"

"I've just called them, sir," Tashan said. "They won't let

me speak to Johnathan Duke or Paige McGuiness, nor will they reveal their source."

"Of course, they won't. Why would they? For fuck's sake!"

"They won't give me anything. Not without a warrant," Tashan added.

"Then get one. I know DSU Smith's at home now but call him. Get him to pull some strings and get one."

"Yes, sir."

DC Jason Scott waved him over.

"What, Jay?"

"Sir, I might have something. Following the article, Tashan and I have been digging into local vigilante groups."

"Okay?"

"We've monitored the usual channels, and Tashan delved into some places; it turns out we have quite an active community of paedophile hunters in the area, sir."

George raised his brows. "Right. Go on."

"It's simple. They hunt down paedophiles nationwide. But that's not all. Not only do they hunt those who have been convicted, but also those who they suspect are paedophiles. I've known some to be pretty violent, too."

"So they're thugs?"

Jason grimaced. "Some of them, sir, yes. For example, last year down in London, these paedophile hunters were involved in assaults on known and suspected paedophiles. The Met couldn't prove anything, and so charges were dropped. If you ask me, it sounds like they intimidate anyone they think is involved with that kind of thing, often coercing people to admit to things to stop the violence."

"How did they know Hancock had been released from prison?"

"I dunno, but from this, they've been working hard across the country to discover his new identity, as he doesn't go by 'Kevin Hancock' any more, for obvious reasons. It seems from this they found out about a week ago."

"So they've put two and two together?"

DC Scott shrugged. "Looks like it, but you usually get three or five when that happens. Thinking about the article, though, I reckon the paedophile hunters are the source."

"And they use violence, even without proof?"

"Yes, sir."

"That's what worries me," George muttered. He scratched his blond beard. "An article in the paper isn't enough for these people, right?"

"Right, sir. They're not done. That's what we think, anyway."

"Okay, Jay. I want you and Tashan on this. I want usernames, IP addresses, home addresses, phone numbers, whatever you can find. If Kevin Hancock abducted Benjamin and they've been tracking his whereabouts, they might be able to help us."

Yolanda lifted her head from the desk across from Jay's, a confused look on her face. "You want help from these paedophile hunters, sir?"

"We have a missing child, Yolanda, and a known child killer and paedophile on our streets. But unfortunately, we have no other leads yet. I hate it as much as you, but vigilantes or not, we need all the help we can get."

* * *

George sat in his office with the door closed; his insides chilled to the bone from the grim information he'd just read.

Kevin Hancock was a monster who preyed on the innocent. Over two decades ago, an eight-year-old girl had gone missing and was not seen alive again. Her name was Angelica Peyton. A picture of the young blonde, her large brown eyes boring holes in him from his computer screen, broke his heart.

She had been abducted whilst playing with a friend in a park in Scunthorpe. A vast search had been conducted, but she had vanished. What had happened only came to light after her body was discovered weeks later, poorly hidden on the grounds of the steelworks. She could have been saved, but a rookie detective ignored a tip phoned in after the TV appeal.

Forensics led back to Kevin Hancock, a monster who had suffered a disturbing childhood filled with sexual and physical abuse. Hancock was known to police in the area, having assaulted a girlfriend in his twenties, but was eliminated from the investigation because of a false alibi given by his neighbour. As a result, he wasn't on their radar as far as being a paedophile.

When Kevin's house had been eventually searched, they discovered a small, hidden hatch to a compartment under the house that Hancock had built himself. It was there that Angelica Peyton died of asphyxiation. During his trial, Hancock explained he'd answered the door to the police searching the neighbourhood for Angelica and left her inside the compartment with a gag in her mouth.

Due to the decomposition of Angelica's remains, they couldn't prove he had sexually violated her. That, along with the fact that Hancock maintained her death had been accidental—even dragging her family through the humiliation of an appeal to get his murder conviction downgraded to manslaughter based on diminished responsibility because of his abusive childhood—meant he didn't have to spend the entirety of his life behind bars.

Hancock's prison record was flawless, and after serving his complete sentence, they signed him off as fully rehabilitated. *So how on earth was he considered safe to be released?*

George slammed his fist on his desk.

How could anyone who had murdered a child ever be safe for release, never mind deserving to be released?

Yet, Hancock had served his punishment as set out by the law, and there was nothing any police officer could do now, not without good reason.

George abruptly stood and grabbed his jacket. He stormed out of his office and told his team, "I'm sick of sitting here with nothing to go on! It's time Luke was relieved. I'm going to head out to the park. After that, I'm going to see Hancock at his home."

* * *

Isabella Wood couldn't help but notice the tired look and anguish on the faces of the volunteers and the search team as they attempted to find DS Luke Mason. "I guess they were expecting to be in the pub by now, celebrating their achievement of finding Benjamin."

"Now they're probably wondering how safe their own children are," George said.

"Saw you on the news," George said. "It'll be good for you. Bet you'll be fighting the women off by next week."

"Fuck off," Luke yelled, a smile on his face. "I was just about to send the volunteers home. Unfortunately, it's too dark for them and," whispering, "they're more of a liability, anyway."

"Good idea," George said. "Dogs still out there?"

"Yeah, I'll wait until they come back before leaving. If it wasn't for us finding the boy's cape, I think everyone would've given up long ago. Honestly, I don't think he's here, though."

Luke's radio burst into life. He hit the receiver and held it to his ear. "DS Mason."

"You need to come and see this, DS Mason. The dogs have found something."

Luke pulled three torches out of a bag on the ground. George could feel the tension in the air. "You're going to need these. Come on, they're not that far, actually."

George felt his stomach knot as they walked along the track, the darkness descending on them every second. All George could think about was that the radio message didn't sound good. If they had found Benjamin alive, they would've told Luke and asked him to call for an ambulance.

Soon, up ahead, George glimpsed artificial light. Then, as they closed the distance, they could see a man standing with a torch, an English springer spaniel sitting at his heel.

"I'm Leon," the officer said. "It's not too far in, but there's a lot of exposed roots, so watch your footing."

Whilst George wanted to ask exactly what they had found, he didn't because he dreaded the answer. But, when he looked at Luke's and Wood's faces, he knew they stayed silent for the same reason.

"I left my team to finish uncovering the earth." Leon had a grim look on his face when he turned to face them. "We're still not sure yet."

They continued in silence. It wasn't a straightforward route, so George trailed his torch on the ground as branches snagged at his jacket and tree roots stubbed at his toes. Dress shoes weren't made for roaming around the woods at night. Finally, they came to a small clearing nearer to Holbeck than Beeston, and two officers could be seen kneeling on the ground, gently digging and brushing away earth.

"Anything, Si?" Leon asked.

"Just these." Si stood and held up an item of clothing.

George stepped forward and shined his torch on the item of clothing: a pyjama top with the letter S in the centre. It was covered in earth but was precisely as Chantelle had described. George explained, "That's what Benjamin was dressed in when he went missing."

He watched as the pyjama bottoms were pulled out together with a pair of absorbent overnight pants. Anger flashed through his veins as he turned to DS Wood.

"Get Lindsey and her SOCOs out here."

Isabella took out her phone and stepped away from the group.

Leon looked down into the hole. "Looks like it's only his clothing. Although, to be honest, when we found them, we thought the worst."

"I don't blame you," DS Mason said. Then, he turned to his boss. "George, I don't think we're looking for a missing child any more."

Leon coughed, and both detectives looked at him. "Mabel here is trained to detect the scent of—" Leon sighed, not finishing his sentence. Both detectives understood the gravity of his words. "If he's here, we'll find him, no matter how well hidden he is."

"Why take off Benjamin's clothes and bury them?" Wood asked once she was back. "Lindsey and her team are on their way."

"Let's bag up the clothes and seal off this part of the woods," George said and looked around the small clearing. "We might be able to get some footprints if not too many people have trampled this way."

Twenty minutes later, Lindsey Yardley and her team arrived, and soon the area was flooded with artificial light, and a tent was erected over the hole to preserve any evidence.

An hour ticked by, followed by a second close behind as George stood and watched the forensic team do their jobs. Now and again, the voice of Leon could be heard giving commands to the dogs. When this happened, George held his breath, expecting a shout that they had found a body, but none came.

"I don't understand," Wood said with a yawn. "The cape was found in the cemetery across a busy road Benjamin would never have dared to have crossed, and now we have a pile of clothes in the woods and nothing else. If Benjamin had been steered this way and then into Holbeck or towards Elland Road, the dogs would have locked on to his scent. It makes no sense. It's like they're leaving a trail."

"It seems exactly like a trail of breadcrumbs, actually," George said.

"Yeah, but leading us to what?" Wood asked.

"I feel like they're leading us away like this is a false trail."

Wood nodded. "Are we going to tell Chantelle about the pyjamas?"

George looked at his watch and shook his head. "Too late at this hour. It can wait."

The dog team returned, and Leon said, "I'm sorry, but they're not picking up anything."

"Start again at first light," George said as an image of the little boy flashed across his mind. Whoever had him was trying to lead them in the wrong direction. He was sure of it. *But, I'm not giving up on finding you, Benjamin—not yet.*

Chapter Thirteen

After watching a repeat of the appeal on the ITV News at Ten, Andy Morris looked across the living room at his children. They were good kids. His youngest, Archie, was watching a video on his tablet, whilst his eldest, Evie, was on her phone, texting her friends and making plans for after school the next day.

They hadn't spoken to him, or each other, for at least an hour. Interactions with his kids were often limited to grunts and groans, every question an intrusion as they fought to stay within their virtual worlds. He longed for the day they would answer a question with a complete sentence and without rolling their eyes towards the ceiling.

There were no issues at school, and they were above average academically. Both kids were polite and had strong friendships. Overall, the pupils and the staff liked the well-balanced individuals. But most importantly, they were healthy and safe, unlike poor Benjamin Davidson.

A phone pinged, and he looked at the two kids.

"Don't look at us like that, Dad. That was your phone for once," Evie said, grinning.

"Was it?" Andy was shocked. He'd never heard his phone ping like that before.

"Yeah, sounded like Facebook Messenger, Dad," Archie said.

Andy pulled a face. As a teacher, he was wary of Facebook and avoided it for obvious reasons, but he had signed up so his wife could tag him in pictures of the kids. He picked up his phone and looked at the message.

Andy Morris, we know about Ciara Adamson, and we'll tell everyone. We will send our information to your employers, the press, and the police. We also know where you live. I'm sure the police will be interested to know a paedophile is living next door to where Benjamin Davidson lived.

Andy inhaled sharply and sat upright, his head threatening to explode from his chest. His kids glanced at him, concerned expressions on their faces.

"You okay, Dad?" Archie asked, putting down his tablet. He eyed his dad, whose skin had turned sallow. It was unlike his dad to be shocked by anything.

"No, no. Everything's fine," Andy said, shaking his head. He sat back and reread the message, trying to keep calm and breathe steadily. He looked at the sender's name, his hands shaking. It had come from a Facebook group called West Yorkshire Predator Hunters. After looking at the page, Andy was sure it was a vigilante group focused on trapping paedophiles online. He'd heard all the stories about men getting arrested when they turned up to meet someone they thought was a child. The page was filled with images of them, men who found out that the person they had been grooming was, in fact, a group of vigilantes who were setting them up.

As Andy continued to scroll through the page with trembling fingers, his mouth dropped open when he saw a low-quality image of a man talking to a young lass. He didn't recognise the place, and he didn't remember the girl, but the man in the picture looked like him, though it wasn't one hundred per cent clear. Beneath the picture was his name, and a message that read:

This paedophile is a teacher from Leeds named Andy Morris. Address to follow. Please share this as often as possible, as we need to stop this predator from being anywhere near children.

Fear seeped through Andy's bones as icy fingers twisted his intestines and squeezed his stomach. The image was fake. It had to be. The more and more he looked at it, the more convinced he was that the man in the picture was somebody else. His heart was pounding, and his head was spinning. It was all a mistake. He replied, *You've got the wrong man; the picture on your Facebook page is not me. Take it off before I report you!*

"Are you sure you're okay, Dad?" Evie asked. Her face was contorted, and her eyes were wet. "What's wrong?"

Andy looked at her and tried to tell her he was fine, but no words came. Then he heard his wife's voice shouting from the kitchen. He was still shaking, unable to believe what was happening to him. They were going to tell lies to his employers and the police. Something like this could ruin him, even if it weren't true. He knew teachers in the past who had been accused of crimes like these and never recovered. He'd once said it himself; there's 'no smoke without fire.'

"Andy," Ella called again, "I need to speak to you in the kitchen." He looked at his phone and swallowed hard, wiping away a stray tear. "Andy?" she shouted. There was an edge to her voice, a nervousness, but he couldn't move. "Andy! Can you hear me?"

"Mum is shouting you, Dad," Evie said, waving her hand across her father's vacant stare.

When Andy continued to sit there, the door opened again, and Ella walked in. She'd tied up her long black hair in a ponytail. She was younger than him by a decade but was lean and fit from their shared workouts. Ella turned heads wherever she went, and Andy thought he had always been lucky that she had chosen him to marry. "Andy!" Ella growled at him through clenched teeth, her piercing, dark eyes looking right through him. "I've been shouting you. Didn't you hear me?"

Andy stared at her blankly. His brain was still frozen with fear, and the words wouldn't come.

"Oh, for fuck's sake, Andy. What the hell's your problem?" Her eyes were wide and condemning, and he could see the friction on her face. She was angry about something.

"Put a quid in the swear jar, Mum," Archie said with a laugh before looking up from his tablet.

A face like thunder met him, and immediately, Archie mumbled, "Sorry, Mum."

Andy stood up from his chair, pocketed his phone, and walked into the kitchen without a word.

The brief journey from the living room felt like it took an age. His legs were like lead, and he could hardly breathe. He was a fit man who worked out daily, yet he felt the way he had done before he met Ella and was twenty stone.

"Close the door, Andy," she commanded.

He closed his eyes and took a deep breath. It took every ounce of energy he had just to reach out his hand and push the door.

"I need you to explain this," she whispered, gesturing to her mobile.

His throat was dry, and his hands were still shaking. "Explain what?" he eventually said.

"I've had a message come through Facebook," she said. "It wasn't a very nice message."

The icy fingers gripping his innards were back, and Andy felt sick. He already knew who the message was from. "What does it say?" he stuttered.

She read it:

Mrs Morris, we have reason to believe your husband is a predator of the worst kind. A child abuser and paedophile. Andy had a relationship with a minor called Ciara Adamson, who came to us after realising your husband had groomed her. We understand you have children together, and Andy works as a teacher. That man shouldn't be allowed anywhere near children. We have shared our information with his employers, the press, and the police. Still, We intend to publicise this information, especially considering you live close to where Benjamin Davidson went missing.

The words bit deep, and every word was a dagger to the heart. Bile threatened to rise up his throat. It was from the same people who had messaged him. Ella watched him for his reaction, her eyes boring into him. He knew what she saw, a shaking man, sweating, unable to speak. He looked guilty. He felt guilty. But he did not know Ciara Adamson.

"Andy?"

"Yeah?" he whispered.

"Why aren't you denying this?" Ella said, her voice strained. She looked into his eyes, and his bottom lip quivered. "This is a hoax, right? Or someone's idea of a sick joke?" Andy looked down at the floor, unable to say anything. "Andy, I need you to tell me this isn't true. Who the hell are these people?"

"I don't know who they are."

"Do you know a girl called Ciara Adamson?" She thought about the missing Benjamin Davidson and how Andy was bisexual but had a preference for women. That, however, didn't make it any easier for her. During past relationships, she'd been jealous of other women, but during her time with Andy, she also had to be wary of Andy checking out other guys whilst they were in the gym. Tears filled her eyes whilst she desperately waited for her husband to deny everything. Yet Andy did nothing. "I need to hear the words from you, Andy. Make me believe all of this is a lie."

Ella's words were interrupted by Archie bounding in through the door. His eyes were wide, his mouth open. He was holding his tablet.

"Dad," he said, an edge of panic in his voice. "Have you seen Facebook? Someone has posted some nasty shit about you."

"No. Facebook? What do you mean?" Andy stammered. "Nasty shit?"

"They're saying you're a paedophile, Dad."

Why had they done this to him? Andy couldn't believe what was happening. He was innocent.

"Block the page immediately," Ella said through clenched teeth.

"I can't," Archie said, shaking his head.

"Of course, you can. Do it now before I take your tablet away from you."

"Mum," Archie said. "It's been posted on the school's Facebook page."

Andy and Ella exchanged glances. There were no words to describe what was happening to them. The school page was highly active, and most parents used it to ask for help or discuss school policy. Ella grabbed the tablet from her son's hands and checked the post. There were over two hundred comments already, and that count increased each second she looked at it. "Andy?" Ella pleaded. "You need to explain what the fuck is going on. Now!"

"I can't," was all he could manage.

"You must be able to—"

"I fucking can't, all right?" he said, his voice raised. He clenched his fists and suddenly slammed them down on the table. "I wish I could!"

Archie's phone beeped twice in quick succession. He looked at the screen and then at his dad before it beeped again. "Is this a joke, Dad?" he asked, astounded. "It's my friends. They're asking me what the post is all about. What do I tell them?" Andy wanted to curl up and die. "Dad?"

"Sorry, son. Ignore them for now. Don't tell them anything," Andy said. He needed to speak to the school and quickly.

"Andy," Ella pleaded. She grabbed his chin and forced his eyes on hers. "For God's sake, will you please answer me?"

He shrugged.

"Andy, do you know that girl?"

"Which girl?"

"Ciara Adamson."

"I don't think so, but I've taught thousands of girls over the years."

"So now you think she was a student?" Ella asked, shaking her head. "Convenient that you can't remember."

"I'm a victim here, Ella. I'm just assuming she was a student, all right. And anyway, it's a lie. All of it. I'd never touch a student, let alone have a relationship with one, so her name is irrelevant."

The kitchen door crashed open again, and Evie appeared, tears streaming down her face. It was apparent she knew. "It's not true, right, Dad?"

Andy said nothing, and Ella lost her patience. "Just fucking say something, Andy!"

"What else do you want me to say?" Three pairs of questioning eyes stared at him. These were the people he loved most in the entire world, yet they looked at him as if he were a monster. How could a random Facebook group fuck everything up? He was innocent. He was sure of it. "I told you I don't know this girl, and I've told you I'd never do anything to a fucking child. What more do you want?"

"I want to know why somebody would do this," Ella said.

"It's obviously just a mistake."

"Then we need to call the police, Andy," Ella said, breathing deeply and pulling herself together. "You need to call them before too much damage is done."

"It's too late for that. The damage is already done. There's no smoke without fire, remember?"

"You sound guilty," Ella said.

"Well, I'm not."

"So call the fucking police."

"Here, Dad," Archie said, holding out the landline. "Mum's right. Call them before people start to believe it."

"Yeah, Dad," Evie said. "The comments are supportive of you so far. They don't believe a word of it."

Ella saw her husband change at the pleading of their two children, and a great sense of relief flooded over her. Andy's eyes focused, and his jaw tightened. Then, finally, he stood up, puffed out his chest, and took his mobile from his pocket. "Everything those dickheads have written is lies. You're right, all three of you. I need to nip this in the bud right now!"

He scrolled through his contacts until he found the number

he wanted, which rang a few times before being answered. "Nichola, it's Andy," he said before listening to her for a moment. "Yes, it's all nonsense, which is why I'm calling. As a page admin, you can remove it. I need it taken down, and that ridiculous group blocked from the school page. Can you do it now?" He listened to Nichola again and nodded. "Thanks, love, I appreciate it. I can't believe the cheek of some people." Andy paused again as he let her speak. "As soon as I hang up, I'll be calling them. See you tomorrow."

He ended the call and looked at his family. "That post is nonsense. It's all lies. Nichola will remove it now, but I want you to promise me you won't engage with your friends about it. Meanwhile, I will talk to the police and see what they can do. Those fuckers could have ruined my career."

Despite the terrible shock, he wrested back some control of the situation. It's what he needed to continue doing because his career was definitely on the line. Everything he had in life was now at risk. He smiled reassuringly at his wife, who didn't return it. She was worried, as she had every right to be. It was his job now to assure her he was innocent. Whilst Ella watched him, he dialled 119, the old number for the NHS track & trace, and said hello. He paused for effect before providing his address and phone number, pacing up and down the kitchen, talking loudly and clearly, as he explained the events of the evening to a disconnected line.

Chapter Fourteen

Tired from the day's events, DS Isabella Wood rested her eyes whilst George drove the short distance to Kevin Hancock's property. He had DC Tashan Blackburn on speaker, who provided George with everything he needed to know about Kevin Hancock, down from his abusive childhood to the grim details of Angelica Peyton's autopsy.

"Thanks, Tashan. Anything else I need to know?"

"Jay found a Facebook group before he left, sir. It's called the West Yorkshire Predator Hunters. I've gained access and have already pulled a list of group members. Josh is running them against the database before Elaine takes over for the night shift."

"Elaine? Brilliant." DS Elaine Brewer had been seconded to a different team to gain experience because of her desire to become an FLO. "DSU Smith said he was putting all hands on deck. Could you send the list to DS Wood's phone?"

"Of course, sir, but remember, there are almost a thousand members."

"A thousand?" DS Wood added.

"Christ. That's a lot of vigilantes," George said. "Thanks, Tashan. Send that list over."

Soon, George pulled up by the kerb on a street lined with the small back-to-back, red-bricked terraces typical of Beeston.

They got out of the car and scanned the long street. Dewsbury Road lay behind them, traffic thundering up and down, despite the late hour. George breathed through his mouth to mask the smell of exhaust fumes, piles of rubbish bags, and overflowing black wheelie bins.

"Here, George," Wood said, pointing to a house beyond a broken gate. Behind the gate was a tiny garden lined with broken flagstones and a tangle of weeds. Two figures loitered, looking busy on their phones, away from the bustling main road, to the detectives' right. It was deserted otherwise. He stared at them, and they seemed out of place.

Wood noticed the two figures and said, "That's not at all suspicious, is it?"

George smiled and entered the garden. He'd thought the same.

The downstairs windows revealed stained net curtains, but it was too dark to see within. Upstairs, one window was broken. Not a single light was on, and there was no movement behind the blackened curtains.

He peered through the letterbox, seeing open doors, stairs covered in a threadbare brown carpet, and a basket of unopened mail. Then, finally, George banged on the door, his police knock echoing through the rooms of the house.

"Place looks deserted. Guess he isn't home," George said, stepping back to look through the letterbox again. "Kevin Hancock. Open up!"

"You think he's done a runner?"

"Looks like it." He tapped his foot, considering their next move before realising they didn't have any. Not without a warrant. As much as he desperately wanted to batter down the door and charge in, they had no probable cause and no evidence. They hadn't even known Hancock was living in the area until a couple of hours ago. And despite coincidence, the law stated he was innocent until proven guilty, no matter what had happened in the past.

"George?" Wood whispered.

The way she said his name piqued George's attention immediately. "What's up?"

"The two suspicious people are heading back this way."

"Let's talk to them, shall we?"

Wood smiled. They exited the garden together to find the couple standing by the Honda, looking inside. Upon seeing the detectives, the man stopped what he was doing, whilst the woman glanced in any direction as long as it wasn't towards them.

They looked suspicious, and they were acting suspiciously. George's instincts told him they were people of interest. Darkness had fallen, yet both wore summer clothes—he, stone-coloured combat shorts and a black tee, her a yellow floral sun dress and black sandals—and a guilty look on their faces. They didn't seem lost, yet they were hovering awkwardly. So what the hell were they doing there?

"Good evening," George said pleasantly, stepping into the light. He recognised them immediately as Mr and Mrs Pickering, Chantelle Coates' neighbours. "What are you two doing here?"

He did not miss how their eyes flicked over his shoulder towards Hancock's property. "It's a free country, is it not, Detective?" Mrs Pickering said with a smile that did not reach her crow's feet.

"Whilst you're right," George said, his eyes narrowed, "I just wondered what you were doing, as you don't live around here. So tell me why you're here."

"I thought that would have been obvious, Inspector Beaumont," Mr Pickering said.

"Enlighten me."

"We're part of the Neighbourhood Watch," Mrs Pickering stated, a defiant edge to her words.

"I see. Isn't this area a bit far away? It's Thora and Maurice, right?"

"Right," Thora said and looked at him with barely concealed venom. Where was this loathing in her eyes earlier? The couple he'd met this afternoon was completely different now.

DS Wood had her phone in her hand and nodded her head for him to come and have a look. They were members of the West Yorkshire Predator Hunters group.

"I understand now. Thank you, DS Wood." He turned to the couple. "You're Predator Hunters." George's voice was clipped, his stare hard.

With eyes filled with defiance, Thora Pickering said, "So what if we are? It's not a crime."

"Being part of a group isn't, but taking the law into your own hands is. Let's pretend for a moment that I don't know why you're here. Be clear and tell me."

Thora's mouth thinned. She didn't like the challenge. "We're watching that monster!" Thora pointed towards Hancock's door. "We're making sure he doesn't hurt anybody else."

"Kevin Hancock?"

"Yes," she spat, her mouth a hideous snarl.

"That man served his full punishment set out by the letter

of the law and is, therefore, Mrs Pickering, a free man. As such, he is innocent until proven guilty. Do you understand?" George hated saying the words with every fibre of his being, but as police officers, they didn't discriminate. "Your surveillance needs to stop. That's our job, not yours. Don't try to take the law into your own hands."

"I can't believe you're defending a guilty man," Mr Pickering said, his hands balled up into fists. George raised his brows and stood up straight. It was enough to stop the man, to remind him who he was speaking to.

When he spoke again, all the fight was gone, though his voice held an edge of annoyance. "You're here, aren't you, Inspector Beaumont? So you suspect him too?" Maurice was clearly referring to the missing Benjamin Davidson.

"As I'm sure you already know, I can't comment on individuals or any ongoing investigation."

"Because he's guilty."

Irritation flared within George, and he ground his teeth. "We will pursue any and all lines of enquiry, especially when an individual is at risk." He glared at them with fury in his eyes.

"How can you protect a predator like that?" Thora cut in.

"It's our job to protect everyone. We don't discriminate," Wood explained, her voice firm. "As DI Beaumont said, our law states people are innocent until proven guilty."

Thora sneered. "He was already proven guilty."

"You're right, but he served his sentence, Mrs Pickering. He is innocent of any further wrongdoing until proven guilty, and that is final," George said.

Thora jabbed a sausage finger at them. "That's exactly what's wrong with this stupid country! We exist because we don't trust you or the law to protect us, especially not our children or our loved ones. We protect people from monsters and make sure they face justice when you don't."

"That's enough!" George snapped. He understood what they were all about, even if he disagreed. "Look," he said, his voice hard and steady. "Benjamin Davidson is missing, and it's critical we find him. We're wasting time here, and I don't want to waste more time by arresting you for harassment. You have no proof Hancock is guilty, so I'm asking you to leave before I do more than just have a conversation with you."

Thora stiffened at the threat like a spring, ready to pounce.

DS Wood stepped forward as Maurice put a hand on his wife's shoulder. "Benjamin Davidson is missing. You know him, and so you know how vulnerable he is." Her voice was pleading, urgent. "We need to find him, so instead of taking matters into your own hands, tell us everything you know to help us. Trust us to bring Benjamin home. Please."

Thora said nothing, but her husband stepped forward. "We've been monitoring this address since last night. Not us personally, but the—"

"The Predator Hunters," George said.

"Yes. He's not been home once in that time."

George shared a knowing glance with Wood, who nodded. If what the Pickerings were saying was true, then Benjamin Davidson couldn't possibly be inside that house.

"Anything else?" Wood asked. Maurice Pickering shook his head. "Thank you." She gave Maurice her card and said, "Contact us if you think of anything else. Trust us to bring that little boy home, all right?"

"Now leave this place," said George, "and don't come back. That's a warning, and you only get one."

He waited as they turned and stalked away, slowly at first

and then more quickly, with Thora giving them a single backward glance, her eyes still seething.

"Well, that was a bit shit, wasn't it?" he said to Wood. "Though I suppose we now know for sure the Predator Hunters know all about Kevin Hancock. And they're watching him."

"Problem is, George, is I think they're hunting him." She pointed towards the broken window.

"Yeah, I agree, but I can't help but think they genuinely were concerned for Benjamin's welfare. Who knows, they could provide information that helps to find him," George said.

"I know what you mean, but if Hancock hasn't been to his house for the last twenty-four hours, then there's little chance of Benjamin being in that flat."

"True, but I'm still going to ask for a warrant so we can search the place."

"I don't think we can trust them." Wood sighed as they headed towards the car.

"You're right, Wood," George said, firing up the engine. "The problem is, asked? anyone."

George returned to the station to drop DS Wood off and rang Tashan.

"Everything okay, sir?" Tashan's voice echoed from the speaker as George drove up Dewsbury Road and turned right down Old Lane.

"Is Elaine in yet?"

"She is, sir."

"Good. Ask her to do surveillance on Kevin Hancock's place. Get her to take a constable with her, will you?" He gave Kevin Hancock's address to his DC. "The Predator Hunters were there already, but we must find him first." He couldn't think about the threat Hancock faced if the vigilantes uncovered him before the police did. "I want her to watch the house. If Hancock comes home, bring him in. If he doesn't, get her to monitor who does. I've warned them off, but I'm not sure they'll listen."

"Yes, sir."

"Any other updates, by the way?"

"No, sir. It's like he's disappeared."

Innocent men rarely disappeared. George's heart sank. "all right. Thanks, Tashan."

"Bye, sir."

George drove past the stadium with Wood and thought about Hancock. Leeds was a big city with many shadows to hide in. The entire day had been a nightmare, and he'd treated every person he had met or spoken to with suspicion, scrutinising their every action. Yet despite that, they were still no closer to finding the boy than they were this morning. And now it was worse. Not only did they have to find a missing boy, but they had to try to protect a convicted child killer from the public. How many Hunters were in the city, living ordinary lives, watching, and waiting? How many marks did they have on their lists? As far as he was concerned, people were innocent until proven guilty, and even though he may not like it, it was his job to protect those people. They needed to protect Hancock from the vigilantes that sought him because if they had found Kevin before they did, they might never find young Benjamin alive.

Chapter Fifteen

Andy pretended to end his conversation with the imaginary police officer and took a deep breath. Next, he went to the fridge and took out an ice-cold can of lager, placing the icy tin against his forehead. But, unfortunately, it did nothing to soothe the growing headache that pounded continuously, and he closed his eyes, wishing that he suddenly awoke to find this had all been a nightmare. But, unfortunately, what he had experienced during the last half an hour was worse than any nightmare he'd ever had. The vigilante group had terrified him despite being innocent. They'd almost convinced his family that he'd done something wrong, and he'd certainly felt guilty, despite knowing otherwise.

"What did the police say?" Ella asked, making him jump.

Andy wanted to open the can and guzzle the contents, but it was a school night, so he placed the lager back in the fridge. It gave him an extra minute to get the story straight in his head. But instead, he saw her swipe away an article and a couple of friends' messages on her phone, blushing when she noticed he'd seen her. She'd been searching for more posts about it, and clearly, she'd been discussing it with her friends despite him asking her not to.

Nosey bitches, he thought. It was none of their fucking business. Not really. He had a couple of messages pop up, too, full of fake concern yet wanting to know the details, but he'd immediately swiped them away.

"What did you say, love?"

"What did the police say?" Ella asked, her eyes cold.

"They said the group hadn't committed a criminal offence, and Facebook has to deal with it. So we should all report the group and the posts." Andy shrugged and looked down at the floor. "They said they would look into it after that, but to speak with Facebook first because they didn't think there was much they could do."

"That's bullshit," Ella snapped.

"What?"

"It's a criminal offence, Andy. They're telling lies about you, so it's defamation. I think we need to take legal advice tomorrow. I've been researching on my phone. How dare those bastards make that kind of shit up! They'll wish they never fucked with the Morris family." Andy noticed Ella had poured herself a glass of wine. She emptied the rest with a long swig and filled it up again.

"It's only a Facebook group," Andy said with a shrug. "I doubt those posts will cause enough damage for it to harm my professional reputation. As I've told you, report it and have done with it."

"We have. All of us have. Some of my friends have, too," Ella said, a grin on her face. But unfortunately, she was slurring her words.

"They won't have any evidence to back up their claims because it never happened, so the page will get shut down."

"It better because if you're lying to me... I warned you

last time what I'd do if you cheated on me again," Ella said, swaying.

Andy thought about Chantelle next door and winced. They had an arrangement, one that Ella could never find out about.

"I told you I was sorry about that, and you said you wouldn't use it in fights any more," Andy said, his tone hard and challenging. "I need you to trust me and your support right now."

"I'm sorry."

"Thank you. And so am I, for the record," Andy said. "This isn't easy on you or the kids. I realise that now. But this isn't my fault."

"I just can't believe they think they can make stuff up like that and get away with it," Ella said, gulping down more wine. "You're a teacher, for Christ's sake. This could ruin you. I just don't understand the mentality of someone doing that without evidence." She realised it sounded suspicious, but she was past caring.

"Well, the post on the school page has been removed, and the rest have been reported," Andy said. "That should be it."

"I hope so," Ella said, opening another bottle. She saw Andy watching her from the corner of her eye. *Was that a look of disapproval in his eyes? How fucking dare he judge me after what I've just had to go through?*

"Something to say?" she asked angrily, filling her glass.

"Nope," Andy answered, shrugging. They would end up arguing all night; it was the last thing he needed.

"No, go on. Tell me." Silence. "If ever I needed a glass of wine, then it's right now."

"Aha," Andy said, turning to walk through the door. "I'm putting Netflix on. You coming?"

"You what? Some dickhead accuses you of being a paedophile online and all you want to do is watch Netflix?"

"What else can I do, Ella?" he asked, shrugging. He felt sick to the stomach with worry, but he wasn't going to share that with Ella. He was innocent. That's how the law worked. All he could do was react to each situation as it came, and dwelling on what a group of dickhead strangers might do next was pointless. "If any damage has been done, then it's been done already. We've done what we can. I can't change anything. I'll explain to work in the morning."

"I wish I were as calm as you," she said. Andy's ability to not be rattled easily was one trait she loved about him. He was her rock when her world was shaken to the core, which it invariably was. "Just tell me this will all blow over, Andy."

"It will, Ella," he said, nodding. "I promise." He quickly kissed her, then added, "They've got the wrong man. Maybe there's another man out there named Andy Morris. Or maybe they got his name wrong entirely." He shrugged. There wasn't much else he could do other than reassure his wife he had done nothing wrong. The problem was, he kept going back to the image he'd seen online. It looked like him. Did the bar start to look familiar, or was he reading too much into it?

Andy plonked himself down on the sofa, and Ella followed, kissing him on the cheek and apologising. "I'm sorry, babe. I guess I overreacted. It was a shock."

It was an understatement, but he kept that thought in his mind. "I understand," was all he said.

"Thank you."

"My body's still shaking," Andy said.

"My hands haven't stopped shaking since I read that message." He grabbed her hand and squeezed.

That night, it seemed like an age before Andy Morris finally slept, and when he did, his dreams were dark and twisted. Images of him standing filming Chantelle and Mitchell whilst they had sex interlaced with memories of him playing football with Archie. Except Archie kept contorting, turning into Benjamin Davidson.

His sheets were damp with sweat when he awoke. It was dark, and the shadows seemed to crowd in on him. People watched and waited for the shadows, hunters who would be out to get him. The sheets were damp with sweat as he rolled over to switch on the bedside lamp. The spot next to him was empty—Ella hadn't come to bed, which she often didn't after too much wine. But tonight, the fact she hadn't come to bed seemed to have more significance.

Chapter Sixteen

The office was silent when George arrived at Elland Road the following day. He made a strong cup of coffee and sat in his office, a pile of statements taken from Chantelle's friends and neighbours and social services reports. George had taken the report home that detailed Mitchell's drug arrest last night and had stayed up until his eyes stung, but nothing stood out. George did the same that morning, draining two large mugs of coffee before he needed the toilet. After relieving himself, he walked into the Incident Room and looked at the incident board.

They had nothing so far. Nothing at all. He suspected that it all came back to Chantelle and Mitchell, but as George ran his hands through his blond hair, he concentrated on coming up with a plausible scenario. It didn't fit. Nothing did. His gut was telling him he'd missed something. But what? Chantelle had woken up to find Benjamin gone and the front door open.

Benjamin had been playing football with Archie Morris when he went missing. *Did Archie know more than he'd let on?* Also, his father, Andy Morris, was suspicious. George understood curiosity and was no stranger to people watching what he was doing, but Andy's gaze was intense. *What was he hiding?*

George's thoughts were interrupted by DS Luke Mason, who

shouted through, "You're in early, George!"

George smiled as he saw Luke plonk himself down at his desk.

"Aye, I slept very little last night. How are you?"

"Same. Hate to say it, son, but you look like shit."

George smiled. "Likewise," he said as his phone rang. Samantha Fields, the office manager's name, flashed on the screen.

"Morning Sam," George said, surprised she called him on his mobile.

"Kevin Hancock is here to see you. I've put him in an interview room."

"What? Seriously?" George looked around. Other than DS Mason, DC Blackburn was the only other detective in the office.

"Yes, sir. He's afraid, says people are after him."

It's the damn vigilantes, he thought. There wasn't much he could do without witnessing the harassment himself, but he needed them to stop. A boy was missing, and they were getting in the way. George exhaled slowly. "I'm on my way." He turned to Tashan. "Come on, DC Blackburn. It's time you got some experience in an interview room."

* * *

Kevin Hancock struggled to settle in the interview room, the cold, hard chair digging into his back. George entered and sat opposite the broken man, the fear evident in his eyes. Fear or guilt, George couldn't decide.

The difference between the mugshots and what sat opposite him was stark. Whilst Hancock was still recognisable, he was thin, and his hair had thinned, his scalp visible through the greasy, black strands. His skin, which had paled to grey, hung from his bones, as did his clothes. Wrinkles lined his face, and his hunched posture only exacerbated Hancock's frailty. He sported a black left eye which looked angry and purple. The right side of Hancock's face was worse. A nasty scar ran from his forehead down to his chin, the result of a sharpened spoon and a fucked off convict. They hated paedophiles in prison, and Hancock had lost his right eye because of it.

George introduced them all for the tape and asked Hancock how he received his black eye. George thought he already knew how but wanted to hear the answer.

Hancock set his jaw and said nothing, eyeing George and Tashan darkly, his beady eye flicking from detective to detective rapidly.

"Mr Hancock," George said, leaning forward in his chair, his elbows on the table, "can you tell me where you were yesterday morning between 9 am and 12 noon?"

"Out."

"Out where?" Tashan asked.

Kevin stared at the young detective. "Holbeck."

"Doing what in Holbeck?" Tashan probed, taking notes.

"I—I. Why do you want to know?"

"Why do you think?" Tashan smiled, his pen ready.

"Look, I don't want to drag anyone else into this. Does it matter who I was with?"

"So, you were with someone yesterday?" George cocked his head.

Hancock gave a nervous smile. "Yes. Look, I know what you think I've done. I've heard about the boy. But I didn't do it."

"What didn't you do, Mr Hancock?" Tashan stared through him.

"That boy. Benjamin whatever. I've seen the news article. I didn't take him."

"Then you need to prove that to us, Mr Hancock. Understand it from our point of view," George said. "If it is a coincidence, then it's unfortunate—you were in the wrong place at the wrong time. But, Mr Hancock, if you took that little boy, you need to make this right and return him. Don't let this be like last time. Like Angelica Peyton."

Kevin's eyes darted away as George spoke her name. Sweat began dripping through his long, greasy strands.

"I'll ask you again, Mr Hancock," George said. "Who were you with yesterday morning? Yesterday was Sunday. Think."

Hancock remained silent, his shoulders hunched and his eye downcast.

"We have a warrant and will search your property shortly. I'm sure I don't need to tell you what that means," George said.

Hancock shrugged. "You won't find anything."

"I hope we don't." George sipped his water before giving Hancock an icy stare.

"Look, I just don't want anyone else getting in trouble," Kevin muttered, yawning.

"If you're innocent, which you say you are, then nobody will get into trouble," Tashan explained. "So tell us."

"I was with a friend—Kylie West. She lives in Morley. Look, there's probably CCTV footage of me getting on the bus. I got on the 200 towards Cleckheaton but got off in Morley. It showed up around quarter to twelve." He chewed his lip. "Got into Morley about quarter past twelve. Check."

Tashan scribbled down the details. Even if they got proof Hancock was on that bus; it wouldn't be enough to prove he didn't take Benjamin.

"Tell us about Kylie." George raised his brow.

Kevin looked away and hesitated. "We're friends. I'm allowed friends, right?"

"Friends?" Tashan asked, looking up. He'd detected the hesitation too.

"Yes. Friends. It's not really any of your business, is it?"

"I suppose it's not unless you're breaking the law," George said. "Are you breaking the law?"

Hancock glared at him and clenched his jaw as he said, "No. Look, I did my time." The glare highlighted Hancock's scar. It amazed him how in prison, criminals had standards. There was no love lost for paedophiles and child killers. "I've done nothing illegal since."

"You did your time, yes," George agreed, though he felt the prison sentence would never be long enough to compensate for the lives Hancock had ruined. The law was not his to make, though he could use it to his advantage to pressure Hancock. "When did you move to Beeston?"

"A couple of months ago."

"You're on the Sex Offenders Register. Why didn't you register your move with us? That's illegal." Yolanda had done more searches on Hancock, and as there wasn't an alert for Hancock, George figured Kevin had missed none of the regular appointments required by the terms of his inclusion on the register. Not yet, anyway.

Hancock cowered before him at the use of the word 'illegal'. "The whole point of coming to Leeds was to give me a fresh start."

George stared blankly at Hancock, inviting him to provide more information.

"I've not missed an appointment." Kevin said nothing else that might damn him further.

George moved on. "But you made friends? You met Kylie?" Kevin nodded. "Why did you go to Kylie's on Sunday?"

Hancock blushed and hesitated once again. "Look, we're involved. Is that all right?"

George raised an eyebrow. "It's not for me to say. Not unless she's underage?" Hancock shook his head, but the fear still lingered in his eye. "So again, where were you yesterday morning, between nine and noon?"

"I just told you," Hancock spat.

"No," George said. "You told us where you were between quarter to twelve and quarter past one. Tell us where you were between nine and quarter to twelve."

Hancock shrugged.

"We need to know so we can eliminate you from our enquiries, Mr Hancock," Tashan said.

Defiant, Hancock folded his arms tightly to his chest and said nothing. It was like getting blood from a stone.

"We'll come back to that then, shall we? When did the Predator Hunters first make contact?"

At the mention of the vigilantes, Hancock went from fierce defiance to fearful in an instant. "Four days ago," he whispered. His eye darted around the room.

"Are you scared of them, Hancock?" George asked, but Hancock said nothing. "That's a hell of a shiner." So instead, he pointed towards the black eye Hancock sported with a grin. "How'd you get it?"

It was difficult to tell whether Kevin's bruised eye widened because of the swelling. "You've no idea what they're capable of. If you knew, you'd be as scared as I am. How do you think I got this?" He jabbed a thumb towards his scar.

"Why don't you tell us?"

Hancock whimpered. "It was one of them. A paedophile hunter. He told me as much before he took my eye. He got out before I did; he told me I needed to watch my back on the outside."

"And they found you four days ago?" Kevin Hancock nodded. "How? You changed your name, right?"

Kevin shrugged. "Right, but I don't know how they found me. I was out, minding my own business, and somebody smacked me in the face, saying that's for—for Angelica." He shuddered at the use of her name. His voice dropped to a mumble. "I knew then that my identity was out. When I got home, someone had thrown a brick through my window. There was a card with a picture of a sword, and a scale taped to the brick. Like the thing on top of the courthouse down south."

George knew the Greek goddess Themis, who personified divine law and presided over the Old Bailey.

"Did anybody witness the assault, Mr Hancock?" Tashan asked.

"No, but that's when I knew the Hunters had found me." George watched as the blood left the man's already pale skin.

"The sword and scale is their logo, sir," DC Blackburn murmured.

"I did my time, yet I'm still paying for it."

"Let's go back to Kylie for a moment," George said. "She's a new friend of yours. Have you shared information about your past with her?"

Kevin opened his mouth but stopped short. He frowned, understanding where George was going with his question. "No.

She doesn't know who I was."

"Because you didn't tell her?" Tashan asked.

"That's right."

"Just because you didn't tell her doesn't mean she doesn't recognise you. You were all over the news."

Hancock shook his head. "No, she would have been too young to have remembered."

Hancock closed his eye and bit his nails. His face had turned beetroot red. George and Tashan shared a knowing smile. Hancock had just messed up. How old was Kylie?

They asked him as much, but he declined to answer. The interview was turning stale, and Hancock wasn't much help. George didn't think he had anything to do with Benjamin's disappearance, but he had to admit it was too much of a coincidence that Hancock was in the area.

"I have done nothing wrong," Kevin mumbled. "I'm only here because it's not safe for me outside. You need to stop them." He took a deep breath, then pleaded. "Please?"

"Unless you put in a formal statement, there isn't much we can do at the moment to stop them," said George, leaning back in his chair and folding his arms. It was true. And with no witnesses, they wouldn't be able to prove anything.

A knock on the door came, followed by a muffled, "Sir?"

George stood and walked to the door, opening it just a crack. "Yeah?"

DC Jason Scott stood outside. "We have some new info regarding Benjamin Davidson's case, sir," he said, passing George a note.

George scanned it and shook his head. "Is this real?"

"Yes, sir. The call was taken yesterday evening, but the DC didn't report it until just now—she's only just made the connection."

"Fucking hell," George said under his breath. "Thank you, Jay." George clenched his jaw as he skulked back to the table and stood there, arms folded. He said nothing for a moment, just staring at Hancock's single, beady eye. "It seems you haven't been telling us the truth, Mr Hancock. Show him a picture of Benjamin Davidson, please, DC Blackburn."

Tashan picked up a blue folder from the floor and pulled out a photo. He slid it towards Hancock onto the desk, and Benjamin's bright, youthful face stared up at them.

George was watching Kevin for his reaction. There wasn't one. "Do you recognise this boy, Mr Hancock?"

"Yes, but only from the appeal," the man said too quickly.

He wasn't wrong. It was the exact image they'd used last night. "For the benefit of the tape, DC Blackburn is showing Mr Hancock a photograph of Benjamin Davidson."

"We have information from two unconnected sources which state they saw a man matching your exact description around Cross Flatts park at the time of Benjamin's disappearance. Can you explain that to us, Mr Hancock?"

"I don't know," he shrugged and retorted. "Whoever it is, it's not me. I told you, there's CCTV of me on the bus—"

"Over an hour later!" George growled.

Hancock shrugged once more.

"Benjamin Davidson went missing between ten and eleven in the morning. I don't give a damn where you were an hour later unless it's connected to the investigation. You have repeatedly stated your innocence, and now it's time you give us proof because all I have at the minute is your word, the word of a registered sex offender and convicted criminal," George spat. "Stop messing about and tell us the truth!"

"You don't have any evidence I was at the park yesterday morning."

"Don't we?"

"I know you don't because I wasn't there. I didn't kidnap that boy!" spat Kevin, suddenly raging. He stood up and met George's glare with a similar ferocity. "I'm only here because I thought you would protect me. Those vigilantes are trying to set me up, and it's your job to protect me from them, not go along with their lies!"

George shook his head. "It's you who is lying, Kevin. You've given me nothing to believe you weren't involved in the kidnapping of Benjamin Davidson. You nearly got away with it last time, but that won't happen again. Angelica died because you were too cowardly to confess. You destroyed her life, as you destroyed her family's lives." George stood up and met Kevin's defiant glare. "Where is Benjamin Davidson?"

Kevin sat down, shook his head, and smirked. "No comment."

* * *

Hancock had said nothing else for the entire interview and had given no clues; absolutely nothing at all. George shook with fury. "Fucking hell!" he roared at the open window. He sank into his office chair, his solace away from the crushing pressure of the case.

Despite it being the early hours of Monday, it was light, and sirens wailed across the city, carried on the warm, stifling breeze. It had already reached twenty-seven degrees, and George felt his shirt sticking to his body. Nevertheless, George breathed deeply and reminded himself that there was hope, bringing him back to himself, prompting him that he had a job to do and that people were counting on him not to crumble. Still, the abyss threatened to overwhelm him, and George knew the pressure would crush him if he succumbed to those depths.

He took another few deep breaths and afforded himself a few more minutes of calm; then, he continued looking through the statements his team had taken. Getting stuck into his work made him realise he could only control himself and not how Hancock responded or even what the man had done in the past. It reaffirmed his resolve, his promise that he would do everything within his power and just hoped it would be enough to find Benjamin. It had to be enough, or else he'd never be able to live with it all. George couldn't let this case be added to the unsolved pile, the ones that left families destroyed whilst the criminals walked away.

George fixed the image of Benjamin Davidson in his mind—those hazel eyes staring at him with all the intelligent purity of childhood—and promised him silently that he would do everything possible to find him before it was too late.

In their bustling Incident Room, George glanced at the burgeoning Board, the image of Benjamin, his hazel eyes staring out pleadingly. At the same time, information and queries wove around it like a web. Kevin Hancock's mugshot showed the man with hate in his eyes, his lips curled in contempt, and he looked every inch the paedophile and child killer he'd been convicted as. Next to Benjamin, it was a stark contrast, one that turned his stomach. Another picture had been added to the board; one George was confused about.

He turned to his team and pointed to the picture.

"Got some new intel," DC Tashan Blackburn said. George

furrowed his brow but said nothing, allowing the young DC to continue. "Last night, Andrew Morris, Chantelle Coates' neighbour, was accused of having a relationship with a minor by the same group who has been harassing Kevin Hancock. So there's a lot of chatter on the Facebook page about Benjamin."

"Get Uniform to bring him in," George said as he looked out the window, surprised to see that the weather had changed. He hoped the rain pouring down wasn't a sign.

Chapter Seventeen

The rain was pouring down when Andy left the house that morning. Ella and the kids were still asleep, and the traffic was light as he drove to school. Andy was anxious, despite it being a journey he had made five days a week for the last thirteen years. He knew he was driving towards a hostile environment where he would have to defend against the accusations. But, in truth, he wasn't too worried about his colleagues. Instead, it was the parents that concerned him the most. Rightfully, they wanted the best for their cherubs, which often meant not listening to facts.

Andy parked his car up in his spot, grabbed his laptop and a canvas bag filled with books he'd marked on Saturday, and exited into the deluge. He followed the bright lights which lit up the school, aware that despite the early hour, most of his colleagues were already in their classrooms, setting up for their lessons or marking.

Inside, Andy was delighted to see that the reception desk was empty. He made his way towards the staff room for much-needed caffeine, where he bumped into an elderly female colleague named Mrs Dempsey. She apologised for not looking for where she was going, but when they met eyes, Andy saw the look of mistrust and uncertainty there. He smiled, but she didn't return it. Andy had known the woman for over a decade, yet he was gutted it seemed she believed a rogue Facebook group over his immaculate reputation. But then, he'd seen the eyes of his family members and understood suspicion was only natural. She mumbled a "Hello," then rushed off as quick as a flash.

Next, Andy bumped into the caretaker, who was mopping up dirty water from the floor. The staff had walked the water in with them, crowding into the staff room. Andy hesitated, unsure whether he could take a brushoff from Neil.

"Morning, Neil," Andy said, looking up.

"Morning, Mr Morris. Terrible weather for June."

"Aye, absolutely shocking."

"Wish your colleagues would wipe their feet on their way in like you do, sir," Neil said. "Then again, give it an hour, and this place will be like a swimming pool. The kids will slip all over the place. Better get the mats out."

"Good idea. You know what the parents are like."

"Aye," Neil agreed. "I'll let you go, Mr Morris. Have a good day, yeah?"

Andy smiled. There was no difference in Neil's manner, although the chances of Neil being online were zero, which meant he probably wasn't aware of any accusations yet.

Once more, Andy hesitated outside the staffroom, his fingers on the door handle for a second. The sound of conversation drifted through the cracks in the old door, and his nerves were on edge as he entered.

Four of his colleagues sat on a sofa around a coffee table, sipping hot drinks. They would undoubtedly have seen the post last night, so there was no point in avoiding them. "Morning," he said. Their gazes bored through him, searching for any signs of guilt. They wouldn't find any. He wouldn't let them.

"Morning," the three female teachers replied in unison. They said nothing else and continued to sip their hot drinks.

The silence was deafening, and the tension was palpable. Andy felt sick and nearly jumped out of his skin when he felt a firm hand on his shoulder.

"My God, Andy, you look like utter shite!" Arthur Clarke said, cutting through the silence. He was a maths teacher and had been at the school since it opened. He wore a three-piece suit and a colourful tie every day, his salt and pepper beard showing evidence of his breakfast—toast with jam.

Andy sighed. "Thanks, mate. I got hardly any sleep last night."

"I saw the post before it was removed," Arthur said. "It's typical of today's society is that. Fancy posting without getting all the facts. They could have ruined your career."

"Yeah, well, it might yet still," Andy said, looking around the staff room. A couple of teachers had entered before immediately leaving when they saw him. Unfortunately, loyalty doesn't exist in today's society. He told Arthur as much.

"Yeah, well," Arthur said, lowering his voice, "it's fucking bullshit. How people are allowed to make ridiculous accusations like that is beyond me. And on a school page, too?"

"I blame Facebook," Andy replied. And the stupid virgin who sat there and made up lies about me, he thought, but he didn't say that to Arthur. Instead, he sat down and put his laptop on the seat. Despite his friend's efforts, the atmosphere was tense. "My name will be cleared soon, anyway. They're an online vigilante group with incorrect information."

"I hope you've reported them to the coppers," Arthur said, frowning.

"Yes," Andy lied. Being at work was more difficult than he had thought it would be. "They're going to speak to Facebook to get the group shut down," he lied.

"Is that it?" Arthur said, shaking his head. "If I were you, mate, I'd press charges. They need to find out who wrote it and put them away!"

"I'm hoping it will all blow over once people realise it's a mistake."

"Do you want me to make you a coffee while you tell us all about it?" Arthur asked.

"Please, mate, though there's not much to tell."

"How's Ella?" a history teacher called Cheryl asked. This was her first year at the school, and Andy didn't think they had exchanged more than a hello, or goodbye since she had arrived. Yet, there she was, asking about his wife, and using her first name, too. *She clearly wanted the gossip first-hand, the two-faced bitch.* He wanted to tell her to do one, but then he knew that alienating people wasn't the best idea. Andy needed as many people as he could on his side.

"She's a bit shaken up, but otherwise, she's fine, thanks," he replied. He smiled, but she didn't return it. Instead, she looked straight through him.

"It must have been a terrible shock for her," Cheryl commented.

"You're right, it was. But, to be honest, it was a bit of a shock to all of us," Andy said.

"So, what happened?" Arthur asked, sitting down next to Andy and giving him a cup of coffee. Unlike Cheryl, there wasn't a hint of suspicion in his voice, and he looked at Andy with sympathy. There's no smoke without fire. Andy knew that. He didn't realise that the deputy head, Charlotte Gleeson, was standing outside, unsure how to handle what she had to do next.

"Andy," the deputy head said, popping her head around the door and smiling. Her perfectly straight eyebrows dominated her round face. She was a good-looking woman, but the worry on her face was evident, and she was blinking at a hundred miles an hour. Also, her usually tanned skin was grey, and the smile she gave him lacked genuine warmth.

"Morning, Charlotte," Andy said, greeting her with a smile. But, this time, it wasn't returned, despite his father telling him a smile would disarm all but the most difficult people.

"I'd seen your car outside and was hoping to catch you early." Andy felt his stomach knot. "Can I have a word with you in my office?" She paused and gestured to the cup. "Bring your drink with you."

Andy stood up and looked at Arthur, who shared his look of concern. Cheryl raised her brow. Andy picked up his bag and laptop, leaving the coffee behind, and no one said a word as he left the room. Andy thought this wasn't going as well as he would have liked as he followed the deputy head to her office. They didn't speak until they were inside and the door was closed. You could cut the atmosphere with a knife.

"I'm assuming you saw the allegations posted on Facebook last night?" Andy said, without sitting down, taking the initiative.

"I didn't see the post personally." Clearly uncomfortable with the situation, the deputy head frowned and cleared her throat. She rarely avoided conflict, unlike the head, who had some aggressive teachers walking all over him. "But I've been made aware of them." She gestured for him to take a seat. "It's awful."

"Yes, it's awful and completely unfounded."

The deputy head didn't answer; the silence was deafening.

"Whilst I appreciate this is hard for you, Andy," she began, "it's also terrible business for the school and—"

"Look, Charlotte," Andy interrupted, "it's nonsense. A vigilante group has got the wrong information and targeted the wrong man. That's all."

"Of course it is, Andy," Charlotte said. "How're Ella and the kids?"

"The accusations have crushed them."

"Of course."

"It's probably the worst thing a man can be accused of, especially one who is a teacher," Andy said, sighing. "My reputation is the only thing keeping me going." Andy shrugged. "My reputation is flawless, as you know, Charlotte."

The deputy head nodded.

"You have no idea what it was like last night. Why they chose me, I'll never know."

"People are shocked, Andy," Charlotte said.

"Not as shocked as I am. They have no right to judge."

"It's probably because of your position."

"Well, that's no excuse."

"Of course, it is. You know what they don't."

"What do you mean?" Andy asked, confused.

"Only you know whether the allegations are true." Charlotte took a deep breath. It was clear the conversation was uncomfortable for her, too. "Your family, your colleagues, and the parents don't."

Fucking hell. He knew Charlotte Gleeson wasn't one to mince words, but those cut straight to the point. Andy snapped, shaking his head erratically. "I gave this school over a decade of service to be treated like this. That's not on. Anyone could post anything about anyone on that page. It doesn't mean it's true."

"Whilst I agree with you when accusations are made, investigations must follow."

Andy should have been expecting it, but he wasn't. *There's no smoke without fire.* He felt sick. He knew it wasn't for the school to prove he was lying; it was for him to prove he was innocent. So what was he thinking, showing up at school this morning? There was no way they'd let him be surrounded by kids daily. The slightest suspicion of wrongdoing had to be investigated.

"I trust you understand, Andy?" Charlotte asked.

He nodded. Charlotte was saying teachers, parents, members of the school board, and the governors had all spoken with her about their concerns. He couldn't blame them, not really. But, on the other hand, he knew he was lucky the police hadn't made contact yet.

"I've also had the police call me this morning because they have received the same information, Andy." Charlotte looked concerned. "They will be, of course, investigating the allegations." There was a long silence, and Andy felt frozen in his chair, unable to breathe. "Have you spoken to them?"

Andy shook his head, unable to form the words to answer.

"Do you know the girl they're accusing you of having a relationship with?" Charlotte asked. Andy shook his head again. "You're sure?"

"Yes, I'm sure!" Andy snapped. How could this be happening to him? How could people listen to a group of strangers rather than a man they had known and trusted for years? He took a deep breath and rested an elbow on Charlotte's desk. "How long have you known me, Charlotte?" Charlotte shifted uncomfortably in her chair. "My reputation is immaculate."

"I'm aware, Andy. Because of that, I checked the list of students who studied here during your service, and it seems they weren't a student, which is good." She attempted to smile, but Andy grimaced at her. "Look, I want to believe it's all lies, Andy. As you say, we've known each other a long time, but after Adam William Harris, we have to be more careful."

Adam Harris was the serial killer the press dubbed the Miss Murderer. He was a teacher with a fetish for blonde female teachers who'd worked at the school.

"But my opinion matters not, especially to the board or the governors, Andy." She turned and looked him in the eye. "I have a responsibility to the parents and pupils of this school. You know that." Andy sensed what was coming next. "Until this mess is cleared up, I need you to take some leave."

"Are you suspending me?"

She shook her head. "No, what we're offering you is paid leave while these allegations are disproved." Charlotte smiled again. "This should prove to you we're on your side. If we weren't, we would have suspended you. However, I'm sure you understand that we cannot take the risk even if we believe in your innocence. It's the best way forward, Andy. Go see the police and clear your name."

Andy nodded, seeing sense in Charlotte's words. The board had backed her into a corner, and she was right—they could have suspended him. But instead, he saw the leave as what it was—removal from the school until proven innocent. Charlotte said as much when she said, "If this is a baseless, malicious attack on an innocent man, then it shouldn't take you long to disprove it. Right?"

"But if you suspend me, everyone will think I'm guilty," Andy said.

"You're on paid leave, not a suspension," Charlotte said. Her voice was calm and composed. "I have no choice, Andy, and to be frank, neither do you. So sorting this out shouldn't take more than a few days, right? You'll be back in no time whatsoever."

"But even paid leave will make people think I'm guilty."

Charlotte shrugged. "Go to the police, Andy, before they come to you," Charlotte urged. "Sort this out so we can put it behind us, and you can get back to what you do best."

"If only it were that simple?"

"What do you mean?" A look of concern spread across her face.

"If you make me leave this building, whether, on paid leave or suspension, the label as a paedophile is fixed." His eyes were filled with tears now. "It doesn't matter how or when I prove my innocence because there's no smoke without fire. So please don't suspend me."

"It's paid leave."

"Bullshit. And everyone will know it's bullshit. They'll know I'm being suspended."

"I don't have any choice, Andy. Neither do you. I had to work hard to get the governors to agree to paid leave."

"Please, Charlotte, I've been here for over a decade. Has there ever been the slightest sign that a child was in danger? No—"

A knock on the door interrupted Andy's words. Charlotte opened the door to see Mrs Baron, the receptionist, standing in the corridor, flanked by two uniformed police officers. The male was tall and thin, whilst the female was short and stocky.

"The police are here, Mrs Gleeson," Mrs Baron said, shaking.

"Thank you, Mrs Baron," she said, nodding to the police officers. "How can I help you?"

"We're here to speak to Andy Morris," the tall, thin male said. "Is he with you?"

Andy heard his name, turned to see the two officers, and his heart hammered, his breath coming in quick gasps. The police had come into the school to talk to him—the nightmare scenario becoming a hundred times worse. There was no way out of this now, no way to save his reputation.

"Yes, yes, he is. Come in." She opened the door and ushered them in. Mrs Baron looked stunned. "Thank you, Mrs Baron. Go back to reception, please. I'll manage this," she said, closing the door.

"Why have you come into school to talk to me?" Andy asked, trying to remain calm. "These allegations are outrageous. I do not know a Ciara Adamson and never have!"

"Mr Morris," the female officer said, shaking her head, "I don't know anything about Ciara Adamson." She paused as she looked at the confused teacher. "I'm here to arrest you on suspicion of kidnapping Benjamin Davidson. You do not have to say anything. But, it may harm your defence if you do not mention when questioned, something which you later rely on in court. Anything you do say may be given in evidence."

Chapter Eighteen

In the Incident Room, DS Williams' notes were neatly lettered on the board, with some in DS Wood's slanting hand too. George refreshed his memory, reading the leads on Kevin—his alibi already queried on the board, and the reported sightings to verify by CCTV, some still waiting for an answer. George knew they would all likely turn out to be dead ends.

He forced down the spike of growing frustration. This ought to have been an open and shut case. Would they have to do the same to Kevin Hancock when he had been caught last time? Would they have to build a case against him, only to find the body by sheer luck more than skill? Would that be the only way to link him to the crime?

George took a deep breath and focused his thoughts. *No, we won't, not on my watch.*

George had already tasked DC Blackburn straight out of the interview with following up on the CCTV from the bus company. It wouldn't exonerate Hancock, but it would mean they could verify where he got on the bus. Perhaps it would show if Hancock had been anywhere plausible to hide Benjamin or dump his body as he had with Angelica Peyton all those years ago in those cold, dreary, and lonely woods.

"Uniform has just called to say Andy Morris is in custody and on his way here," DS Wood said, interrupting George's thoughts.

"Great news. I knew there was something odd about his behaviour," George explained. "Yet he wasn't giving off any vibes. It's strange."

"Yeah, I know what you mean. I have an update for you if you have a minute," Wood said. George nodded.

"Dr Yardley and her team got some good footprints from the site where we found the clothes. They eliminated ours and the search teams, which leaves a size eleven trainer and a size four boot. Dr Yardley should be here in a moment."

"They must have been working all night."

"Yeah, well, I told them we needed something," Luke said, appearing from behind the pair, mugs of coffee in his hands. "Practically begged them to find something."

The door swung open, and a rather dishevelled-looking Lindsey Yardley walked in. George wasn't used to seeing her in such a state.

"I'm afraid I've got very little for you, George."

George smiled. "I'll be happy with anything you've got."

"This print is a size eleven, with a well-worn tread. A popular brand, probably worn by half of Leeds." Lindsey handed a photo to George.

"We've taken images of a few partials as well, but that's the best one. Interestingly, the cast we took is deeper at the front." She handed over another photo with measurements on it.

"Looking for a guy with a limp, maybe?" Luke said, leaving his desk to come peer at the photograph.

"Yeah, or he's wearing shoes that were too big," George suggested.

"Could be either," Lindsey said, "but that's your job to work out."

"And the other footprints?"

"Looks like a ladies' chunky heeled boot, size four, well-worn tread. I'd guess an ankle boot, but we'll check out the make and style. I'll let you know when we find out."

"So, it looks like one male, one female," George said. "The male shoe is too big to be Benjamin's. I'll speak to Cathy and see what size Chantelle is."

As they discussed the prints, the rest of his team filtered in.

"What about Benjamin's pyjamas?" George asked. "Did you get anything from them?"

"We're testing for DNA. We expect to find the child's and the mother's, probably Claire's too, but hopefully, there will be something to work with. There're no visible bloodstains."

"Well, that's good news," George said.

"Do we think he's still alive?" DC Scott asked.

Luke shook his head. "It doesn't seem likely."

George looked at his mentor and frowned. Whilst he was probably right, George didn't want to give up hope. "Let's not give up hope yet. There may be some other reason the clothes were removed and buried."

"What, like illegal adoption?" Tashan said.

George nodded. "Exactly. If someone offers to pay enough money, they can get a child to order." He looked around the team, who all looked doubtful. "Look, it's a better alternative than Luke's and one we must consider. Anything else?"

"Plenty, sir," Yolanda said. "The ANPR footage of Henry's car leaving Hull matches the exact hour and minute Henry provided both Saturday night and Sunday morning. So there's no way of him getting from Hull to Leeds and avoiding every camera."

George nodded. "Just to be safe, speak to the DVLA and get the details of all vehicles Henry could have had access to. That's close friends and family. Work colleagues. The lot. Let's be thorough. Then cross reference those plates against ANPR footage. If you need help, Tashan is at your service. all right?"

"Thanks, sir. DS Fry has been working away all night. We're cross-checking the members of the Hunters' group on Facebook with the dark web forum members Josh found. He says it's slow going, trying to match up usernames, IP addresses and stuff, but he feels there may be something there to help us pin Hancock for this."

"Right, okay. Keep me informed, yeah?" George said.

"I sent Josh your interview transcript, and he's been able to cross-reference the information Hancock gave you with information on the forums. It looks like the Predator Hunters have been after him."

"Go on."

"The perpetrators aren't shy in admitting the responsibility of giving Hancock his black eye. Two others have replied to the thread congratulating the person and have boasted of putting Hancock's windows through."

"Can Josh track them?"

"No, sir. He's tried. They're using VPNs, which disguise your IP address when you use the internet, making its location invisible to everyone, including us. Josh is contacting the VPN companies as we speak."

"Good." George meant it. The Hunters could smell blood in the water. "I'm not sure how they're connected to Benjamin's disappearance—whether it's a coincidence, whether they can help us, or whether they're just getting in the way, but we need to identify as many of the Hunters as we can. Especially because they seem to have identified Andy Morris as a person of interest, too. It could be either. Or it could even be neither. Are they working together? Who knows?"

"We're on it, sir."

"Any update on Chantelle's accounts?"

"Going by her financial records, she seems to have some financial difficulties. Her credit rating is poor, and she is on an IVA but is making payments on all her accounts every month, and there are no large or unusual transactions that we've found in her accounts. I don't think there's anything there."

"Right, that's good then. And her mobile?"

"Chantelle's been making a lot of calls and texts to Mitchell since Benjamin disappeared, but it looks as if he is ignoring her. That strikes me as unusual, sir because before Benjamin vanished, they were in regular contact."

"That is unusual. Monitor their mobiles and let me know if you find anything else suspicious. Anything else for me?"

"Yes, sir, the community is back out in force, looking for Benjamin, and so are we. Uniform is still up in the area, mainly door-to-door in the Noster and the Parkfield areas, looking for witnesses and whether anyone saw anything suspicious. I'm collating the statements as they come in, but we've already done hundreds of houses, and there's—there's nothing."

George could hear the edge of despair in Yolanda's voice. "You're doing a great job, Yolanda; keep it up." He squeezed her shoulder, then turned to Lindsey Yardley, who, luckily, was still in the office. "What did you find at Hancock's?" he asked.

"A filthy hovel." George snorted. "The place hadn't been cleaned or cared for. I don't think he'd ever used the stove or oven, more an instant noodle and microwave meal kinda guy."

George flinched. That struck a little close to home; he was an 'instant noodle and microwave kinda guy' right now, despite living there for nearly a year. It was sad because he enjoyed cooking.

"Hancock's a big drinker, too—found a stack of beer cans that could have built The Great Pyramid of Giza," Lindsey continued. "The living room was messy, with only a dirty sofa, a small TV, and an old laptop, which we've seized. There was nothing untoward in the bathroom though we took water samples and swabs in case any matter was passed down the drains. We used luminol but got nothing. Now, the bedroom—" Lindsey shuddered "—Well, let's put it this way, made the rest of his house look like a model home. Christ, I can still smell it." She closed her eyes and pinched her nose before taking a deep breath as though to steel herself. "There was plenty of DNA in the bed, mostly semen. We took samples from each room and dusted them for prints. The usual. It'll be enough to confirm Kevin Hancock lived there, but that's likely it, to be honest. It wasn't a nice place, George."

George nodded, attempting to put a sympathetic look on his face, and said, "So you didn't find anything of Benjamin?"

Lindsey shook her head. "You'd have been the first to know if we had. There was nothing obvious, but perhaps the DNA will turn something up. No possessions belong to Benjamin, and he's certainly not there. We turned the place upside down, and believe me—we didn't leave a stone unturned. I'm sorry, if there were something to find, we would have found it. The laptop is probably your best bet of finding out what Hancock's been up to, but I don't think he took Benjamin there."

George's shoulders sank. He had come to a similar conclusion, especially after speaking with the Pickerings. However, he'd still hoped that Benjamin would be inside that flat and that, unlike Angelica Peyton, they would have found the child in time this time. Alive.

"I'm sorry." Lindsey sounded genuine—and she was. Probably not for George, but for the little boy's life that was at stake.

"Anything else from the park or the woods?" George checked his watch and stood tall. There was no time to mope; it hadn't even been a full twenty-four hours since he vanished, and whilst there was no trace of Benjamin, and he knew time was running out, George wouldn't give up hope just yet.

"Sorry, nothing," Lindsey said. "It's bad enough that we're searching parks and woodland, to be honest. It makes it difficult as the local search party had trashed everything we could have hoped to find by the time we got there."

"Well, let me know what the laptop turns up and anything else you find."

Lindsey smiled and left the office.

"Anyway, Andrew Morris is being brought in," George said. "I think it's time we brought this lot in." He pointed to the list of names on the board.

"All of them?" DS Yolanda Williams asked. "Including Henry?"

"Yeah, one of them knows what happened to Benjamin if not all of them. He didn't walk out of that park on his own. If they don't cooperate, arrest them. DS Wood, organise a search warrant as I want a thorough search of every property." He thought back to the prints Lindsey was still holding. "I want their clothes and shoes, as well as any laptops, computers, and phones."

"You think Henry would sell his own son?" Tashan asked.

George shrugged. "He doesn't want Benjamin brought up by Chantelle, and if he thought he wouldn't get custody, then maybe he would rather see him brought up by somebody else. Also, according to Claire, Chantelle has no interest in Benjamin and is struggling for money. So that's enough motive for her to sell her son, too. And Mitchell Cook, well, I don't want to imagine what he's capable of."

George let out a breath; he could feel the tension building in his head which was already throbbing from lack of sleep. It was going to be another long day, and he still hadn't seen Jack.

"Okay, let's get to it," Wood said.

"Good. First up, DS Wood and I are going to interview Andy Morris. Once we've done that, we're going to see Claire. I'm sure she was holding back on us yesterday. As soon as the warrants are signed, Luke, please pick them up. Yolanda, can you call Cathy and tell her to bring in Chantelle. Ask her to find out Chantelle's shoe size, too."

"Thanks, boss; I'm sure the magistrate will love being dragged from his breakfast," Luke said with a grin.

"It's what you're best at," George replied, mirroring Luke's grin as he walked into his office.

"Are you okay?" DS Wood entered George's office behind him.

"Yeah, why?" George turned to look at her.

"Well, I don't think I've ever seen you so wound up."

"I just keep seeing that picture of Benjamin, and he reminds me of Jack. He's got his whole life ahead of him. He should be home, safe and loved, not alone, afraid, or even dead. Someone knows what happened to him; a child doesn't just disappear," George said. "While there is a chance he's still alive, no matter how small, we must keep trying."

"It doesn't look good, though," Wood said.

"No, it doesn't, but I just feel that he's out there somewhere."

Chapter Nineteen

Being arrested changed everything, especially for a different offence entirely, and Andy Morris felt his world disintegrating as he was handcuffed and led away. He'd seen the look in Charlotte Gleeson's eyes, the way she immediately changed her mind from possibly guilty to definitely guilty. He'd seen her pick up the phone as he was marched away, no doubt to the governors.

As they paraded him down the corridor, the door to the staffroom opened, and his colleagues filed out, watching with accusing eyes and muttering to each other as he passed, their heads shaking.

Being arrested made him guilty, whether he was guilty or not—the police didn't arrest people for no reason. Their suspicious looks were like daggers to the heart. Neil, the caretaker, was bemused. He was clueless. As they passed reception, Mrs Baron looked scared. She shuffled papers while he was led away. Andy didn't glance at anyone; he felt too much shame. No one was listening; he couldn't defend himself. To them, the online allegations appeared to be true. Before first break, the entire school would know that Mr Morris was arrested for being a paedophile. He felt tears gathering. He felt for his kids. They'd be bullied. Kids are cruel. When word spread, Archie and Evie were fair game. The other kids would destroy them. Yet he was powerless to stop this injustice.

Andy didn't respond earlier when the officer read him his rights. He knew saying nothing was better than saying something wrong. Andy felt nervous, frightened, confused, and anxious, which was no state of mind to be in when answering questions. Yet, despite his innocence, Andy neither protested nor fought the law.

The officers were abrupt and aggressive when putting him in the van, bashing his head on the roof. Andy wondered whether it was intentional. It probably was. Like his colleagues, the officers thought he was a paedophile. *What happened to being innocent before being found guilty?*

They confined him to a tiny cell at the station that stunk of vomit and piss. Andy sat down on the grubby vinyl-covered mattress and thought about what Ella would say about him being arrested at work. She suffered with her mental health and was insecure at the best of times. The arrest would pour fuel on the fire. They must have had evidence of his wrongdoing; otherwise, they wouldn't have arrested him. But what evidence did they have? He had never crossed the line with a student and hadn't taken Benjamin Davidson. His stomach twisted, and he felt bile rise up his throat.

There was a sudden wailing sound coming from the room, and Andy realized the sound was coming from him. Luckily, no one was there to see him sobbing. He let the tears flow, choking, unable to breathe. He'd done nothing wrong, so why was he being treated like an animal?

The thoughts rattled around his head. What did they have on him that was so clear-cut they arrested him for it? Yet he came up with two answers every time: either they had the wrong man, or someone was telling lies.

Two hours ticked by painfully, the time dragging until he heard the door unlock, and a uniformed officer stepped inside, gesturing for him to step out. She led Andy in silence to a row of small interview rooms, where she opened a door, nodding for him to enter. Inside sat a grey-haired man immaculately dressed in a grey suit, clearly a solicitor sent by Owen, whom he hadn't met before. The man stood and shook his hand, and Andy was relieved. He was half expecting Owen to be sitting there, scowling. It wasn't a secret that Owen disliked Andy.

"The detectives will be along to speak with you shortly," the officer muttered. She met Andy's eyes with a look of disgust. The morning's events had taught Andy not to expect sympathy.

"Thank you," the solicitor said politely. He turned to Andy and nodded. "I'm Christian Blakley."

"Andy. Thank you for coming."

"Owen asked me to represent you." There was a calm manner about the man. "How are you coping?" he asked, noticing Andy's distress.

"I'm not," Andy said, shaking his head. "I've been treated like a criminal, yet I've done nothing wrong." Then, finally, his voice cracked, and he stopped speaking to compose himself.

"It's easy for me to say, but don't take it personally—everything they've done is designed to rattle you and unsettle you. How you're feeling is completely normal." His voice was warm and gentle, and Andy realized this was the first time he'd been spoken to in such a way since yesterday afternoon when the kids took him out for Father's Day dinner. "You've never been arrested before?" Christian asked.

"Never," Andy said, frowning. "What did Owen tell you about me?"

"Nothing much," Christian said, smiling. "I appreciate you may be worried about the fact I work with your brother-in-law, but what you say will be in confidence unless you decide otherwise."

Andy nodded. "Thank you."

"Good," Christian said. "Now, before we start, I have a question."

"Okay."

"Are you aware of any evidence the police may have?"

"No. They shouldn't have anything because I have done nothing."

"Good, then we won't be here very long." Christian paused and lowered his tone. "We'll be as cooperative as we can while they are asking questions, but it's my job to protect you, so whilst I want you to answer anything they ask if they produce any evidence, we're not happy with, I may advise a different course of action."

"What does that mean?"

"If they throw something at you I don't like, I'll advise you to say 'no comment' to every question, but only as a last resort. Okay?" The icy fingers gripped Andy's guts again, twisting and squeezing them. He knew he should be asking Christian a million questions right now, but his mind was blank.

A pair of detectives walked in when the door opened. The male was of average height but athletic, with a blond beard and messy blond hair. The man had broad shoulders, a thin waist, a firm jawline, and looked the business. Whilst he'd given off an air of authority yesterday, the detective's presence was intimidating today. Andy hadn't spoken with the female detective at all yesterday, and she said nothing as she sat down. She was attractive, wearing a white blouse and dark trousers, with brown ringlets that fell to her shoulders. As she took her seat, a hint of vanilla and coffee perfume wafted toward Andy. The detective ran a manicured hand through her hair and met Andy's eyes. They were dark brown, intelligent eyes that seemed to suck him in and made even more beautiful by the light touch of makeup she wore.

He felt like those dark eyes were searching for chinks in his armour, studying him. Still, she said nothing. Andy struggled to pull away from her gaze, desperately wanting to be swallowed up by the beautiful detective.

Christian coughed and patted Andy on the back, releasing him from the woman's spell. "This is my client, Andy Morris. A man with no criminal record and a previously impeccable reputation."

"Nice to see you, Mr Blakley," the man said, smiling with no warmth. It was a challenge instead. He pointed to a camera mounted in the corner above them before pressing a button. "This interview is being recorded, Mr Morris. I'm Detective Inspector Beaumont, and this is Detective Sergeant Wood," George Beaumont said. "You're still under caution, Mr Morris. You understood what the uniformed officers told you earlier?"

"About harming my defence if I fail to mention something I may later rely on in court?"

"Yes, Mr Morris. Do you understand?" he pushed. Andy nodded. "Speak for the recording, please."

"Yes. I understand," Andy mumbled.

"Do you know this girl, Mr Morris?" DS Wood asked, placing a photograph on the table.

"What does this girl have to do with my client's arrest?"

Christian asked. "He's here to answer questions relating to Benjamin Davidson."

Andy took the photograph, anyway. The girl was in her early teens, maybe younger—it was hard to tell these days. Andy looked and shook his head. Was there something familiar about her eyes or the way she smiled? No. He had never seen her before. Was he sure? *Yes.*

"It's fine, Christian,"

"Do you know her, Mr Morris?"

"No. I've never seen her before."

"Are you sure?" DI Beaumont said.

"Yes, I'm sure." Andy was relieved—they had got this all wrong. He looked at his solicitor, Christian, and shook his head. "I don't know this girl," he said clearly. He looked up at the camera and repeated his statement. Christian smiled thinly. Andy got up, a smile on his face. "Can I go now? I told you this was all a mistake."

"Sit down, Mr Morris," DI Beaumont said. "Her name is Kara Adams." He pushed the photograph closer. Christian looked at his notes.

"Who is Kara Adams? As I said, my client is here to answer questions about Benjamin Davidson," Christian challenged.

"The minor your client is accused of grooming."

"I thought her name was Ciara Adamson?" Christian said.

"So, someone spelt something wrong on Facebook," the sergeant said. "This is the real world, Mr Blakley, and your client needs to realise that."

"This is Kara Adams, Mr Morris," the Inspector said, ignoring the look from Christian. He tapped the photograph. "Do you know her?"

"My client has clearly stated that he doesn't know her."

"This is another picture of Kara Adams, Mr Morris," DS Wood said as she placed another photograph on the table. It was a picture of a pretty young woman with curly brown hair, her face full of make-up, and wearing a low-cut top. The sergeant tapped the new photograph and said, "Do you recognise her?" Andy looked between the two photos, and it became clear he was looking at the same girl. Yet the difference between the two images was stark. In the first image, she looked like a typical year eight or nine student, whilst in the second, she looked dressed up for a night out. The name Kara bounced around his head. *Kara.* There was something about her eyes and the way her lips curled into a smile. He felt his guts clench, and bile threatened to come up again—Kara Adams, not Ciara Adamson. A distant memory, one hidden deep within his mind, spoke to him and an icy chill spread through his bones. *Kara.*

The sergeant placed another photograph on the table, and when Andy looked at it, he was floored. Literally. He fell back into his seat, which gave way, and he fell to the concrete floor, the chair legs sticking in his back. The image unlocked a cascade of memories which flooded his mind. The DS had a smile on her face. *Kara Adams.* He knew her. "Do you remember Kara Adams now, Mr Morris?"

The third photograph was of him standing next to Kara Adams, his arm around her, her lips on his cheek while she took a selfie. They were both holding shot glasses containing a clear liquid. *Lick, shoot, suck!* Tequila. He remembered the pair downing them and him buying more. *Kara Adams. Lick, shoot, suck!* The name echoed around his mind, dulling his senses. His throat felt dry, and he needed to be sick. Christian helped his client up, a concerned expression on his face.

"This is Kara Adams, Mr Morris." DS Wood tapped the photograph again and looked into his eyes. "Can you tell me who the other person in this photograph is, Mr Morris?"

Christian fired his client a warning look and shook his head.

"You said you had never seen Kara Adams before." The detective sergeant picked up the photograph and handed it over. "Take a good look, then tell me if this is you."

"My client has been arrested for the kidnapping of Benjamin Davidson, and from now on, will only answer questions regarding this charge," Christian said. "I'd like a moment with my client before we continue."

"No," DI Beaumont said. "You had enough time earlier."

Christian was used to detectives being this way, especially once they smelled blood in the water.

"Tell us about yesterday morning. Sunday," DI Beaumont said.

Andy looked at his solicitor, who nodded. "I got up early, as usual. Archie was up, excited about it being Father's Day. He asked me if he could go out and play football with Benjamin in the park. I said yes. I didn't think anything of it."

"Then what happened?" DS Wood asked.

"I worked out in the garden and talked to the neighbours. The next minute, Archie comes back. Alone. He asks me if I've seen Benjamin, and I tell him I haven't. I continue working out, not clicking about the situation until I see Chantelle outside, panicking about Benjamin being missing. I asked her if she needed help, and she said no."

"And what? That's it? You didn't help?" DI Beaumont asked.

"Well... Of course, I did. I asked Archie where they were playing and went into the park to look. There was nobody around, so I went back home."

"How close are you to Chantelle Coates and her family?" Wood asked.

"Not that close. Telle's a single parent, so I help when I can. I guess that's the teacher in me. I hate to see people struggling when I can help, even when they don't want me to."

"Yet you call her Telle. That's odd for somebody you don't consider as close." She looked at her partner, who nodded. "Is that what happened with Kara Adams? Did you overstep the mark? Did you try to push her too far, do something to her she didn't want you to?" Wood asked.

Andy looked at Christian for help, who shook his head at his client and said, "We're here to discuss Benjamin Davidson, not Kara Adams."

"Yes, but getting an idea of what Andrew Morris got up to in his past will help move our inquiries forward," Beaumont said. "Do you know this girl? Kara Adams?"

"Yes," Andy said. There was no point in lying about it. They couldn't prove anything happened because it didn't."

"You said before you didn't know Kara Adams. What's changed?" Wood said.

"I didn't connect the name with the face, especially a name that was initially wrong."

"Can you explain why you're hugging a fourteen-year-old girl in a bar?" the sergeant asked.

"Excuse me?" Andy nearly choked.

"You heard me, Mr Morris." She held the image up again. "Kara Adams. In this image, she was fourteen years old."

"Fourteen?" Andy said, stunned. He glanced at Christian again, who shuffled uncomfortably in his seat. "To answer your question, I had no idea she was fourteen because she told me she was nineteen," he protested, looking between the two detectives and then at Christian. He couldn't read either of the detective's faces, but it didn't matter—the photograph of him with his arm around her said it all. "Anyway, it doesn't matter how old she was because I never touched her. To reiterate, I didn't know how young she was. She lied to me."

"So, you can remember Kara now?" Wood asked, her eyes wide.

His hands were shaking when he said, "Vaguely." In truth, his memories of that night were foggy and difficult to recall. The amount of alcohol he'd consumed during the night blurred the images, but at least the memories were steadily coming back. "I only knew her as Kara. I never asked for her second name."

"Do you remember where this photograph was taken?"

Andy thought for a moment, wanting to be sure before he answered. The detectives sat and waited. They were used to it, and Christian, it seemed, wasn't, as he was shuffling around in his seat. "Look, can I get a drink, please? It's hot in here."

"Stalling for time to create a story, Mr Morris?" DI Beaumont asked.

"Certainly not. I remember everything, so I don't need to make anything up!" Andy shouted. Christian grabbed him by the arm and squeezed. It was a warning.

"Go on then, Mr Morris. Tell us your story," DS Wood said.

"Yeah, tell us what you remember, Mr Morris," Beaumont said. The blond man looked incredibly smug as he sat there, surveying him. The man was probably judging him, too, judging him for somebody else's lies.

"I'd gone to Blackpool for my mate's stag do, and I was the last one standing. They'd all returned to the hotel, but I'd started chatting with a group of people."

Andy closed his eyes in an attempt to fight against the immense pressure that was building in his head. As he replayed the memories in his mind, he knew it didn't look good. In a way, he didn't blame them for arresting him—she was fourteen, and he had bought her drinks intending to seduce her. However, whilst they didn't need to know his intentions, they needed to know the outcome, which was her falling asleep on his bed whilst he slept on the sofa. At first glance, the situation was dire, but he had done nothing and had to make them understand. "I can't remember the bar's name, but she came over and asked me if I wanted to buy her a drink."

"It was at The Lancaster bar," the sergeant said. "And this was eighteen months ago?"

"Yes, that's right."

"She approached you and asked you to buy her a drink?" Beaumont asked.

"Yes," Andy said to the floor. He shifted uncomfortably in his seat. "I'm married. I don't approach women, even during stag dos." He glanced at Christian, whose face was impassive. "I don't go to bars at all. It was a one-off."

"What happened next?" Wood asked.

"She told me about her boyfriend dumping her and how she wanted a rebound. She asked me if I was interested. I said no because I was married. We chatted for a bit, and I bought her more drinks." *Lick, shoot, suck!* It was Kara's voice he was hearing. "Then— "

"That's a rather detailed account for somebody who initially claimed to have no memory of the person or the event, Mr Morris."

"It's hazy. I had no idea the accusations launched against

me last night were about Kara Adams. I wouldn't have clicked anyway, as she never told me her surname."

"Yet you were provided with an image of Kara?"

"What?"

"Here's document five," DS Wood said, pushing another image across the table. "Document five shows a screenshot of the West Yorkshire Predator Hunter post on the Hunslet Park Academy Facebook page last night. Do you recognise the image under the post?"

"Yes."

"And you recognise the two people in the said image?"

"Yes."

"For the tape, please tell us who the two people are."

"Me and Kara," Andy said. "But I only remember that now. I didn't last night. I didn't know when you asked me earlier."

"That sounds strange to me, Mr Morris," Beaumont said. "A group accuses you of being with an underage girl, and you didn't connect it with Kara, the minor you met in Blackpool?"

"My client has already insisted he did not know she was a minor. So let's move on, shall we?" Christian said, matter of fact.

George smirked, seeing how visibly shaken Andy was.

Andy could see how this looked; all he could do was explain himself. "Look, Kara told me she was nineteen, and I had no reason to think she was lying. I did nothing with or to her. Period."

"Really?" DS Wood said a sly grin on her face. Andy held eye contact with her, determined not to get lost in those huge brown eyes. "You did nothing with, or to, her that night?"

"No. That's the truth."

"We have evidence that says otherwise," DS Wood said.

Chapter Twenty

"What evidence?" Christian asked. He wasn't happy with where the interview was going and thought it might be best to advise a no-comment interview. "I'd like a break."

"I'm sure you do," DS Wood said, nodding. She looked at the DI, who nodded back. "Before you do, we'd like to disclose this evidence. This is document seven," she said, handing over an image. Christian nodded and sat back whilst Andy took the image. It was a picture of him kissing Kara Adams. "You just told us you did nothing, yet it looks like things were getting steamy in this one," she said. Andy had one arm around Kara's neck, his other hand grabbing her bum.

Andy buried his head in his hands and fought back the tears. "I don't remember that," Andy muttered.

"How do you remember this moment?" Beaumont asked.

Andy was about to tell the detectives that he remembered Kara Adams forcing her tongue down his throat for a few seconds before he pushed her away. How somebody photographed him, he didn't know and wondered for a moment whether he'd been set up. But he knew it would be virtually impossible to convince people it had happened for just a few seconds. This picture would be the end for him because the hard facts were that she had been a fourteen-year-old girl, and he was a teacher.

"Deepfake," Andy eventually said. "We were dancing, I'll admit, but I never kissed her."

"You expect us to believe a teenager faked this image?"

"No. But someone did. Who that is, I don't know?"

"We've had it analysed, Mr Morris," Beaumont said. "It's legit."

A tear dripped and splashed on the table. How was Andy supposed to explain this to his family? Despite him not knowing Kara's age, Ella would leave him if she found out he'd kissed another girl. It wasn't a grey area. It would bring all the years of his unfaithfulness into question again. The photo was damning, and that was a fact. And then there was Chantelle to think about. The woman he loved more than his wife, the woman he desperately needed to be with right now, consoling her whilst her son was missing.

An image of him kicking a football with Benjamin in the park flashed across his mind.

"Explain this photograph, Mr Morris," DS Wood said.

"We were drunk and dancing together. I don't remember kissing her." He shook his head. The detectives had that picture and denying it only made him look guiltier. "I can only explain it by stating she must have grabbed me for the photograph and kissed me to trap me. You should look at Kara and her accomplice, not me!" He turned to his solicitor, who shook his head. Everybody in the room realised that Andrew Morris was simply trying to get out of it, and he would keep pulling out excuses from his arse until one stuck, or so he thought.

"So you're accusing Kara of framing you, Mr Morris?"

Andy shrugged, saying, "She must have grabbed me because I wouldn't have kissed her. I'm a married man."

"So you're not denying kissing her?" George said.

"I don't remember, but you said that image is legit. So Kara must have forced me."

"That is convenient. Drunk. Memory loss. Being under duress. Sounds like nonsense to me." George Beaumont raised his brow.

"They're just excuses," Wood agreed.

"As I've said, we were dancing. She tried to kiss me, and I pushed her away," Andy protested. "That photograph is staged."

DS Wood smirked. "So, you remember kissing her?"

"Sort of, but my memory is foggy."

"Yet a moment ago, you said you didn't remember," George said. "Explain to us what happened, Mr Morris."

Andy looked at his solicitor, who shrugged. "We had tequila shots."

Lick, shoot, suck!

"Then we danced, and she was flirting, so I needed to put her straight," Andy said, his eyes pleading. "I told her I was married and had a daughter not much younger than her." He licked his lips and coughed. His mouth was dry, and he needed a drink. He looked at Christian again, who nodded that he should continue. "She kissed me, and I pushed her away. That picture was just a snapshot, a second out of the two hours we spent together." He shrugged. "She told me she was nineteen, remember?"

"I'm struggling to believe a word you say, Mr Morris," DI George Beaumont said, "especially considering you denied ever seeing Kara before."

"Okay, we've had enough," Christian said, standing up. "Andrew, say no comment until the end of the interview." He turned to the two detectives. "Mr Morris won't be saying anything else until I've spoken with him alone."

"Wait a minute," Andy said, turning to Christian. Beads of sweat and bulbous tears were dripping onto the table. His entire body was shaking, and his leg was hammering up and down on the floor. He was desperate for the detectives to believe him. "I want to answer your questions because I need you to believe I'm innocent." The detectives' accusing eyes bored into his. "I can explain this if you let me. Please?"

"I'm advising you to stop and not to say any more," Christian said firmly.

"I need to clear this misunderstanding up," Andy said, turning to his solicitor. Then, he turned to the detectives. "Please?"

"We're waiting," George said, sitting back and folding his arms.

"It was a drunken moment, nothing more," Andy said.

"Nothing more?"

"No."

"Nothing else happened?"

"Nothing."

"Are you sure?"

"Yes, I'm sure."

"Did you take her back to your room after this photograph was taken?"

Christian looked at Andy, anger in his eyes. He placed his hand on Andy's arm and leaned closer, whispering in his ear. "Stop talking, Andy," Christian said. "If you can't follow instructions, then consider every word you say. It doesn't matter that you thought she was nineteen."

Andy took a deep breath. "She came back to the hotel," Andy said. Christian sighed in exasperation, and the DI smirked. "Look, get that look off your face, Inspector, and let me explain what happened," Andy stammered as sweat trickled down his forehead.

Christian shook his head and looked horrified. He sat back and listened intently, ready to intervene. Andy was digging a big hole for himself; Christian knew he was, and the detectives knew he was.

Yet, for Andy, his only intentions were to convince them of his innocence. The evidence was damning, but it painted a picture of a sordid encounter that never happened. He had to try to explain. "It isn't what you think. I'll explain."

"Please do," DS Wood said.

"Look, we were drunk, but at no point did I do anything inappropriate to her. She told me she was nineteen, remember?" He paused. It didn't sound good, no matter how he said it. Even he thought he sounded like a pervert.

Christ.

"As I told you already, she told me about her boyfriend dumping her and how she wanted a rebound. She asked me if I was interested, and I said no because I was married."

"Yet she came back to the hotel with you?" DS Wood said.

"Just let me finish!" Andy shouted.

The two detectives grinned. They were interrogation experts, and Andy had never been arrested in his entire life. Christian looked at his client and pleaded for him to stop talking.

"All I wanted was for her to get home safely. So we asked reception for a taxi, but they had all been booked."

"Why?" DI Beaumont asked.

"There was a football game on, I think. Blackpool was busy. They—they said they had no taxis available, and I wanted to help her."

"Why?" DS Wood asked.

"She was all by herself."

"So?" Beaumont said. "She could have stayed in the hotel reception until a taxi became available," the sergeant suggested, shaking her head. "Why did you get involved?"

"Look," Andy said, raising his hands, palms out. "I know how this looks."

"You do?"

"Yes." Andy tried to compose himself. "She said she had no money, so I wanted to make sure she got into a taxi so that I could pay for it."

"So why didn't you give her the money and leave her in reception, or were you hoping for more from her?"

"No, it wasn't like that."

"What was it like then?"

"She was drunk and kept saying she wanted another drink," Andy said. "I didn't want her walking off, putting herself in danger." He shrugged and looked from one detective to the other. "I dread thinking about what she would have been involved in if I'd left her alone. You've got to believe me." The detectives looked at each other and shook their heads.

"But if she was nineteen, then why care? She was an adult."

"That didn't matter to me."

"Fine," the detective sergeant said. "So, what happened next?"

"We tried to get a taxi for an hour or so with no joy, so I said she could sleep on the sofa in the hotel room and get a taxi in the morning."

"So, you took her back to your room?" Beaumont asked.

"Yes, but not like how you mean."

"What do I mean?" George said.

"I know what you're implying, but nothing sexual happened." Andy shook his head. The detectives were trying to trap him. He could feel them reeling him in, and he was as helpless as a fish. All he could do was keep pulling, hoping their line would snap. "I was trying to help a vulnerable young girl, that's all."

"She was vulnerable, all right. She was fourteen."

"Look, I didn't know she was fourteen for the thousandth time," Andy stressed. The sergeant raised her eyebrows and shook her head. "Mike was in the other bed as we were sharing. I slept in mine, and the girl slept on the sofa. Honest." Andy tried to remain calm as he explained.

"Mike, who?"

"Mike Flanagan," Andy insisted. "It was perfectly innocent. I did not touch that girl."

"Kara Adams."

"Yes. Kara Adams."

"That isn't what she says."

"What?" There was a look of fear in his eyes.

"That isn't what Kara said," the sergeant said calmly.

"Then she's lying," Andy said.

"She said you had sex with her on the sofa."

"Nonsense!" Andy shouted. "She's lying."

"Why would *she* lie?" the sergeant said, her comment landing like a hammer to the back of his head.

Everything else could have been independently verified and forgiven, but the police had a girl saying she'd had sex with a man when she was fourteen years old. No one would believe him; this was the end of everything: his marriage, family, friends and career. He had to convince them he was telling the truth, but how? "Why would *I* lie?"

"You tell us," the DI said.

"I did not have sex with her, believe me." Andy sighed, wanting to crawl under the table and die. But instead, the resentment he felt towards the police was increasing. Not only did they have the wrong man in custody over the statutory rape of Kara Adams, but they were wasting time in here with him when they could be out there finding Benjamin Davidson.

Andy took a deep breath and then reflected upon his situation. The detectives didn't say a word. *A girl has accused me of having sex with her when she was fourteen. What else could they do but arrest me and ask questions?* He thought about what had been said; the photographs backed up her story, but what could he say to prove he was telling the truth? His mind was numb. "Ask Mike."

"We've tried. Unfortunately, Michael Flanagan passed away a month ago," DI Beaumont said.

The news hit him like a sledgehammer. He was telling the truth, yet there was nobody to vouch for him.

"She's lying."

"Why would she lie?" DS Wood asked.

"I don't know."

"She's given a very detailed statement of what you did to her. If you'd like, we could read out how long you lasted and how many times you did it?"

"Fucking hell!" Andy shouted. "It's all lies!" His mind was a tornado, making it difficult to comprehend what the fuck was going on.

"Shall I read her statement to you?" DS Wood asked again.

"No," Andy said, turning to Christian. "I'm innocent. What can I do to prove it?"

"My client categorically denies having sex with Miss Adams."

"Okay," George said coldly. He sat back. "Let's go back to Benjamin Davidson. When was the last time you saw him?"

Andy shrugged. "Saturday. He was in the park with his dad, Henry, playing football. I was playing with Archie when they arrived, so we played 2v2, adults in the goals. We set down our jackets as goalposts."

"What time was that?" DS Wood asked.

"I don't know for sure. About five."

"How did Henry and Benjamin seem to you?" DI Beaumont asked.

"Same as always. We play football in the park a lot. No difference."

"Okay," DI Beaumont said. "So on Sunday morning, you said Archie asked you if he could go out and play football with Benjamin in the park. You said yes as you didn't think anything of it. Does that sound right?"

"Yes," Andy said.

"What time was that?"

Andy shrugged. "No idea. I worked out in the garden. Talked to the neighbours. The next minute, Archie comes back. Alone. He asks me if I've seen Benjamin, and I tell him I haven't. So I continue working out, not clicking about the situation until I see Chantelle outside, panicking about Benjamin being missing. I asked her if she needed help, and she said no."

"Yet you went and looked for him, right?"

"Yes. I asked Archie where they were playing and went into

the park to look. There was nobody around, so I went back home."

"You said earlier you weren't that close to Chantelle Coates and her family," Wood said, "yet you've admitted to playing football regularly with Benjamin. That again strikes me as odd. I'd say you were close, especially to Benjamin. I can't imagine many other adults playing football with a child they didn't consider close."

"We're neighbours. My son, despite being eleven, enjoys spending time with Benjamin. What's wrong with that?"

"Nothing's wrong with that," DI Beaumont said. "We're just trying to find a little boy, and we need you to be honest with us."

"I am being honest with you! About everything."

"Including Kara Adams?"

"Especially involving Kara Adams. Nothing happened," Andy said, "and that's final!" He looked from one detective to the other and realised they didn't believe his words. He could see it in their eyes.

"Okay, Mr Morris. Tell us what happened after you invited Kara up to your room."

"I covered her up and went to bed," he said. "When I woke up in the morning, she had gone."

"That's it?"

"Yes."

"You didn't have sex with Kara Adams?"

"No, I told you already. She's lying."

Christian had had enough and raised his voice. "Kara Adams' story, whilst tragic, is just that—a story. It's becoming far too common in our society, and you have no proof to back up her story." Christian steepled his fingers. "Let's be frank, detectives; Kara Adams may have been fourteen, but what was she doing in that nightclub. She approached a man, much older than herself, and declared herself as nineteen." He shook his head and pointed to a photograph. "I am sure she's admitted to lying about her age. If she had told my client the truth about her age, he would never have behaved the way he did; in fact, I'm sure he would have pointed her out to the management for her own safety." He looked at Andy, who nodded. It was the truth, the teacher in him. "No one in their right mind would have entertained a fourteen-year-old girl in a nightclub, especially not a teacher. She lied then, and she is lying now."

"Ignorance is no defence," DS Wood said. "Whatever her motives, she was a fourteen-year-old child and didn't deserve what happened to her."

"Whatever happened to her," Andy interrupted, "wasn't anything to do with me."

Christian stood up this time. "The fact of the matter is, even if he had sex with her, you can't prove it with what you have." Christian sighed. "It's his word against hers. You have no forensic evidence whatsoever. Terminate the interview, or ask whatever questions you have left regarding Benjamin Davidson."

The custody sergeant approached the door. "Release Mr Morris on bail for now, please," DI Beaumont said.

The two detectives left the room, and Andy was in a daze as he was discharged. Christian made small talk, his tone positive, but Andy wasn't listening. The custody sergeant was abrupt but polite, politer than on Andy's way in, as he handed him his belongings, and they were shown out of the front by a uniformed constable.

"I'll take you home," Christian said, but Andy didn't hear

him—he was still shocked by the accusations thrown at him. "My car's in the car park opposite."

"Andy Morris?" a voice said from behind them. He turned around and stared at a young woman with golden brown hair, wearing a black skirt and a white blouse. He couldn't guess her age—he wouldn't, not any more. That single mistake he made before may have just cost him his future.

A flash blinded him, and he staggered backwards, scraping his shoulder against the wall. "Paige McGuiness, South Leeds Live. Have you been charged, Mr Morris?"

"No comment," Christian said, leading Andy away by his shoulder, away from the journalist.

"Give us a quote, Mr Morris," she said, following them. She took another picture on a digital camera.

Why was a reporter here? Had the vigilantes tipped them off, or was it the police? If it were the vigilantes, then how did they know he'd been arrested? Regardless, the last thing Andy wanted was anybody writing an article about the accusations against him—the fewer people knew, the better because, irrespective of the facts, people made up their minds. Currently, he was guilty until proven innocent.

"Give me your side of the story, Mr Morris, or we can only tell the other side. I'm here because I'm trying to do you a favour," Paige McGuiness said. She followed them to Christian's car. "Have you been charged, Mr Morris?" she shouted. Customers from the ice-skating arena were staring at the trio, and Andy's face turned beetroot red.

"Just leave me alone. I never touched her. She's lying about everything, all right?" Andy said, pulling desperately at the passenger door.

"Andy!" Christian scolded. "Stop talking. Come on." He

unlocked the door, and Andy got inside. "She's worse than the detectives, Andy. Don't give her anything."

The problem was, he already had. Paige was there because of a tip-off she'd received stating Andrew Morris had been arrested in connection with the missing Benjamin Davidson. Yet Morris had said *she* was lying and that he'd never touched *her*.

Paige sauntered up to the side of the car and bent down. "Tell us your side, Mr Morris. Tell us about the lies *she* told." A shiver ran down Andy's spine. "People need to read both sides, or they'll make their minds up, anyway." Christian got in the car and started the engine. "My number's on the website," Paige said as Christian pulled away. "Don't make this worse for yourself by listening to her advice. She doesn't care about you; you're just a statistic to her."

As Christian drove Andy home, all Andy could think about was the fact that he'd had a shitty day, the worst he'd ever had on the planet, and it would only get a million times worse. But what Christian said next threw him.

"You need to decide what to tell your family," Christian said. "What was said in your interview is confidential, so it won't get back to Owen, or Ella, from me."

They stopped at some traffic lights, and Andy cowered in his seat, paranoid that people walking on the pavement were watching him.

"If this goes to court, then what was discussed today will become public information later on. I can't advise you what to do, but I know what I'd do if I were in your shoes."

"It's not as if things could get worse, is it?"

Christian signalled right at the end of a busy junction and glanced at his client. "Don't be daft, Andy. It can always get worse," Christian said. "The press will find out about this, hence why McGuiness was sniffing about. They'll have a field day with this story. You, a teacher with an immaculate reputation, accused of raping a minor, not to mention the accusations of you being a child snatcher. Your shitty day is far from over, mate. You need to prepare yourself for what's coming." Christian looked at his client, who was shaking erratically. There was no way he was going to recover from this. "My professional advice would be to stay home, turn off the phones, and speak only to your wife and kids."

"But why?" Andy said. "They didn't charge me, so they must have believed me."

"You're wrong, Andy. Inspector Beaumont wasn't comfortable with what they had on you and was probably pressured from above to bring you in. I've seen it a hundred times. They bring people in and reveal enough to make you panic, hoping you cave under pressure and admit everything. But, instead, they wanted a confession out of you, which they didn't get, which reassures me as your solicitor that you're telling the truth."

"That's because I am... Telling you the truth, I mean."

"I believe you, which is why we need to discredit their evidence."

"How do we do that?"

"Well, you need to stop bullshitting and start being completely honest with me."

Chapter Twenty-one

DI Beaumont and DS Wood drove in silence to Claire's house. They had nothing on Andy Morris, and the entire interview felt like a waste of time. It was probably because of the lack of prep, George thought. Elaine Brewer only had a brief conversation with Kara and her parents that morning, but it had been enough to go on. They were due to arrive at the west division of Lancashire Police Headquarters any moment, and he'd tasked Yolanda to interview the Adams family via live link.

George hammered on the door, and when Claire opened it, he noticed that she visibly paled when she recognised their faces.

"We don't have any news," George quickly reassured her, "but we need to ask you a few more questions. Can we come in?"

Claire breathed a sigh of relief. "For a moment, I thought you'd come to tell me—I thought it was bad news." She stepped back to allow them to enter. "Would you like a drink? I've just poured myself a tea," she asked as she led them into the kitchen.

Both detectives asked for coffee, and whilst Claire made herself busy, George said, "Even though we haven't found

Benjamin yet, we have found evidence that he was in the woods at some point."

"Chantelle said you found his cape in the cemetery?" Claire said.

"Yes, and we've found a lot more than that, but I can't go into it. I got the impression that you wanted to tell us more yesterday. So I need you to tell me everything you know, no matter how insignificant it seems."

"I've told you everything." Claire handed them their drinks.

Did I misread the situation? No.

"Has Chantelle ever talked about giving up custody to Henry or putting Benjamin up for adoption?" George asked.

Claire shook her head. "Not to me, no. She wasn't best pleased when she got pregnant, but then she seemed to enjoy the attention. You know how I feel about her parenting skills or lack thereof, but she's never said anything like that to me. Why?"

"Why don't you like Mitchell? Is it more than the fact that he takes drugs?" Wood asked, ignoring Claire's question. Wood, like George, had noticed Claire hesitate yesterday.

Claire bit her lip. "It's more of a feeling I get when I'm around him, I guess."

"Feeling?" George asked. She nodded. "Go on."

"Last summer, we took Benjamin swimming, and Chantelle brought Mitchell. I didn't like how he looked at all the little girls and boys in their swimsuits."

"You think he has an unhealthy interest in young children?"

She shrugged. "As I said, it's just a feeling. Mitchell was staring a lot. I didn't want to say anything in front of Telle because, well, you can imagine what her reaction would be."

"We have a warrant to search his mother's house, so if there is anything like that, I'm sure we'll find it," George said. "I didn't see a lot of his possessions there, though. I have to ask, do you think he's living with Chantelle?"

"His mother's house?" Claire frowned and shook her head. "He has a flat in Holbeck, above the chippie opposite the basketball court. You haven't searched it?"

George felt a twinge of hope. Benjamin could be there.

"Are you sure he still lives there? We searched and found no record of Mitchell renting a flat."

"You wouldn't; the flat is a sublet in his mate's name."

George felt a sudden rush of adrenalin and a need to move fast. He thanked Claire, and he and Wood hurried to the car.

"Call Luke and ask him how they are getting on with the warrants. Then, get Uniform to meet us at the Holbeck flat."

He pulled the car onto the main road as Wood made the call.

"Warrants are signed," Wood said. "I can't believe we missed it; the kid could have been there all along."

"We'll go straight in and knock down the door if we have to."

George gripped the steering wheel as he sped towards Holbeck. The flat wasn't far from the Holbeck entrance to the park and woods where they'd found the pyjamas. A police car was already parked outside the chippie as they pulled up.

"He's here." Wood pointed to Mitchell's car, parked up a side street.

"Let's go." George climbed out of the car and was met by PC Sally Fletcher.

"We've got the paperwork," Fletcher said.

"Good." George pressed the buzzer for the flat, counted to ten, and then pressed again, keeping the buzzer pressed. Finally, impatient, he said, "Mitchell's had enough time." He turned to Fletcher. "Break the door down."

Fletcher moved quickly to the car and returned with another officer. George and Wood stood back as they hurled the 'big red key' at the door. With another two hits, the door gave way, the noise echoing through the street.

"Police!" Fletcher kicked the door in and continued shouting as she and the other officer entered the hallway.

As George stepped over the threshold, he heard the top door open and clunky footsteps on the stairs. He stepped in front of PC Fletcher in time to see Mitchell rushing towards them, eyes wild, brandishing a baseball bat.

"Don't be an idiot, Mitchell," George shouted.

The words had no effect, and Mitchell launched himself at George, swinging it back like he was trying to hit a home run.

George moved quickly, knowing he needed to kill the speed of the bat, so he stepped in, whilst it was still slow, and caught the bat in both hands, low down in front of his gut. There was no power during the first foot of the swing, and all George felt was just a harmless smack in the palms. He saw Mitchell attempt to draw the bat back, but the momentum of the failed earlier swing worked to George's advantage, and George pulled the bat towards him, grabbing Mitchell's wrist and twisting as he knocked Mitchell's feet from beneath him. The baseball bat clattered to the floor as Mitchell fell backwards. Fletcher and her partner took over, turning Mitchell onto his front and cuffing him as he screamed a string of obscenities.

"Get him out of here," George said, his hands shaking. He wanted to hurt the man. He took a deep breath.

"Pig scum!" Mitchell yelled as Fletcher's partner hauled him to his feet and dragged him from the house.

"You okay?" Wood asked.

"Fine." George smiled and rubbed his palms together as he headed upstairs.

"That was rather impressive," Wood whispered in his ear. "It kinda turned me on."

George laughed and turned red. "You coming to mine tonight?"

"As long as you're not in pain." She pointed at his hands.

She liked it when he used his hands. George grinned. "I'm a bit stiff; I could do with some relief."

"Yeah, I bet," she said with a wink.

They heard footsteps behind them on the stairs, so George said, "Come on, we've got to search this place." George hurried into the living room, his eyes darting around. "Benjamin?"

Nothing.

He moved to the bedroom.

"Benjamin's not here." Wood followed George in, and his hope disappeared as he scanned the room. "I guess I was hoping for too much."

His eyes caught sight of a power cable taped to the wall and disappearing into a hole in the ceiling.

"The loft." George rushed out of the room; his eyes fixed on the ceiling as he looked for the hatch. "There." He stood atop the steps and pointed upwards. "Benjamin!" Nothing. "There's a stepladder in the kitchen, Wood."

Wood disappeared and returned with the ladder, positioning it under the hatch.

"I'll go up," George said. "Hold the ladder for me."

George climbed the ladder and lifted the hatch. Warm air and the whirring of fans greeted him as he pulled himself through the hole and upright, keeping his head bent to stop it from hitting the rafters.

The floors had been boarded, and the walls insulated. A soft glow emitted from the black tents that took up most of the space, and George knew what to expect before he unzipped the first tent. Rows of cannabis plants sat below a light with a built-in fan circulating the air. He breathed in the sweet, heady aroma.

"Anything?" Wood's voice drifted up.

"Looks like he's trying to start up a cannabis farm." George climbed back down the ladder where a group of officers stood. "Search every inch of this place. I want his shoes and clothes bagged and the computer sent to DS Josh Fry. There are a few plants up there, which, irrelevant to the Benjamin Davidson case, should be enough to get him sent down for a couple of years." He turned to Wood. "Come on, let's head back to the station and question the others."

Chapter Twenty-two

"Got them all, boss," DS Luke Mason said, grinning at George. "They're waiting in separate interview rooms. PC Fletcher says Mitchell is still kicking off in his cell, demanding a phone call and solicitor. Sally reckons Mitchell was off his face when they brought him in."

"I think she's probably right," George said, thinking about Mitchell swinging the baseball bat at him. "We'll leave him to come down before we talk to him. Have the duty solicitors been called?" George asked.

"Yep, they're waiting downstairs," Said Luke. "Henry doesn't want one."

"Neither does Chantelle," Yolanda said. "Cathy brought her in, and whilst I explained that this would be a formal interview, she still declined."

"Claire hasn't said whether she wants one," Yolanda said.

"What are we doing about Andy Morris?" Luke asked.

George frowned. "Not much. We have nothing to go on. He kept to his story despite the pressure. I don't think he has Benjamin, but we still need to liaise with the Lancashire Police and help investigate the accusations raised by the Adams family. I've not cleared him yet, so keep digging, all right?"

His team nodded and was about to get back to work when

George added, "Do we have anything yet from the stuff brought back from Mitchell's?"

"Yes, actually. We got a match to the male footprint found in Holbeck Park woods," Luke said. "File's on my desk." Luke got up to fetch it.

"You've been busy this morning," Jason said. "Makes a change."

Luke gave him the finger, and they both laughed.

"So we have forensic evidence to link Mitchell to the woods?" Luke nodded and handed over the file. "Great result, Luke!" He turned to Yolanda. "I take it Chantelle's house is being searched?"

"Lindsey Yardley and her team are there now. This time, they will check all the rooms to see if there are any signs that Benjamin was injured," DS Williams said.

"Good. We don't know whether Benjamin returned to the house after playing football with Archie."

"Maybe Chantelle gave him a right bollocking for going out without permission, and he hit his head, and she panicked?" Luke speculated.

George nodded. It was a sound theory but unlikely. Andy Morris would have heard the commotion, and with the pressure they put on him, Andy would have said. "You don't think Andy and Chantelle are in on this together, do you?" He looked at his team.

"Don't know, boss," Luke said. "What we know is we have Benjamin's parents ready and waiting to be interviewed."

"True, the forensic search could take hours, so we're just going to question them with what we've got. But you're right that we don't have time to sit around, so hopefully, one of them will let something slip. Luke and Jason, you can interview

Henry. Yolanda and Tashan, are you okay with interviewing Claire?"

Yolanda's eyes lit up. "I'm ready, boss."

"Good, your job for this morning is to keep reviewing their statements for inconsistencies. Chantelle lied about Mitchell being there, which I think is extremely important, so I'll talk to her. We'll leave Mitchell until last. Let him stew for a while."

"Can I have a word?" Cathy asked as she entered the office.

"Yeah, do you want to do this in my office?" George smiled.

"No, here's fine. It won't take a minute." Cathy sat down. "I was cleaning away some stuff this morning in the kitchen and found a partially smoked joint. I've bagged it and sent it for testing. Hopefully, we can get some DNA."

"Good work. Do you want to sit in on the interview with Chantelle? I think it may be useful."

"I'm happy to do that. I think she trusts me."

"Good." George picked up a file and headed downstairs with Cathy.

* * *

Chantelle sat in the interview room, chewing her nails, a cup of untouched coffee on the table in front of her.

"Hi, Chantelle." George took a seat and laid a file on the table before turning on the recording device and dealing with the formalities. Cathy sat next to Chantelle.

"Chantelle, do you understand that this is a formal interview?" George asked.

Chantelle nodded, and her eyes rested on the file. "Cathy said it was normal for you to interview everyone during cases like this."

"Yes, we're interviewing everyone that was at your house on Saturday night. I must remind you that you are entitled to legal representation."

Chantelle shrugged. "I don't need one."

"Okay, but you can change your mind during the interview, and we can stop. So just let me know."

Chantelle nodded.

"You need to answer for the tape."

"Yes, I understand."

"Good." He smiled. "So, I'm going to disclose some evidence to you now." Chantelle nodded. "We found items of clothing that we believe belong to Benjamin." George took a photograph from the file and pushed it towards Chantelle. "This is document thirty-two. Are these Benjamin's pyjamas?"

Chantelle ran her fingers over the photo as if trying to clean away the dirt. "Yeah, they're Benjamin's. Where—where did you find them?"

"They were buried in Holbeck Park woods."

George watched Chantelle's eyes widen. Then, shaking, she pulled her knees up to her chest and wrapped her arms around them. "Why would his clothes be buried? I don't get it. Did someone take them off him?" Her bottom lip trembled, and a bulbous tear fell from one eye. "You've found him, haven't you?"

"No, we haven't found him."

"But you think he's dead, which is why you've brought me here," Chantelle said.

George watched Chantelle's movements. Her face was drained of colour, and her whole body continued to tremble. She looked sad, not guilty. Either she's an excellent actress, or she has nothing to do with Benjamin's disappearance.

"Chantelle, you were seen leaving the house at half ten on Sunday morning. You had your denim jacket on, the one with the skulls on the back. Where did you go?"

"I've answered this question already." She looked at Cathy. "Whoever left the door open must have taken it. I was still asleep at half ten." She had always assumed Mitchell had been the one to leave the door open. Had he taken the jacket? And if he had, why? Mitchell was pissing her off because he wasn't answering her calls or replying to messages.

"What size shoes do you wear?"

"Size four."

"Do you own a pair of ankle boots?"

"Yeah." Chantelle looked confused. "Why?"

"Do the boots have a chunky block heel?"

"Yeah." She looked at Cathy, confusion on her face.

"We found footprints near where Benjamin's clothes were buried, a size four chunky heeled ankle boot and a size eleven trainer. Mitchell is a size eleven, right?"

"Dunno." Chantelle shrank into the chair, sucking her thumb.

"CSI is at your house as we speak, which means they will match the footprint to your boots, and any samples they take from the material will be matched against the soil in the woods. So, if you went to Holbeck Park woods, we'll find out."

"I didn't go into the woods. Why won't you believe me?"

"Because you haven't been very honest with us from the start, Chantelle. You lied about Mitchell."

"I told you why."

"So start and tell us the truth, mainly why you were seen leaving your house, wearing your jacket, at around the time

Benjamin went missing?"

"I can't." Chantelle sniffed and wiped her eyes with the back of her hand.

The timings made no sense, and George made a mental note to interview Andy Morris again. Perhaps he'd been mistaken. Still, George put the pressure on. "Can't, or won't?"

"I can't because I was still asleep." She turned to Cathy. "Tell him. Please. We searched for my jacket, but we couldn't find it. Remember?"

George also wondered whether they'd soon find a denim jacket with skulls on the back buried in the woods. He sat back in the chair and took a sip of water.

"Okay, Chantelle, tell us your theory of how Benjamin disappeared."

"It's Henry. I'm sure of it." George said nothing, inviting Chantelle to speak. "He—he could have easily come to mine earlier, kidnapped Benjamin, and then took him somewhere. His excuse doesn't add up. He's never late picking Benjamin up."

George had a similar theory, but the only ANPR footage of Henry's car leaving Hull matched the exact times Henry had provided. He disclosed that information to Chantelle, who looked back at him, defeated.

"What if he used a different car?" Chantelle said.

George had thought about that, and Yolanda and Tashan were already working on it. He said, "We have detectives working on information relating to that scenario. So far, we have nothing."

"Nothing?"

George nodded and then said, "Talk to us about Mitchell." In his eyes, Mitchell was more of a suspect than Henry at the moment.

"What about him?"

"What time did he leave? You told us he left yours around eleven pm on Saturday night, but that isn't right, is it?"

"No, he stayed over."

"So Mitchell could have got up and taken Benjamin?"

"No, absolutely not. We fell asleep on the sofa. I would have felt him get up and come back later."

"So when you woke up, Mitchell was still on the sofa with you?"

George saw the hesitation. It was only slight and extremely well masked, but it was there. That meant he was gone when she woke up. George just knew it.

"Yeah."

"Right, so let's go back to last night. What did you and Mitchell get up to?"

Chantelle hesitated again. Was she buying time to make up a story, or was she genuinely afraid to tell him?

"We got drunk."

"And you had a joint?" George asked.

"A joint?" She shook her head.

"Come on, Chantelle, we know you like to smoke and were smoking last night."

"Okay." Chantelle huffed. "I shared a joint with Mitchell." She looked at Cathy.

"Did Mitchell bring it?" Cathy asked.

Chantelle shot Cathy a scathing look. "I don't think I want to say anything else. You said we could stop. I want to stop."

George leaned forward and pushed the photo of Benjamin's pyjamas further towards Chantelle.

"Your son is missing. Do you want to help us find him, or

is all this just a game to you? Did you get angry at Benjamin for leaving the house by himself? Did he have an accident that forced you to take Benjamin into the woods? And did that accident make you panic enough to make up a story about him being taken?"

"No—no, that's not what happened."

"Then what happened, Chantelle," Cathy coaxed. "All we want to do is find Benjamin."

"I got up in the morning after eleven, and he was gone. I'm telling you the truth."

"What happened, Chantelle?" George asked, venom in his tone.

"I don't know. I'm telling you the truth."

"You don't know, or you won't tell us."

"I don't—" Chantelle put her head in her hands. "I don't know what happened," she sobbed.

"Your door was unlocked and open," George said.

"Yes."

"Why?"

"I don't know."

"Did Mitchell leave?"

"No, we woke up on the sofa together."

"Are you sure?"

"Yes."

"And he couldn't have left you for half an hour?"

Chantelle shrugged. "What does it matter?"

"Because Mitchell could have gone outside, abducted Benjamin, and hidden him before coming back and pretending he was asleep!"

"No, he wouldn't do that."

"Why do you constantly feel the need to protect Mitchell?

Isn't your son more important?"

"Yes, he is, but Mitchell wouldn't do that. I didn't feel Mitchell get up, and I know neither of us would ever hurt Benjamin."

"You didn't feel him get up? So there's a chance now he could have?"

"No." Chantelle shook her head.

"Make up your mind! Are you two working together? Are you alibiing each other to get away with this crime?"

"Oh, God." Sobs wracked Chantelle's body.

"Chantelle, we'll keep you here at the station until we've finished searching your house. In the meantime, I suggest you think hard. I also suggest you take some legal advice. We have a duty solicitor on standby. Cathy will take you to them."

George stood and ended the interview, leaving Chantelle with Cathy.

Luke came out of the opposite interview room, his face thunderous.

"Get anything out of Henry?" George asked.

"No, I pushed as hard as possible, but he's sticking to his story. We have nothing to link him to this, and that smug bastard knows it."

"Chantelle isn't being honest with us. She's slowly revealing more and more information, but by the time she reveals the truth, I fear it might be too late."

"You think she did it?"

"I don't know. Chantelle probably didn't abduct the kid, but that doesn't mean she wasn't involved in Benjamin's disappearance."

"Great, well as it stands, we have the clothes, a missing child, and footprints." Luke sighed. "It's not enough to go on,

George. Let's hope CSI find something."

"I agree. I wonder whether I should speak to the Super and see if he'll agree to charge them all with abduction. One of them is bound to crack. Then again, I'm convinced Mitchell is involved, but whether that's with Chantelle's knowledge or not, I can't decide."

"Mitchell's involved, George. I can feel it. Let's see if he's come down from the drugs."

"You want in on the interview, don't you?"

"Do I ever," Luke said, grinning.

Chapter Twenty-three

Mitchell sat with a scowl, his fingers drumming the table when DS Mason and DI Beaumont entered the interview room. A female solicitor sat beside him, scribbling notes on a writing pad.

Luke turned on the recording device, announced the time and date, and asked those present to identify themselves before sitting down. George nodded at Luke, who glared at Mitchell and said, "Where's Benjamin Davidson?"

"How do I know? I told you I was only there to borrow Telle money on Saturday night. Didn't even see the boy." George frowned at the incorrect use of borrow whilst a smile played on Mitchell's lips. "Look, detectives, if I knew anything, I would tell you."

"Except you're lying to us, Mitchell. You were at Chantelle's house all Saturday night and woke up in her house on Sunday. We have witnesses," George said.

Mitchell shrugged. "Your witnesses are lying." He looked at the solicitor. "I've answered your questions, so you've no reason to keep me here."

The solicitor cleared her throat. "As I understand it, you haven't charged my client."

"Not yet, but your client *will* be charged with an assault on a police officer," Luke said.

"Assault?" Mitchell smirked. "I thought someone was breaking into the flat. I'm allowed to defend myself."

"Officers clearly identified themselves when they entered your property," George said. "There was sufficient light, and you were facing me when you attacked me with the baseball bat. You then tried to hit me with it again," George said.

"You nearly broke my wrist," Mitchell retorted.

"I used reasonable force to disarm you. But, as I said, you attempted to assault me again. There were witnesses present."

"I assume you had a warrant to enter the property," the solicitor said.

"You assume correctly." George took a copy of the warrant from his file and handed it to her.

The solicitor scanned the document and furrowed her perfectly plucked brows. "This is in connection to the missing child, Benjamin Davidson."

"Yes," Luke said. "Now, let's get on with it. We have witnesses that placed your client in the home of Chantelle Coates on the day her son Benjamin went missing. Trainers were taken from your client's home, which matches prints found where the child's clothes were buried in Holbeck Park woods. The soil deposits found inside the tread also match deposits taken from the woods. See documents forty to forty-two."

"That's fuckin' bullshit." Mitchell's fist slammed into the table. "You're setting me up."

Luke took two photographs from the file, laid them side by side and shoved them towards Mitchell. He pointed to the first photograph. "This is document forty, the print taken from the woods, which is a size eleven, the same as you wear. This one, document forty-one" – Luke jabbed at the second photo – "is from your trainer. It's an exact match. Document forty-two is a soil analysis."

Mitchell's eyes narrowed as he stared at the photos, then his face relaxed, and he sat back in the chair. "Yeah, I was in Holbeck Park woods yesterday. I told you yesterday that I went out with my mates looking around Beeston and Holbeck for Benjamin. Loads of people saw us."

How convenient, George thought. *Mitchell probably went into the woods to cover his tracks and to monitor things. Slimy shit was no doubt laughing at us behind our backs.*

"That's funny," Luke said, "because the thing is, I was leading the search parties yesterday, and I didn't see you. Plus, the volunteers' search was nowhere near where we found the prints."

Mitchell shrugged. "Yeah, well, I may have wandered off for a bit with my mates. We went in pretty deep."

"Stop messing us about," Luke snapped. "You took that little boy into Holbeck Park woods, stripped him of his pyjamas and—"

"No! I'm not a fucking paedo!"

"What were you doing with Benjamin, then?" Luke's eyes furrowed dangerously.

"Nothing, I didn't take him." Mitchell turned to the solicitor. "Are you listening to this bullshit? Are you going to do your job, or what?"

"My client has given you a reasonable explanation why his footprint may have been in the woods. It looks like a popular trainer to me, and size eleven is a popular size. Wouldn't you agree?"

"It was an exact match to the print. That, along with

Mitchell's constant lies when questioned, doesn't look good," George said. "We know you were at her home Saturday night and Sunday morning, Mitchell. There's no point in denying it."

"Look, I didn't want to get Telle into trouble. She struggles as it is, never mind having to listen to bullshit from social services," Mitchell said.

"What time did you leave Chantelle's on Sunday morning?" George asked.

"Just before she rang you. We searched for Benjamin for a bit, but he wasn't anywhere. It was well after eleven, though."

"What time did you wake up?"

"Dunno."

"Who woke up first, you or Chantelle?"

"Dunno. What did she tell you?"

George could see Luke's anger rising—a vein throbbed in his forehead, and he was grinding his teeth.

"Did you leave the door open when you left?"

"Dunno." He looked at his solicitor. "Look, is there a point to this?"

"Quite the factory you've got in your loft," George said, changing tack. "Must have cost a bit of dosh to set up."

"Ah, I see now. I thought this was dodgy. You use Telle's kid as an excuse to have a brief look 'round my place," he said, tutting. "That wasn't on your warrant, was it?" His solicitor shook her head. "I don't think you're allowed to do that, detectives," Mitchell smirked.

"We weren't there to find drugs," Luke said. "Finding them was just a bonus, but I have to ask, did someone pay you off to snatch the kid? Is that how you funded your factory?"

"You sick fuck!" Mitchell snarled. "Anyway, it's not my

place. I was just house-sitting for a mate. I've no idea whether there's a factory, or whatever you just said, up there in the loft."

"I'm sure forensics will prove you wrong." Luke smiled. "So, I'll ask you again: where did you get the money to set up the factory?"

Mitchell shrugged, but the grin had disappeared. "I don't know what you're talking about."

"Saturday night, you had drunk alcohol and smoked drugs. Don't deny it; Chantelle has admitted it," Luke said. "In fact, she told us you brought the weed to the house."

Mitchell grinned. "Don't think so. I may have smoked it, but I didn't supply it."

"Cut the bullshit," Luke barked. "You two were off your faces all night. It's why you slept in."

"Just tell us what happened on Saturday night, Sunday morning, Mitchell," George asked.

"I already told you I don't know what happened to Ben. Telle made him go to his room just before I arrived, so I didn't even see him on Saturday night." Mitchell sat back in the chair, his right leg bouncing up and down. "I'm not saying anything else, so either let me go or charge me."

This is just a waste of time.

George stood up. "Charge him with the cultivation of cannabis and the assault of a police officer, then put him back in the cell."

"What! You can't do that." Mitchell leapt from his chair and looked at his solicitor. "They can't do that, right?"

"Sit down, Mitchell!" Luke said, his eyes boring through Mitchell. "You can tell your fictional story to the magistrate. But, in the meantime, I suggest you think long and hard about what happened. A little boy is missing, and it doesn't look good for you."

* * *

George left the interview room and headed back upstairs into their Incident Room, where he gathered the rest of the team. "Please tell me you got something from Claire?"

"Nothing we don't already know," Yolanda said. "I asked about the shoe, and Claire wears a size five."

"He's back in his cell and kicking off," Luke informed them as he walked in, followed by DSU Smith.

"Carry on," Jim Smith said and took a seat.

"We've got Chantelle's clothes, footwear, and her phone and laptop," Yolanda said. "So far, there hasn't been a match to the boots."

Maybe she has another pair of boots which have conveniently gone missing, George thought, *just like her denim jacket.*

"Okay, I want Mitchell's finances checked, see if he was in debt and if he's received any unusual payments. The money for his cannabis venture must have come from somewhere. Claire also suggested that he may have an unhealthy interest in children, so get the tech guys to give his laptop a thorough search. DS Fry can liaise on that. Get him to check the search history on Chantelle's laptop to see if she searched any adoption sites."

"We have something from Hancock's laptop," Yolanda added

George glanced at the clock, realising they only had a few more hours left before they would have to release Hancock without charge. While they had twenty-four hours to question him, it was far less because, even as a suspected criminal, Hancock was allowed breaks and eight hours of uninterrupted sleep. "Yeah?" George's eyes lit up.

"Hancock's laptop contained no forensic evidence, so Lindsey handed it to digital forensics, which yielded interesting results. There were no internet searches for kidnap, concealment, murder, or anything in Benjamin's name. Whilst it doesn't connect Hancock to Benjamin, they found a lot of porn—plenty of young women George considered girls but all of legal age and consensual. Just. They were found on the hard drive, recovered from deleted files and salvaged deleted Internet history."

It didn't mean the man was innocent. Still, all they had so far was a wildly inflammatory press article and a couple of anonymous sightings, which was hardly enough to ask the CPS for an extension, especially when the kidnap, or murder, may not even have happened. Whilst unlikely, Benjamin could have wandered off on his own and come to entirely accidental harm, or he could even be safe and well. But he knew it was wishful thinking—a young boy with a hidden disability wouldn't last too long in the world alone.

"We got nothing from Hancock's phone due to it being a dumbphone, but I've asked for the numbers in his contacts to be traced as you requested. We're still waiting for the results."

"Good, thanks, Yolanda."

George suddenly felt overwhelming fatigue. He walked to the incident board and massaged his temples.

Smith clapped George on the shoulder before looking around at the team. "You've done a flawless job so far, but I think it's time you all went home and got some rest."

"I think there may be a chance that he's still alive, sir,"

George said, "so I can't go home just yet. But, unfortunately, he's already been missing for about twenty-eight hours, so his chances are diminishing by the minute."

"The search teams are still in the woods, and we are following up leads on the appeal," Smith said. "You can't work to your full potential when you're all shattered. How much sleep did you get last night, Beaumont?"

I didn't.

George shook his head before looking around at the team. Smith was right. They all looked exhausted. "DSU Smith's right, go on, all of you, go home and get some rest."

Smith nodded but said, "Same goes for you, DI Beaumont."

"Yeah, I will, sir, but hopefully, Hancock's ready to talk again."

Chapter Twenty-four

George left the interview room, slamming the door on his way out after another hour of Kevin Hancock saying "no comment" to every question. They could keep him overnight, but there was no point, as George had nothing to charge Hancock with.

After the custody sergeant returned Hancock's belongings and signed him out, George escorted Hancock from the station. They'd advised Hancock he was on bail, not to go far, and that they would monitor him.

Kevin turned to look at him, his eyes full of malice. George mirrored it right back at the bastard. Yet, George did not miss the flicker of fear in those eyes. Hancock might not have wanted to be in custody, answering "no comment," but there had been a reason Hancock had come willingly to Elland Road. George watched as Hancock paused on the main road, seemingly not so eager now to leave. It was obvious why. He still feared the Predator Hunters.

The moment soon passed, and Hancock soon disappeared. Of course, he was innocent until proven guilty, but George hated Hancock had left the station as a free man.

* * *

DI Beaumont stormed out of the station shortly after Hancock's release that Monday evening, rage pumping through his veins. The more George thought about it, the more he doubted the coincidence. Kevin Hancock, a convicted paedophile and child killer, had appeared in the right area at the right time to abduct Benjamin Davidson. Whether he planned it or whether the abduction was opportunistic didn't matter. Yet George couldn't do a damn thing about it, not one damn thing to help little Benjamin.

He understood the Predator Hunters' fury and their crusade, though if asked, he would never admit it. What he didn't like was how they went about their business. They were vigilantes. Some were hardened criminals. George thought some criminals could be rehabilitated but did not believe that to be the case for anyone who had committed the crimes that Hancock had.

And now it was up to George to stop Hancock from doing it again before it was too late. It was hard not to feel like the justice system had failed when he had a missing child, especially when Hancock lived in the local area. What made it worse was they had no evidence to connect the two—or at the very least, keep Hancock locked up and under pressure until he cracked and admitted what he had done.

George was confident Hancock had done it. His alibi was poor, but as the law dictated, Hancock was innocent until proven guilty.

George got into his Honda, slammed the door, and fired up the engine. He allowed himself to calm down for a moment before he slid it into gear and drove it out of the car park. Mia wouldn't be best pleased if he turned up at the house in a bad mood.

George turned right out of the station towards the M621. He rarely drove this way to his old house, preferring to cut past the White Rose Shopping Centre, but he needed the extra miles to think. It was dead at that time of night, even as the M621 changed to the M1. Mia would no doubt moan about the late hour, but he wasn't in the mood to hear it. Jack would be up, anyway, so he wasn't sure why it mattered.

They still weren't on the best terms, especially after what the Blonde Delilah had put Mia through. George knew Mia was back on medication, and he knew she was struggling, but she'd refused all help, wanting to get over the trauma herself. It wasn't the first time George's job had affected Mia, but he hoped it had been the last.

And as he pulled up outside his house that Monday night, it felt like a stranger to him. He didn't mind living in the shitty flat, not if it meant Jack had a nice place to grow up in, but it hurt George that he couldn't see his son every day.

* * *

"I thought you were coming around last night?" Mia hissed as soon as the door opened.

"I told you I couldn't. I had to stay at work late."

"Is your work more important than us—than Jack?"

"You know that Jack is the most important person in my life, Mia. I was knackered, just like I am now. I've had a shite few days, and I'm in no mood to argue. So believe me when I say I came as soon as possible, okay?"

She glared at him and then summoned him inside with a rude gesture.

It still felt strange to be invited into his own home, but the only way he would be allowed to live there was to become romantically involved with Jack's mother, which George didn't see happening again.

He loved Isabella, probably more than he'd ever loved any woman—even his mother.

"I was just about to put Jack to bed," she snapped, her eyes flashing in anger. Mia was controlling by nature and had been during their entire relationship. George thought that by ending it with her, they would have become equals, but George still felt as if she controlled everything and had power over him.

"Fine, Mia. I won't be long. I just want to see him."

"You're lucky, George," she said. "Five more minutes, and you'd have missed him."

"Don't be like that, Mia," he said. "Jack's my son."

"I know that, but I'm his mother. If you want to see more of him, come back to me. To us. I mean it. Just think, George, you could wake up to him every morning." She tried to hold his hand, but George pulled it away.

"Christ, George, no one would ever think you'd loved me with how you act now. I'm not a monster, you know? I just miss you. Jack does, too."

"You know I want to move on, Mia."

"I suspected as much, but it's the first time you've said it aloud." George was confused by the statement. "You've found someone else already. Somebody to replace me." She had changed instantly, suspicion and bitterness contorting her beautiful face.

George shook his head. "It's none of your business; anyway, I could never replace you."

She said nothing and then stormed into the house.

"Fine. I'm going to bed at eleven." George checked his watch to find it was already well after ten.

Holding his son was a relief he desperately needed, especially after the two days he'd had. But George couldn't help but feel guilty. Two parents out there couldn't hold their son like this, and it was his job to find Benjamin.

When Mia announced she was going to bed and George had to leave, he stood up, gritting his teeth as the familiar dark anger surged through his veins. He kissed his son, got up, and left without another word, storming down the driveway towards the pavement where he had parked. He heard the door close and the lock twist behind him. It wasn't until he got to the Honda that he shook with anger and frustration, but Mia knew what she was doing. She knew how George would react.

It seemed to George that everything Mia did now was to hurt him like it had been his fault the relationship had broken down. They had fallen in love quickly and passionately. They had tried hard, and they had failed. But they hadn't failed because of him, despite what Mia told people. They had failed because she had cheated on him with the first serial killer George had hunted, who he'd been convinced had impregnated Mia rather than himself.

Chapter Twenty-five

Andy was sitting at the dining room table with his wife, Ella, across from him, Archie to his right and Evie to his left. Evie was sniffling, her eyes red raw from crying. It had been a terrible day at secondary school for his kids today, and whilst he sympathised with them, Andy knew it was her reputation she was grieving for, not his. That didn't make her a bad kid; she was just susceptible to how her peers perceived her. He understood that. The ordeal they had suffered at school wasn't lost on him or their mum, yet Andy could feel the tension coming from his family. They blamed him; no matter what the circumstances, it was his fault they were being teased. He wanted to scream his innocence from the rooftops, but he knew no one was listening. Everyone he knew was now questioning him.

"I realise this has been a tough day for you," Andy said, looking at his two kids individually. Only Archie held his gaze, but there was suspicion in his dark and angry eyes. "I need you to understand that this has been a hard day for me, too." He paused. There didn't seem to be much empathy in the room. "This is a nightmare situation. I need you to know none of it's true."

"Are you going to tell us what the police said to you at the station or not?" Ella asked angrily. Her husband's solicitor, Christian, had mentioned nothing to her brother, which didn't bode well in her mind. Instead, it showed there was substance to the allegations, which meant their marriage was over.

"Yeah, of course I am," Andy said, nodding. He didn't know where to begin. There was no way to tell the story without sounding guilty. "That is why I've asked for us to sit down together, so I can explain what has happened and why."

"I don't think I want to know," Evie said quietly. "I feel like I'm going to be sick."

"I haven't done anything wrong, Evie," he said. "If I had, they would have charged me."

"My friend Bisha said the police must have had solid evidence to arrest you," Evie countered. "And her mum is a constable, so she knows."

"They have nothing solid," Andy said. "All they have are lies."

"They have nothing solid?" Ella snapped. "So they do have *some* evidence?"

"What lies?" Evie asked.

"Give Dad a chance," Archie said, irritated.

"Well?" Ella said. "Tell us."

Ella's mobile phone began ringing. She stood up and crossed to the kitchen worktop to answer it. Archie and Evie rolled their eyes and sighed. The interruption was unwelcome, but Andy felt relieved to be given a few more minutes; he didn't even know where to start.

"Hello, brother," she answered. Andy hoped Christian hadn't broken his promise. "No. I haven't seen it," she said, glaring at Andy. "I'll take a look now and call you back. Thanks for letting me know. Bye."

She put down the phone. Andy felt the tension rising, and he could sense something was about to happen. Ella turned around and smiled coldly before looking and smiling at her two children.

"Apparently, your father is all over the front page of this evening's South Leeds Live," she said. Andy felt icy fingers gripping his stomach, and he wanted to scream. The children ran to get their tablets and laptops to read precisely what the newspaper said their father had done.

Andy watched in horror as his family read the news article online. He walked behind Archie, who was reading it on his tablet.

The headline read: Leeds teacher arrested on a statutory rape charge.

He wondered how much Paige McGuiness knew and how much she had divulged. It soon became clear she had everything and had told a damn good story.

"So, it's true," Ella said, reading the article at warp speed. "Who is this Kara Adams?" she said, looking up. "I thought her name was Ciara Adamson?"

"They got her name wrong last night," Andy mumbled.

"It doesn't make any difference what her name is if the allegations are true." She was reading the article as fast as she could. "How could you do this to me? To us?"

"It isn't true, Ella," Andy protested. "It's fiction."

"Fiction?"

"Yes. Made up—"

"I know what fiction means, and that photograph on page two is not fucking fiction, is it, you thick fuck!" she screamed. Archie and Evie each found page two on their electronic devices to find the photograph of their father kissing Kara Adams.

Archie looked up at his dad, his eyes full of disappointment. Andy smiled and shook his head to reassure him, but the doubt didn't budge.

"Calm down, Ella," Andy said. "It isn't what it looks like."

"Is this you, Andy?" she snapped. Andy looked down. "Answer me."

"It looks like me."

"And this is Kara Adams?"

"Yes."

"Fiction means there's no proof." She picked up her iPad and pointed to the picture. "This is a picture of you with your tongue down a fourteen-year-old girl's throat. What part of that is fiction?"

"Oh my god, Dad, she was the same age I am now," Evie wailed. "That's sick! How could you?"

"How could you, Dad," Archie asked, shaking his head. He looked at his mother, knowing she was about to go psycho. "You can't explain this picture, Dad."

"You said it wasn't true," Evie said, sobbing. "This picture says otherwise."

"It isn't what it looks like, princess," Andy said, touching Evie's hand.

"Don't touch me," Evie shouted. She pulled her hand away and tucked it under her arm. "You're a pervert! Stay away from me!"

Andy recoiled, "Evie, please, I'm not a pervert." Andy tried to calm the atmosphere, but the picture said a million words. He could not deny him kissing a fourteen-year-old girl. He could explain so much about the circumstances around the photograph, but he could never deny it. "I was very drunk, and she grabbed me on the dance floor. She kissed me, and I pushed her away. Whoever took that photo was lucky. And I didn't have sex with her."

"She was fourteen, Dad," Evie cried. She wiped snot from her nose with a tissue. "I can't believe it's in the newspaper. Everyone reads it. You've ruined my life. No one will ever speak to me again at school. She was fourteen; you are so sick!"

"I didn't know she was fourteen; she told me she was nineteen."

"I hate you. You're a paedophile. You've ruined my life." Evie ran out of the kitchen, and Andy fell to his knees as tears ran down his cheeks. He could hear her storming up the stairs to her bedroom. "I hate you," she shouted again as she slammed the door. "I hope you rot in hell!"

"You had sex with a fourteen-year-old girl," Ella said. She was incredibly calm. Too calm. "It says here that she came up to your hotel room."

"I didn't touch her, Ella. I promise."

"I have never been more disgusted in my life. You need to leave. Leave this house right now."

"It's all lies, Ella."

"She was pregnant, for fuck's sake!" she snapped, venom in her voice and hatred in her eyes.

"You what?" Andy asked.

"Page three. Here."

Andy read the story and felt sick.

"How can a girl possibly lie about being pregnant, Andy?" She closed her eyes and breathed. "You tell me how she lied about being pregnant or get the fuck out of this house."

"There's no proof that she was pregnant," Andy said, clutching at straws. "And if she was pregnant, it was nothing to do with me."

"Get out!"

"Ella, please."

"Leave," Ella said calmly. "Now."

"Ella," Andy pleaded. "I know how this looks, but—"

"How did you not know she was fourteen, Dad?" Archie looked at him, confused.

He'd forgotten his son was still in the dining room. Andy rubbed his head and tried to explain. "I was drunk, and she came up to me at the bar. She asked me if I wanted to dance. It was a stag do, and dancing isn't illegal. Anyway, she told me she was nineteen."

"So fucking what?" Ella said. "Even if you thought she was nineteen, what the hell were you doing inviting her to your hotel room and fucking her on the sofa?"

"I know you're angry, but that kind of language doesn't help," Andy said to maintain the fragile peace.

"Angry?" Ella snarled. "Oh, I'm more than angry, you pervert. You had sex with a child!"

"I didn't have sex with her."

"This photograph tells me otherwise. Get the fuck out!"

"I didn't know how old she was; that photograph is a snapshot. A millisecond. I pushed her away when she kissed me."

"Oh, she kissed you?" Ella snorted. "Your hands look as if they're enjoying her body. You know, the body of a drunk fourteen-year-old girl. Is that why you took her back to your hotel room? You enjoyed the kiss and the grope that much?"

"Will you just give it a fucking rest?" Andy screamed. "I'm telling you, I had no idea she was only fourteen. I offered her the sofa to sleep on because she struggled to get home. When

I woke up, she was gone. That is all!"

She appeared calm on the surface, but he could tell she was at boiling point. "I'd say her age is irrelevant because, in a way, it is. She could have been nineteen," Ella said, "but you are a married man with children of a similar age, and you took her back to your room, drunk. You fucked her and made her pregnant. You disgust me!"

"I know it looks that way, but it's not true."

"Tell me how to look at it another way, Andy?" she asked. Her voice was calm, but he could feel her anger; she was teetering on the edge. "Cat got your tongue?" Andy couldn't answer. "Here's what I think, then. I can see you kissing this young girl, and then, according to this article, you invited her back to your room, where you had sex on the sofa, and she became pregnant. That is what I can see. It is what everyone else will see. The police, the judge, our kids, family and friends will all see the same thing." She stared through him, shaking her head.

He couldn't find the words to explain; everything he thought to say sounded weak and unbelievable. "You wanted to tell your story, Andy, but you've stayed silent." He couldn't find the words to form an answer. "Get your things and get out of this house. This is our family home; you don't deserve to be in it."

"I didn't have sex with that girl," Andy said. His chest was tight, and he was finding it hard to breathe.

"Then why is she saying you did, Dad?" Archie asked. He was searching his eyes for the truth, almost sympathetic to his plight. His son was dutiful like that, innocent until proven guilty, and not the other way around. "Why would she say that?"

"I don't know, Son. I wish I knew."

"But it says she was pregnant, Dad."

"I know, Son, but that changes nothing. The fact is, she may have been pregnant, but it wasn't anything to do with me. To be clear, Son, I did not have sex with that girl."

"And what about Ben, Dad? Darcy from school told me you were arrested for his abduction."

"That was all a mix-up, Son. They arrested a known paedophile called Kevin Hancock for that. They didn't even ask me many questions about Ben because they know I wasn't involved."

"How can we be so sure, Andrew?" Ella said. "Paige McGuiness has just posted an update. Kevin Hancock was released from Elland Road an hour ago!"

"Please lower your voice, Ella. Chantelle can hear us!"

"I don't fucking care what she hears! Get out of this house now, Andrew!" Ella snapped. Archie jumped to the side just as Ella threw a plate across the room, shattering against the wall, showing Andy with sharp shards. One nicked Andy's cheek, and he winced. "Leave now and never come back. Don't even consider contacting the kids or me until you hear from my solicitor."

"I'm their father, Ella."

"No, Andrew., you lost that title when you fucked a young girl and got her pregnant!" Ella shouted. Andy looked at Archie and shook his head. "Don't you fucking dare look for sympathy from your son, you bastard! Get the fuck out! Looking at you is making me feel sick. You—you disgusting paedophile!"

"Ella, please?"

"Get out now! Before I call the police."

"The police?" Andy said, astounded. "Why would you call

the police?"

"Because you won't leave and I'm concerned for the safety and welfare of my children. You're being investigated as a paedophile. They'll be here like a shot if I tell them that. So get the fuck out!"

"Don't be absurd," Andy pleaded. "I would never do anything to my kids."

"I didn't think you would fuck a kid, but you did," Ella said nastily. "Who the fuck have I been married to for all these years? What else have you done behind my back? It's over. Get out!"

"Mum," Archie said, getting in the middle of his parents. "If Dad says he didn't have sex with her, then I believe him."

"Shut up, Archie," Ella snapped. "You've no idea! This is adults talking."

"I'm eleven, Mum."

"Three years younger than the girl your father fucked and made pregnant, Archie," Ella screamed. "She was younger than your sister." Ella turned to Andy. "Get out, Andrew or I swear to god I'll call the police." She picked up her mobile. "I'll call 999 and tell them you are threatening us. I mean it."

Andy looked at his son, who had tears in his eyes. Archie was a good kid, and it felt good that one person believed him. If Archie believed him, then others might, too. Then, with fresh resolve, he held up his hands in surrender. "Okay." He walked towards the back door and picked up his car keys.

"I'll call you tomorrow after you've had a chance to calm down," Andy said as he opened the back door. A second plate hit the doorframe above his head, telling him it might take a little longer than overnight. "I love you all."

Chapter Twenty-six

It was pitch-black when Kevin Hancock stepped off the bus in Beeston, but that was how he liked it. Whilst in the light of day, new identity or not, he felt the judging glares of society. It was as though everyone watched him, as though everyone knew who he was and what he'd done. After the attack in prison, he'd been unable to stop looking over his shoulder, and now the Predator Hunters knew where he was; he had only gotten worse.

The darkness hid him.

A car raced past, and Kevin jumped. A few people were milling about, so he ducked his head further, shoving his hands in his pockets and continued down Beeston Road. He took a right onto Parkfield Avenue, entering the convenience store on the corner. Cross Flatts Park was opposite him, his destination after the shop.

Hancock found the alcohol section and picked up a bottle of vodka, shuffling to the counter and paying with a tenner. He had two left in his wallet and wouldn't get any more until next week.

"You got any ID, mate?" said the cashier, a teen lad with bright white teeth.

"What?" Hancock said.

He nodded towards the vodka. "ID?"

A look of fear stretched across Kevin's face. "Are you serious?"

Another customer entered the shop, a cap on his head. The teen looked between the man and Kevin, then said, "No mate, course not," with a cackle. "Just havin' a laugh."

Hancock grunted as he received his change.

"Having a party?"

"Sure." He wasn't, but the lad didn't need to know that. He was off to buy drugs from the knobhead dealing in Cross Flatts Park. He desperately needed it after the day he'd spent in custody. It was warm enough for him to sleep in the park, especially with the tent he'd stowed in the bushes, as he couldn't face going home again. Not yet. Not in the dark. Those vigilantes would be waiting for him, and he dreaded to think what they'd do if they caught him.

Hancock grabbed his vodka from the counter and left without thanks or goodbye.

"What a fucking loser," he heard the teenage lad mutter behind him. Kevin assumed he was talking to the stranger in the hat, not that he cared.

Hancock pocketed the vodka and stepped across the road to the park entrance. He knew Mitchell dealt near the graffiti mural. Hancock could have gone to one of the other dealers—there were plenty in Beeston, but the prices varied, and more times than not, he couldn't afford to be choosy—but it was his addiction and morbid curiosity that drew him to the park. This is the place he'd been accused of committing a crime.

He wandered through the deserted park. The playground to his right was still and silent, devoid of boisterous laughter. The darkness, the shivering swings, and the creaking and rattling of metal spooked Kevin, but not enough to curtail him from his mission.

Mitchell wasn't by the mural like normal, but Hancock knew he varied where he dealt, sometimes dealing in the bushes to the west of the park. The foliage was close enough to the paths to deal and close enough to the park boundaries to run in any direction he needed to. Hancock coughed in the usual place. Despite that, it was silent.

"For fuck's sake," Hancock grumbled under his breath. Mitchell was there every night. Perhaps the police presence in the park had scared the knobhead off? He could see the fluttering remains of the police tape and wondered whether this was where the young lad had been abducted. He could see a street sign with Back Cross Flatts Avenue on it.

Still, with morbid curiosity, Hancock approached the bushes, stepping into the pitch-black shadows.

Inside, a twig snapped. "Hello?" Hancock said, jumping back. He edged back north towards the exit. "Mitchell?"

"Mitchell's not here," a male voice said from the shadows of the bushes.

"Where is he?" Hancock took a step closer into the darkness, his heart hammering.

"Dunno, mate. I was asking the same question myself."

"Right." Hancock turned to leave. "Thanks." The shadow in the bushes terrified him. Maybe the police had put a tail on him, and they were waiting for him to fuck up?

"Wait, mate. You smoke?"

Hancock paused for a second. "Yes."

"Ah, good, you got a lighter?"

He didn't want to admit to having one because the man

clearly wanted to borrow it, but the way he had survived prison was by giving in and not refusing people.

"I do." Hancock rummaged in his pocket and wandered back towards the bushes. "Here." He sparked the flame and held it out, the light illuminating a man wearing a cap, his eyes flashing as the cigarette caught fire.

"Cheers, mate. Mitchell should be back another night."

Hancock grunted and turned away, frustrated, shoving the lighter back in his pocket.

The force of the impact on the back of Kevin's skull knocked him to the floor. Deep, fiery pain burned at the base of his neck, and he could taste copper in his mouth.

"Not that you'll ever see Mitchell again, Kevin Hancock."

The man in the cap leaned down and turned Hancock over, not wanting to touch the monster but having no choice. The paedophile stunk, and the man heaved. It was definitely Kevin Hancock.

Kevin's attacker let out a low whistle. "What a catch." Paige McGuiness had been right after all. The news had both disappointed him and excited him in equal measure. Whilst it meant the useless police hadn't charged Hancock, which made his blood boil, he now had the chance to hunt Kevin himself.

He was the predator, and Hancock was the prey. He could spend his time exacting righteous vengeance that the police had failed to do. The man in the cap smiled, wondering how Hancock felt right now, after everything he'd done to that poor child. So, he dragged Hancock into the bushes, away from prying eyes. But the very touch of the monster repulsed him, and every cell in his body felt dirty, having come so close to a paedophile and child killer.

* * *

Hancock's attacker felt a mix of emotions: the rush of excitement, the thrill of the hunt, and the fear of discovery as he wrapped several cable ties around Hancock's hands and ankles. The man in the cap wasn't a butcher, but he trussed him up as he imagined a butcher would truss a pig on his belly, with his ankles and wrists bound near the small of Hancock's back.

He took in the monster's form before him, and it was hard not to think of Angelica Peyton and what she had suffered at Hancock's hands. That sick bastard had laid those very same hands upon the girl, and his eye, which was now closed, had watched her in her dying moments. The man wondered whether he put that mouth upon her too and whether he had touched her in other ways? He thought of poor Benjamin Davidson, who was now tied up in this demon's ongoing, gruesome legacy.

The man's skin crawled just looking at the dirty bastard.

"Kevin," he spat, leaning closer. "Kevin—Kevin, wake the fuck up!"

When Hancock did not respond, the man slapped him across the face. It was a hard slap, and his palm stung from it. He hoped Hancock felt the pain.

Hancock groaned. He took Kevin's vodka and poured it across his head, which made Hancock gasp with shock. Hancock's eye blinked open, and he stared at his attacker.

"Who the hell are you?" Hancock asked, struggling against his bindings.

"You don't need to know who I am, Kevin." The man smiled.

Hancock's stomach roiled at that cold, calculating smile. The back of his head throbbed, and his mouth felt sticky.

"What do you want from me?"

"What everybody in this world wants, Kevin. Justice. I want you to pay for what you've done," the man said, waving a spoon in front of Hancock's face.

"I haven't *done* anything," Hancock said quickly. "Please, I haven't done anything. I didn't take that little boy, Ben, whatshisname. Please, let me go." He flailed like a fish out of water, struggling against his bonds.

The man's smile only deepened, and he laughed. The darkness meant Kevin couldn't see the features of his attacker, just the ferocious glint in his eye from the fiery cigarette end.

"You're going to pay for what you've done. We both know the police are useless, and that's not true vengeance, anyway. Not really. You deserve so much more than the pigs can provide." The man continued brandishing the spoon. "Recognise this?"

"Please. Not again."

"This is my first time, Kevin. I've never been in prison, but I knew about the spoons the Hunters fashioned. I've done my research, you see."

"Please, let me go."

"No. I'm going to take your other eye so that you can't feast your eyes on children ever again. Then we're going to play a game. You're going to tell me every nasty little thing you've ever done, Kevin. The more you tell me, the less I chop off." The man waved a long, sharp boning knife in Hancock's face. "I suggest you tell me the truth."

"Fuck off!" snarled Kevin. "Leave me alone! I've done my time. I paid for my sins."

"If only that were true, Kevin. I'm sitting here wondering how you abused poor Angelica Peyton." Hancock visibly recoiled at her name. "I'm going to ensure that you'll never violate anyone again. So tell me, did you use your fingers on the child?"

Kevin opened his mouth to deny his attacker's accusations, but the man thrust a balled towel into his mouth—one hand stuffing it between Hancock's jaws mercilessly, the other fingers pulling his hair back to stop Kevin from moving away. Next, the man in the cap wrapped silver Duct Tape around and around, ripping the end with his teeth.

"I guess you need me to show you how serious I am, Kevin?"

Kevin's muffles cried out into the night, his body twitching as the grinning man grabbed Hancock's left ear and pulled it away from his head. Kevin tried to move his head, to fight the man, but the blow to the back of his skull meant he couldn't lift it from the floor and was now at the man's mercy. The man sliced the knife down, and Kevin Hancock's muffled scream pierced the night.

Chapter Twenty-seven

A loud tone shattered George's nightmare, and he reached over to his phone. It was 6 am. "DI Beaumont."

"It's me." Isabella. "There's been a development in the Benjamin Davidson case." There was a tone to her voice he didn't like.

"Go on?" He sat up, alert.

"I'm at Cross Flatts Park, parked outside Chantelle's. Meet me here?"

Icy fingers splayed across his chest. "Have you found Benjamin?" he asked gruffly, phone to his ear lodged by his shoulder as he attempted to find a clean suit.

"No, George. It's better if you see it for yourself." George heard sirens in the background.

"I'll be there in half an hour." Shit. It was unlike Isabella to be shaken so much?

George took a quick shower and put on his clothes, fumbling with the buttons on his shirt in haste. "More speed, less haste, George," he said. When he was finally dressed, he pulled his fingers through his hair, grabbed his car keys, and exited his flat without thinking of coffee or breakfast, adrenaline pumping through his veins.

George pulled up behind Isabella's car, surprised by the amount of police presence. The already tattered cordon from Benjamin's disappearance was replenished with extra tape. An ambulance waited, silent and empty.

What the hell had happened?

After not seeing Wood anywhere, George made his way into the park, flashing his warrant card to quash the protest from the guarding constable. Officers stood in a group ahead to his left, with the dark green paramedics amongst them.

"DS Wood," George called, spotting her amongst the group.

She walked over to him. "Sorry for the early call, George, but you needed to see this."

"What's going on?"

DS Wood grimaced. "Kevin Hancock's dead."

George halted. "What?"

DS Wood gestured for him to follow her towards a grizzly scene. The smell hit him first. George's empty stomach roiled. On the already boiling morning, the stench of decay and the copper tang of blood carried on the soft breeze.

Within the bushes where Benjamin Davidson had lost his football lay a body; the dark clothes torn and covered in blood, the head wrapped in a black bin bag. The body lay on its front, its hands outstretched, its bare arse up in the air, with its trousers and pants around its ankles.

"How do we know it's Hancock?"

"His wallet was still in his pocket. There was a bank card and a provisional driving license with his new name on it."

"He's wearing the same clothes he left the station in last night, to be fair," George said with a nod. "He was scared when he left the station," George said. "With good reason, by the looks of this." He glanced around at the officers milling around. "When was he found? Who found him?"

Wood pointed at a man George recognised sitting on a park bench a short distance away. An officer stood looking down at him. Henry Davidson looked traumatised. George knew the discovery of a body took a toll on most people, especially the first time.

DS Wood said, "Davidson was searching for evidence of Benjamin and called it in. I was due to start at seven, so the Control Room instructed me to come here."

George glanced at the broken body and then at the dozen officers around him. "Right," he said, clapping his hands together, "I'm DI Beaumont, and I'm taking charge of this cordon." He took their names and ranks and ordered them to man the cordons at all entrances around the park.

"Crime Scene Investigation is on its way, George."

As the officers got on with their orders, George inspected the body, avoiding the foliage. The bin bag dehumanised Hancock as if he were just a pile of rubbish and not once a living, breathing person.

"Can you see Hancock's hands, George?" Wood prompted.

George peered closer, taking tiny breaths through his mouth to handle the rising scent of decay. He grimaced. All Hancock's fingers had been removed. They were just bloody stumps with white bones peering through the darkened blood.

He couldn't be sure how Kevin Hancock had died, but the man had clearly suffered brutally before he'd been strangled or stabbed, or God knows what. Hancock had gone from suspect to victim overnight, and George shuddered as a chill crawled down his spine. First, he'd allowed Hancock to go free, and then this had happened. George only hoped that Hancock's death, as he was George's prime suspect, didn't mean a reduced chance of finding Benjamin Davidson alive.

* * *

Lindsey Yardley and her team of SOCOs arrived, fully kitted up in their paper forensics suits and masks, making the park even busier.

George watched as her team meticulously took samples and photographs before allowing the paramedics to remove the body for formal identification and a post-mortem. They'd erected a huge white tent over the bushes to provide cover from the increasing heat, and the locals who were clamouring like crows for a look through the railings. George knew the crowds would only increase as the word escaped and rumours grew.

* * *

"Briefing now, everyone!" George snapped. "Come on; we haven't got all day!"

The lack of coffee made George mardy as he led his team towards the Incident Room. The frustration caused by the new setback they had encountered didn't help, either. He was worried they'd lost their only lead.

A few minutes later, DS Wood entered and stuck some prints and information to the incident board, the whiteboard pen ready and waiting in her hand.

"This morning, at the site of Benjamin Davidson's kid-napping in Cross Flatts Park, the body of Kevin Hancock was found deceased by Benjamin's father, Henry Davidson." George detailed what he and DS Wood had encountered and the information they were awaiting from Lindsey Yardley.

The room was suffocatingly silent. They all knew what Hancock's death meant for their investigation.

"From the silence, I see you all realise the gravity of the situation," George said, a mixture of despair and anger fighting within him. "Our prime suspect is dead, so whatever small lead we may have had regarding Benjamin Davidson's disappearance, we've now lost. We've got fuck all, to be honest with you. I'm sorry for the language, but we need to find out who did this to Hancock and why. These two cases are connected, so finding out what happened to Hancock might be our only lead in locating Benjamin."

"Where do we go from here, sir?" DS Williams asked quietly. "Benjamin's been missing for nearly forty-eight hours." The silent implications hung heavy in the air.

George sighed, closed his eyes, and ran a hand through his hair. "The only thing we can do, Yolanda—we go back to the beginning. I need you, Tashan, and Jason to review everything and see what we missed. Josh is back on days, so once he's in, he'll go through the initial forensics from the park and the new forensics from Kevin Hancock's murder for any similarities. I want you to help him, Luke."

DS Mason nodded. "It's got to be something to do with the family," Luke said.

George said, "I've been thinking about Shannon Matthews again."

"Aye, I know what you mean. I was involved in the case, George." George nodded for his mentor to continue. "In 2008, like Benjamin, a young girl went missing without a trace. It was the biggest West Yorkshire Police operation of its kind since the hunt for Sutcliffe. Finally, after thousands of paid hours, thousands of house searches, nationwide media appeals, the lot, she was found in Batley Carr, safe and well, four weeks later. The poor girl's kidnap had been arranged and staged by her mother to claim the huge reward money for finding her."

"We cannot afford to let this happen again; DSU Smith will have all our jobs if we do," George said. Shannon Matthews was hidden in plain sight. He knew his team was all thinking the same. "DS Wood and I will see Chantelle again. Now, before I continue, I have some news. We have a recruit that some of you may have worked with before. DC Holly Hambleton. She's coming in later, and I expect you all to welcome her. all right?"

His team nodded. *Good.*

"Holly will reread all the witness statements and analyse all phone calls and tips we received after the appeal. To repeat, everything we have needs to be re-evaluated, in case there's one small thing we missed."

"Once you're finished on the priority jobs, go over Hancock's flat. Did we overlook anything? Yolanda has already agreed to read through his interview transcripts to see if she can pick up on anything I missed. Tashan has also agreed to track Hancock's movements on CCTV after leaving here. I've spoken with Juliette Thompson to get an appeal out there to look for witnesses from the park from last night. Is there anything I've missed?"

George paused as Tashan's cautious hand rose. "Go on, Tashan?"

"What about the Hunters, sir?"

"We're pretty sure Hancock was murdered, and he looked terrified when he left here last night. We're waiting on forensics, but there's foul play involved. I think it's wise to look at the hunters. They're involved in Hancock's abuse, anyway, what with the stalking and the assault, and Thora and Maurice Pickering live opposite the foliage where Hancock's body was found. So, Jay, get on the internet and find out if anybody has claimed responsibility for Hancock's murder. Keep an eye out for anything important."

"On it, sir."

"In the meantime, I'll chase pathology and forensics and find out exactly what killed Hancock before seeing Chantelle Coates." He nodded his head towards the open door. "Get on with it, then. I want answers—today!"

Chapter Twenty-eight

"DI Beaumont," George said as he picked up on the second ring, his heart rate rising as he saw Lindsey Yardley's name flash up on the screen.

As he waited for Lindsey to call, he paced his office. He hadn't been able to get in touch with Dr Yardley or Dr Ross down in pathology, but a SOCO had told George she'd ring him back with any updates. The open window offered no respite from the hot day as he loosened his collar and removed his tie.

"Hi, George. As we speak, Dr Ross is doing the post-mortem, so the full report will be a few hours."

"Thanks for calling me so quickly, Lindsey. I appreciate it."

"I can confirm it's Kevin Hancock. His death was dreadful and incredibly brutal." George could hear the shock in Yardley's voice. "Hancock was tortured before he was murdered. A significant amount of bruising on his body suggests he took a real beating, as does the presence of cracked ribs that occurred before his death. Hancock's lips, tongue, and ears were removed by something sharp, like a boning knife. We don't know where they are. His fingers and thumbs were removed before his death. Dr Ross thinks the culprit used a kitchen cleaver. Do you remember how his hands were splayed palm down on the floor?" She didn't wait for George to answer.

"They weren't found at the scene. Kevin's other eye was also gouged out. The culprit gave Kevin a scar to match his other."

George grimaced. This was the part of his job he hated the most because they dealt with such a different world than most people.

"Shallow cuts to the wrists suggest Hancock's hands were bound at some point, probably with cable ties. Also, Kevin—" she stuttered, unable to finish her sentence. George wondered how bad it was to shock somebody as experienced as Lindsey Yardley. "—Kevin's testicles and penis were cut off, and Dr Ross suggests it was the same knife on his lips and ears. But, again, those body parts are missing."

"Christ," George said. He was lost for words. Whoever had killed Hancock intended to cause him severe pain and elongate the suffering as long as possible. It was a personal attack, one in George's opinion, designed to humiliate Hancock and to remove his five senses. George thought about the people who had it in for Kevin Hancock. Angelica Peyton had no family members left alive, so George figured it must have been the Predator Hunters. If it was anybody else, then George knew nothing about them. He thought about the Hunters and what he knew. Thora Pickering's angry, defiant face appeared vividly in his mind. Only the vigilantes had a motive, and out of the group, the Pickerings were interesting.

"Indeed. Just be grateful you didn't have to see the body, George." George had never heard Lindsey Yardley like this before.

"What was the cause of death, Lindsey?"

"Exsanguination. Hancock has a wound to the back of his head, but Dr Ross says that occurred early and probably incapacitated him."

"Really? I'd have assumed asphyxiation." He thought about Angelica Peyton and how she'd died. If the Hunters wanted revenge for Angelica, then George thought how they murdered him would have been symbolic. Was he wrong to suspect the vigilantes? Could it be somebody else? Somebody related to the Benjamin Davidson case?

"We thought that at first, especially because of the bin bag. However, Dr Ross says no fibres are in his lungs, so the bin bag was added post-mortem. He was gagged, though."

"Time of death?" George asked.

"Somewhere between 12 midnight and 3 am this morning. Dr Ross will know more later. What I can tell you is the bushes were the kill site. We found fibres from a separate set of clothes, but they could belong to anybody. As I told you before, because it's a park, it's challenging to isolate the killer from everybody else."

George sighed. The questions seemed to be mounting, but they weren't coming up with any concrete answers. "We have nothing yet, either," George said. "No witnesses, and nothing from the house-to-house searches."

"Sorry, George. I do have something else for you, though."

"Go on," he said.

"We've found a shoe, which we think might be Benjamin's."

"What?"

"Yeah, but don't get your hopes up. We can't match it to Benjamin because it's been scrubbed so clean that there's no DNA on it."

"So nothing to match it to Benjamin or the culprit?

"No."

Shit!

"You're suggesting it was deliberately cleaned?"

"Yes."

"Why?" He chewed his lip.

"I don't know, but I do know that Kevin Hancock was a complete slob. We found no cleaning products at his house, so I'm concerned it was planted."

"Planted by the killer or somebody else? Benjamin's kidnapper, maybe?" Maybe Benjamin's kidnapper and the killer were the same person? Were they trying to frame Hancock?

Lindsey's reply was soft—softer than she usually spoke to him. "That's your job, George—not mine."

"Thanks for ringing me. I'd appreciate it if you could let me know as soon as you find anything else." She said she would, and George hung up.

"Fucking hell!" George screamed at the ceiling, letting the awful details of Hancock's murder echo in his mind.

Kevin Hancock hadn't just been murdered; he'd been tortured and cut to pieces. As his thoughts echoed, he realised the symbology of the kill. It was the Hunters. It had to be. Predators used their senses to catch their prey, and the Hunters had removed those senses from Hancock.

He quickly called his team into the Incident Room to brief the team on Dr Ross and Yardley's findings.

"Any update on those bloody Hunters?" George asked DC Blackburn and DC Scott.

"We're still working on the identities of those who claimed responsibility for the attack on Hancock," Tashan said.

"We've got a murder to investigate now as well. It surprises me the Hunters aren't clamouring about it."

"True, sir," said Jason. "But I don't think anybody will take responsibility for a murder."

"They might not admit it, Jason, but they could incriminate

themselves by knowing details only the murderer would know. Somebody from that group wanted to kill that sick bastard! The vigilantes were watching him, so they'll know his movements. That information could lead us to Benjamin. This is a double enquiry now. It all connects. I need this. We need this. We could save Benjamin."

"Yes, sir," the two constables said in unison.

"Got anything else for me?" Then, George turned his full attention to DC Williams, who was updating the board with new information.

"Not really, sir. We have CCTV of Hancock in a shop at the top of the park. A member of staff recognised him. Says he bought a bottle of vodka at approximately 11 pm. CCTV loses him as soon as he goes into Cross Flatts Park."

George nodded for her to continue, his fists clenched.

Yolanda shook her head. "I have a couple of officers conducting house-to-house searches. There was one other person in the shop when Hancock entered. He left shortly after and followed Hancock into the park. The cashier couldn't give a description, and the footage from the shop is too dark."

"So that man could be the killer or a witness?"

DS Williams nodded. "That's right, sir."

"Okay, ask the officers searching house-to-house to keep an eye out for CCTV."

"Will, do. What are we doing about the press, sir?"

Shit. George hated dealing with the press.

"Well, people have seen the tent in the park. As it's where Benjamin went missing, we're getting a lot of enquiries about whether Benjamin's body's been found," Yolanda said.

George hadn't thought of that. "That's not ideal." George chewed his lip, thinking. "We can't tell them Hancock's dead yet, and we have no updates on Benjamin." He scratched his head. "Speak to DSU Smith. Maybe he and Juliette Thompson can come up with something. Anything new from the appeals?"

"Will do, sir." Then she shook her head. "The public is doing their best, but no."

"Are they?" he said irritably and then shook his head. "I don't think they are because they've given us no useful leads yet. The public and the press are getting in the way. All they've given us is a damning article on Hancock with absolutely no basis of truth that most likely contributed to his death and us losing our most promising lead."

Chapter Twenty-nine

George walked into the office feeling exhausted and stressed after the morning's events. DSU Smith gestured for him to enter his office.

George smiled as he approached the desk. "Morning, sir."

"Morning." Smith looked up from his paperwork. "I'm afraid there were no new developments overnight. The financial reports and laptop analysis you requested are on your desk. We've ended the search of the woods, extending the search to Holbeck. I'm sorry to say this, George, but I don't hold much hope of bringing him home safely. It's been over forty-eight hours now."

"There's still the possibility that he was handed over to someone. It means he could be anywhere in the country. Any more sightings reported?"

"No, the phone calls have tapered off."

"Shit!"

"Shit indeed! Well, I'll leave you to it," Smith said, looking down at the paperwork on his desk. "Keep me updated."

George made a cup of coffee in the kitchen, carried it back to his office, and started reading through the financial reports and laptop analysis. Then, he called his team back into the Incident Room to update them.

He explained to his team about the shoe Lindsey and her team found. They were tense as if they had all reached the same conclusion; that the Benjamin Davidson case was no longer a missing person inquiry but a murder investigation.

"Did Hancock kidnap Benjamin, or did somebody plant it there? I want answers."

His team nodded their heads at him.

"Okay, I've also finished reading through the reports on Mitchell's and Chantelle's finances and laptops." He took a large sip of coffee. "Chantelle is heavily in debt. She has arrangements with Yorkshire Water and council tax recovery resulting in an attachment of earnings and benefits. This takes a chunk of her wages and benefits, meaning Chantelle barely survives. Her credit cards are maxed, she has a maxed Very account, and other payday loans are spiralling out of control. I can't see many supermarket transactions suggesting she's paying cash. Find out where she's getting the cash from because her wages and benefits cover debts and bills; that's it."

"So, if someone offered her a large cash sum for an illegal adoption, it looks as if she might be tempted?" Wood questioned.

"Yes, which would be her motive," George agreed. "It's not good if it's true."

"The buried clothes could've been put there to distract us," Wood added. "You did say you felt as if they were leading you, George."

"Yeah. Our main suspect is Mitchell, given the match to the footprint in the woods. Unfortunately, it is insufficient evidence, but he's due before the magistrates on assault and drug-related charges this afternoon. The IT technicians found some pornography on his laptop, and although he appears to watch young women, they apparently appear to be of legal age. There were also several videos of him and Chantelle, filmed by a third person. We need to find out who this third person is, all right?"

DS Luke Mason entered the room. "Got the report you asked for." George nodded. "Forensics found no indication that Benjamin sustained any injury in the house. So we have fuck all."

"There's always the chance that someone will come forward with new information, especially as DSU Smith is going national," Wood said.

George smiled at her but turned to his mentor. "I know, Luke, but we have to keep digging. We're looking into the Hunters, as well as looking into known paedophile rings. Benjamin's face is all over the newspapers, and posters are on every lamppost. If someone has him, they aren't going to be able to keep him hidden for long. There are now over a hundred officers involved in the case, so we will find him if he's still in the area."

"If he's still alive," Jay said.

"Agreed, but it's our job to have hope. Chantelle needs speaking to again, and I feel it's time to put some more pressure on her." George grabbed his phone and keys before heading out of the office with Wood.

* * *

"I'm sorry we haven't had much time together recently," George said as they drove towards Chantelle's house.

"You don't need to be, George." She leaned over and kissed

his cheek. "Finding Benjamin is the priority. If we don't have a date, so what. And anyway, I haven't felt like it, either. I'm worried about this kid."

"Me too. And thanks, babe. I keep thinking about Jack. I can't imagine what Chantelle and Henry are going through."

"You still think she's innocent?" Wood asked.

"Yes and no. I think Chantelle's involved, but at what level, I don't know yet. Mitchell stands out. Most of Beeston will know that he's being questioned now, so we better hope, for his safety, that the magistrate doesn't grant him bail. The last thing we need is the Hunters taking matters into their own hands again."

"Yeah, well, it would serve him right if he's done something to that little boy," Wood said.

"I know what you mean, but we don't have any proof. I'd rather see Mitchell convicted by a jury and made accountable for his actions."

"It's got to be him. He was there, and we matched his footprint," Wood said.

"Yeah, but his explanation would make sense to a jury. And remember, the cast we took is deeper at the front, and Mitchell doesn't appear to have a limp."

"So his trainers were too big?"

"That was my thought, Isabella, but all the footwear taken from the house was the same size, so the trainers weren't too big."

"Maybe he was off his face and staggering about?" Wood said.

George thought that was most likely the case but wanted to play devil's advocate. "What if someone took his trainers to frame him."

"Really?" George nodded. "By who?"

"I don't know, but I think Hancock was a red herring. I think the shoe was put there to frame him. Maybe the culprit thought we'd tie him, Benjamin, to Hancock by the shoe and shut the case. Whoever left that shoe could have taken Mitchell's shoes to frame him, too."

"What you're saying makes sense, but I think only one person could do that. Chantelle. But then, she's been trying to protect Mitchell the whole time."

George stopped the car outside Chantelle's and sighed. "I just don't know what to make of Chantelle. She seems genuine but doesn't appear to feel guilty. Most mothers would be hysterical with worry and full of remorse if they'd left the door open and their child went missing. Maybe she initially intended to frame Mitchell but killed Hancock."

"There's no way she could have murdered him alone," Wood said.

"I agree, so she must have an accomplice. Mitchell was locked up, so who else do we have?"

"What about Andy Morris?" Wood said.

"Yeah, we need to speak with him again," George said. "His wife may not like it, but we have precedent to search their place. It's a shame Kara Adams wasn't well enough to talk to Yolanda, but I'm glad they've rescheduled the meeting."

When Cathy opened the door after George's knock, raised, voices could be heard coming from the living room.

"Can tell they're sisters," Cathy grinned. "They've been at each other's throats for the past half hour."

George entered the living room and saw Claire sitting in the armchair, her eyes dark and her lips in a hard line. Chantelle was beside her, puffing on a cigarette.

"Sorry to bother you, but we have a development," George said as he took a seat in the remaining chair.

DS Wood stood next to George, and Cathy sat next to Chantelle.

He passed an evidence bag over to Chantelle. Her eyes went wide with shock as soon as she saw what it was. "This is Benjamin's trainer."

"How can you tell?" Wood asked.

Claire snatched the bag from Chantelle's hands. "It's Benjamin's. You can tell by the lack of laces. These trainers have laces and Velcro, but we had to chop off the laces because Benjamin didn't like them on his shoes. He has three other pairs just the same upstairs."

Chantelle nodded, and Cathy went up to check.

"We need to ask you some more questions, Chantelle," DS Wood said.

"You what? Do you still think I'm involved in all of this? All you lot need your heads testing!"

"What do you mean?" Claire glanced at Chantelle, then turned to look at George. "Chantelle's a suspect?"

"What? Even me?" Claire fumed.

"Yes, Claire. Even you. We haven't ruled anybody out yet."

"But I told you where I was. At home. You have my alibi."

George looked at Claire, whose fists were clenched and eyes narrowed. She looked guilty. Could she have taken Benjamin? If so, why?

"You seem upset for somebody who says they're innocent," Wood said, turning to Claire.

"It's because I'm innocent that I'm upset. I didn't do this. None of us did. Not me, not Henry, not Chantelle—"

"Not Mitchell either," Chantelle added.

"Don't start with that again!" Claire threw her hands up in the air. "They've arrested him. He must be guilty."

"I'm glad you're here, anyway," Chantelle said. "I've heard rumours that the body found this morning was of a convicted paedophile. Is that true?"

"We can't comment, I'm afraid," George said with a smile.

Claire shook her head in frustration. "But the body was found in the same place where Benjamin went missing. That's not a coincidence."

"Whilst I agree with you, Claire, we can't comment. If, and I say if," George said, enunciating the word. "If there's a connection, then we will inform you."

George could sense that Claire was close to losing her temper and walking out. It was as if she was grasping at straws. He thought about the description given by Andy Morris of Chantelle when he thought he saw her. The sisters did look similar from a distance. George filed it away to speak to Wood about later.

"How do you pay for your food?" George looked at Chantelle.

"What?" Confusion crumpled her face.

"We noticed your bank statements have no record of purchasing essentials," Wood said.

"What?"

"No record of visiting a supermarket or shops where you can purchase food and clothes. That sort of thing," George said. "Money from benefits and wages come in regularly, with the same amount going out for credit cards and online catalogues."

Chantelle scowled. "So you do think it's me who kidnapped Benjamin." It wasn't a question.

"Don't be so bloody ridiculous," Claire snapped. "Answer

the question."

"We just need to know where you're getting the money for essentials," Wood said.

Colour rose in Chantelle's cheeks. "Mitchell."

"Don't lie," George said, his tone sharp. "We've checked his, too."

"He gives me cash. Honestly." Chantelle lit another cigarette.

"It's clear somebody is giving you cash, but we don't think it's Mitchell. So tell us," George said.

Chantelle shook her head. George wanted to try another tack. On the way over, he'd considered the videos on Mitchell's laptop. "Are you aware that Mitchell has pornographic videos of you on his laptop?" George looked at Chantelle, who had a puzzled expression on her face.

"I knew he sometimes filmed us, yes."

"The videos we saw were filmed by somebody else. You and Mitchell were in the video. Who filmed you?"

"Somebody was filming us?" Chantelle puffed her cigarette, keeping her eyes downcast.

"Yes. Did you consent to that?"

"No."

"Look, Chantelle." George sat forward in the chair. "Are you getting cash for appearing in pornographic videos?"

"No." Chantelle inhaled deeply.

"And you can't remember somebody else filming you?"

"I've already said, haven't I?"

Claire laughed. "You're being defensive, sis."

"Some of the videos were hardcore," Wood said.

Claire turned to her sister. "You better tell me now, Telle! Are you selling porn?"

"No, I'm not!" Chantelle leapt up from the sofa. "Just fucking leave me alone!" She ran from the room, and George could hear her footsteps thumping up the stairs.

"I'll go up and talk to her in a minute," Cathy said with a smile.

"I wouldn't, Cathy; she won't speak the rest of the day. She always sulks like this when she's been caught out lying," Claire said. "I must say I'm shocked you think she's involved. Could she have done it?"

"I don't know for sure," George said, "but if I'm honest, it doesn't look good."

"Then I can't stay here." Claire stood up. "I can't be anywhere near her." She turned to George. "How can I clear my name?"

George got up, too, and nodded for DS Wood to leave the room. "Thanks for having us," he said to Cathy. "Claire, we'll come back and see your sister with any updates." Unfortunately, George couldn't help her clear her name because she was still a suspect high up on his list.

Chapter Thirty

When George and DS Wood entered the office, his team were busy on the phones or clacking away at their computers. He walked through to the small kitchen off the side of the office and made two cups of coffee. By the time he returned to the open office, Isabella Wood was already sitting at her desk, delicately picking at a sandwich, a spare chair pulled up for him.

"I need you to look into Claire's movements, Yolanda," George said.

"Okay," she said. "Is Claire a suspect now?"

"Yes. I need to know where Claire's been driving to," George said. "Check the DVLA for any registered vehicles she'd have access to, and run the plates through ANPR. Extend it to close friends and family members of both her and her husband. If you find anything, come straight to me."

"I'll look into it, sir," Yolanda said. "But it's not going to be easy. She told me she drives a lot because of her husband."

"Whatever it takes, Yolanda," George said. "Once I have a list, I can speak with Kyle Murray." He turned to Luke. "I want the Murrays' financial details, too."

"Will do," Luke said.

George looked around until he spotted Tashan and Jason.

"Tashan, Jay, got any more info for me about those vigilantes?"

Tashan cleared his throat. "Yes, sir. I'm close to tracking down the people admitting to assaulting Hancock, but so far, there's nothing on there about his death."

"How strange. If the Hunters were responsible, then you'd expect a lot of chatter, right?" George asked.

"Right."

"Okay, lads, keep on it. Good work, you two."

* * *

There was a knock on George's office door. "Sir, it's urgent," Tashan said.

"Come in, DC Blackburn."

"Kevin Hancock's death is out. I don't think we have a mole here, but the Yorkshire Post, the Morley Observer and Advertiser, the Wakefield Express, the Bradford Herald, and the South Leeds Live newspapers all know about it. It's spreading like wildfire.

"Shit. What info do they have?" George hoped they didn't have all the gory details—that Tashan was right and no one inside had leaked it.

"Thankfully, not as much as we know," Tashan said. "Most state that Hancock is dead and was found in Cross Flatts Park. They have pictures of the forensics tent but nothing else. The problem is, sir, is they're wondering if it's connected to Benjamin Davidson's disappearance because of the location."

DC Jay Scott knocked on the open door and popped his head through. "Juliette Thompson has just called—she's being hounded for updates on the Kevin Hancock murder. Are we issuing a statement, sir?"

"Fucking hell," George said, a scowl on his face. They were always going to tie Hancock and Benjamin together, but maybe it had worked in their favour. If they could find out where the story had come from, if it wasn't a mole, then only somebody involved in the murder could have leaked it.

"Yes, ask DS Mason to pass this on to DSU Smith. He loves being in front of the camera. Meanwhile, I need you two to speak to the newspapers and ask them where they got their information. Is that clear?"

"Yes, sir," Tashan said, visibly uncomfortable. "There's something else."

"Go on?"

"The Hunters are buzzing about the death, sir. Before I came over, a new user posted details of Hancock's death on the public forum. People create new accounts for anonymity. Anyway, this person knows more about the murder than the papers. They know things that no one would know unless—"

"Unless they killed Kevin Hancock."

"Yes, sir. Or, they're police. As they're using a new anonymous account, I reckon we are looking at the culprit or one of them."

"Are they taking credit for Hancock's murder?"

"No, sir, for obvious reasons. It's unfortunate, but I'll keep looking."

"Right. Monitor the forum, Tashan. Stay on it, and tell me if you see anything credible."

"What about me, sir?" DC Jay Scott asked.

He was more confident now that the Hunters were responsible for Hancock's death. But where did that leave Benjamin? Trapped alone, waiting to die? It reminded him too much of

Angelica Peyton. "We need names, Jay, and quickly. Trace the people who are posting. Find out who they are and where they live. The anonymous user is likely the killer, but one of the others may know more than they're letting on."

* * *

"Do you think DI Beaumont will, you know—" Jason Scott trailed off.

"Give you a bollocking?" Tashan Blackburn answered. Jay nodded. "Nah, not for this. The DI likes to get things done."

Jay grinned, then he leaned forward and hit the button. "all right. It's done; there's no going back."

"Shit, shit, shit!" Tashan said with a creepy wink. "I hope he doesn't sack us for this!"

Jay groaned. "You just said he—"

Tashan burst into laughter.

"You two sound happy for people supposedly working on a missing child case." DS Luke Mason appeared, a cup of coffee in his hand. He slammed it down next to Jay's monitor and looked at the screen.

"Sorry, sir. Jay's just signed up as a Predator Hunter," Tashan said.

"He did what?" Mason raised an eyebrow.

"DI Beaumont wants results, sir, so I thought thinking like one might help us to find them, right?" Jay said.

"So you've identified the Hunters who claimed responsibility for Hancock's attack and murder?"

Tashan sighed. "Murder, no. Attack, kind of. We're waiting on a warrant to request IP addresses from the user's VPN servers. The owners of the servers are tricky shits, so they won't give us any info without it. The problem is that the magistrate doesn't see it as a high priority considering Hancock's dead."

"Right, you put pressure on them by telling them about the murder, and I'll speak with DSU Smith and see if he can get the warrant prioritised. I still don't understand why you've had to create an account and log in.

Jay and Tashan knew their DS didn't understand, so Tashan explained. "As most forums are private, we can't access them without signing up. There wasn't another way that we could think of, sir. What we did know, however, was if we could get in, we could find something—"

"Tash," Jason interrupted, pointing excitedly at the screen. "Look at that!"

The three detectives squinted at the screen.

Jason grinned. "Oh yeah, baby!"

"I can't see what the excitement is all about," Mason muttered. "One of you explain. Now!"

"They accepted us, sir," said Tashan. "The vigilantes chat in here on different boards in this user-only forum. Look at that—they have one exclusively for Kevin Hancock's death. We should be able to get some juicy stuff from this, sir."

Mason slapped the two young detectives on the back as he realised the gravity of what they had uncovered. "Right, lads. Great work. Get as much information as you can, and keep the team updated. I'll speak with George; let him know what you've uncovered."

"On it, sir." Tashan turned to the keyboard, his fingers playing an arpeggio on the keys.

* * *

George returned to his tiny flat late that night, concerned that they were nowhere near finding the poor kid. He retrieved a microwavable curry from the fridge, peeled back the plastic, and set the timer on the microwave. He stood, eyes transfixed on the spinning plate within, breathing in time with the hum.

What were they missing?

There was no forensic connection between Kevin Hancock and the missing Benjamin Davidson, and their anonymous sightings couldn't be verified. All they had was a damn shoe that was as clean as a whistle, conveniently placed at the murder scene. They needed more. A lot more. There were two sets of prints in the woods, so if Claire was a suspect, who was her partner? Certainly not her husband, not with his illness. So who?

The microwave pinged, interrupting his thoughts. He grabbed at the carton, hissing when it burned his finger.

Spooning the meal onto a plate, he headed for the sofa and plonked down, going back over everything he knew while he waited for his food to cool. *What are you missing, George?*

His instincts were usually good; now, they were screaming at him that he'd missed something important. But what? And how? Was it Andy Morris? Was he and Claire Murray working together? It would make sense why he said he'd seen Chantelle before Benjamin went missing, especially if they were trying to frame Chantelle. But why would Andy do it? Claire's motive was apparent—she wanted Benjamin away from Chantelle, the unfit mother. But Andy? George wasn't so sure. Andy liked teenage girls going by Kara Adams, not little boys like Benjamin Davidson.

George turned his attention to the window where darkness had fallen at last. *What time is it?* He checked his phone. *Jesus.*

Ten past eleven. No wonder I'm so tired.

He hadn't stopped until DS Luke Mason had insisted he pack up and go home, but the five minutes George had promised he'd only stay for after Mason's departure turned into another two hours before he finally realised the time and called it a day. Jay and Tashan had needed his help searching through the forums.

George finished his curry, drained his beer and flicked off all the lights in the living room before making his way to the bedroom to get ready for bed.

It wasn't thoughts of Benjamin Davidson that hounded him into slumber. It was Jack and Kevin Hancock. What lengths would he go to if his son was ever in danger?

* * *

After being haunted by the phantoms of his imagination, George was glad to return to work the following day. It was early, but George focused on the case with fresh determination.

More details of Hancock's death had leaked to the press overnight, and DC Tashan Blackburn waved George over to his desk to provide an update, having seen the growing chatter on the forum and Facebook page.

"Whoever killed Hancock provided the press with this information," George said.

"I agree, sir. It was on the South Leeds Live website first, then spread to the others, so I think McGuiness got the tip first—just like last time. As for the forums, there's no one claiming direct responsibility yet, but as Jay is a new member, he doesn't have access to all the threads."

"Okay, when he comes in, tell him to get access. I'll handle South Leeds Live." But, first, George would have to speak with Johnathan Duke, the six-foot-five Falstaffian American.

George stormed to his office and rang through. "Can I speak to Johnathan Duke?"

"I'm sorry, sir, but Mr Duke is busy. Please may I take a message?" a young man's voice replied.

"I'm Detective Inspector George Beaumont from the West Yorkshire Police. I'm known to Johnathan. Put him on."

"I'm sorry, Inspector, but he's in a meeting right now. I've checked his calendar and the earliest date I have for a meeting is next week as he's swamped."

Blood flushed through George's veins, and he clenched the fist, not holding the phone. George knew how awkward Duke was but also knew just how much he liked to protect his reputation. "Fine then. Tell Mr Duke I'll be down to bring him into the station for questioning if he prefers. You can get Paige McGuiness to print it in your paper. A reputable editor gets brought in by police for questioning. I even wrote the headline for her. I'll be down soon—"

"There's no need for that, Inspector," the young man interrupted. George grinned. "Please hold."

The line went silent, and a ridiculous pop song played in George's ear as the ruffled secretary tried to get hold of his boss. Then, the young man's wheezy voice returned after a couple of minutes. "Mr Duke will take your call."

"Of course he will," said George with a laugh. A call from the police made people free up their schedules quickly.

"Ah, Inspector Beaumont, how are you, my friend?"

"Forgive my manners, Mr Duke, but I don't have time for pleasantries. So instead, I have questions about the articles you've been publishing about Kevin Hancock and Benjamin Davidson."

"Ah yes, Inspector. Well, if it's all the same, it's a pleasure to speak to you. Tell me how I can help."

"I need your source."

"Ah, that puts me in a bit of a predicament, Inspector. I couldn't possibly do that. It's a matter of respect; I'm sure you understand."

"I think you'll find I don't, Johnathan. You published an article linking Benjamin Davidson's disappearance to Kevin Hancock quite unnaturally soon after the lad's disappearance—and that article led to a violent assault on Kevin Hancock and then his subsequent murder due to your paper's publishing of his whereabouts."

"Poppycock!"

"You didn't publish the story our press office asked for—which was to highlight the search for Benjamin Davidson. Instead, you printed an entirely self-serving, clickbait pile of shite that led to a man being assaulted and murdered, and an ongoing police investigation seriously impeded Johnathan."

"Now, there's no need for that language, Inspector," replied Duke.

George could hear the worry in Duke's tone, despite him trying to hide it.

"Tell me your source, Johnathan. I can't help you if you don't help me."

"I don't think I understand, Inspector?"

"Paige's most recent article regarding Hancock's murder is filled with details only known to the police and the murderer. As a result, you have published information about a highly sensitive investigation, which you should not have done."

"We tell the truth, Inspector. What else would you like me to say."

"Give me your source unless you'd like to visit the station? If you didn't receive the tip-off personally, we could bring in all your staff for questioning on the matter."

Johnathan Duke said nothing, so George continued. "This is the biggest story you've had for a while, Johnathan. There's no way Paige is working alone on this, but if she is, then tell me, and put her on the phone! Stop wasting my time. There's a kid out there who needs saving, and you might have the answer I need!"

Silence greeted him.

"This is your last chance, Johnathan. Tell me, or I'll come down there and arrest you personally for obstruction."

"Okay, Inspector. I must say, however, that I don't like you like this. The old Inspector Beaumont would never have spoken to me like this."

"Shit happens, Johnathan. You're in the way of me finding a five-year-old boy. Give me your source."

Duke provided a mobile number and hung up.

George strode into the open office, aware of his team's blearily eyes, to find Jay and Tashan.

When he found the pair at their desks, he pulled up an office chair behind them and said, "Jay, can you run a number for me, please? I think it might be connected to the Hunters."

Jay grinned and said, "Of course, sir."

George explained where the number had come from, and Jay typed the mobile number into a window on his screen. "Right, I've got the network, so I'll get in touch and request details. This network's pretty good when we ask for details. Shouldn't be long, sir."

"Great. I'll be in my office. Call me when it's done."

As soon as DC Scott shut the door, George's phone rang.

"DI Beaumont."

"George, it's Lindsey. We've found Hancock's body parts, and the murder weapons."

Chapter Thirty-one

"Where?" George asked.

"In the Morris family black bin."

"Great job." He texted DS Luke Mason to get Uniform to bring Andy Morris in ASAP. "Dare I ask what you found?"

"It was grim, George, I'm not going to lie. In one bin bag, which were in the process of matching to the one wrapped around Hancock's head, were lips, tongue, ears, testicles and a penis along with a boning knife."

"Christ. You'll be testing for DNA and prints, yeah?" George asked.

"Of course. Once I get confirmation they're Hancock's; I'll let you know."

"Anything else?"

"Aye, we found a second bag with a kitchen cleaver in it. Inside were also eight fingers, two thumbs, an eye, and three cable ties. We're checking them for DNA and prints as usual, but there's no way we can track the cable ties. They're sold everywhere."

"Understood. Thanks, Lindsey."

* * *

George swore under his breath in the open office. "Another dead end."

"Yep." Jay looked as miffed as George did.

The number Johnathan Duke provided had been a burner, not registered to a known address or individual, and inactive since last calling the paper; either destroyed or the SIM card removed to make sure any local cell towers couldn't triangulate it.

George sat in a chair next to Tashan and Jason, discussing everything they had—the doubts forming in George's mind.

"Lads?" he said during a brief silence.

"Sir?" They both looked up.

"Whilst I'm hopeful Andy Morris will confess, I know he won't. Why? Because I'm not sure if he was involved. I also think Hancock had nothing to do with Benjamin's disappearance. I think the Hunters are behind it and were trying to at first frame Hancock, and when that didn't stick, they're now trying to frame Morris. It's a hunch, but finding those body parts in Morris' bin is too easy. He wouldn't hide the evidence at his home if he killed Hancock. The man's not stupid."

"We agree, sir," Jay said. Tashan nodded. "It's why we're working so hard trying to find out the Hunter's identities."

"Good lads. I'm lucky to have you." George clapped them both on the shoulder.

Tashan grinned at the praise and explained, "We know the usernames and the IP addresses of the people who claimed responsibility for the assault on Hancock. We're waiting for another warrant to pressure the internet provider to get the customer details, sir."

"Also, lads, because I think Hancock, and possibly Morris,

are being set up, I want you to check the sightings of Hancock reported to the anonymous helpline. We don't have names, but we have the numbers that called the sightings in. The sightings are the only other things tying Hancock to Benjamin. If I'm right, then the Hunters are behind those calls."

"I can do that now, sir," Jay said, clacking away at his keyboard, flicking through different screens so fast George couldn't keep up. "There. That's the list." Then, after a short pause, Jason said, "Sir?"

"Yeah?" George said, leaning forward to look at the screen.

Jay squinted. "I know this number."

"Go on!"

"Well, sir, one of the numbers belongs to the Pickerings, Morris' neighbours and the pair you saw outside Hancock's place. Mrs Pickering gave her number to DS Wood. I remember the number because it had '377' at the end, just like mine, but it's a landline rather than a mobile number. So the Pickerings must have made one of the calls about Kevin being spotted near Cross Flatts Park on the morning of Benjamin's disappearance."

George's blood chilled. "They were in the garden the morning Benjamin disappeared. They alibied Andy Morris, and he alibied them, but the timings didn't add up. They went inside around the time Benjamin disappeared. They could have looped around from the front of the house."

"You think the Pickerings took Benjamin to frame Hancock?" Tashan asked, a look of dread on his face.

"They also live opposite where Hancock was murdered," replied George. "They could have put Hancock's body parts in Andy's bin to frame him. It would have been easy for them."

George got up and pulled his mobile from his pocket. Despite only having a hunch and a potentially fake tip, George knew the Pickerings were guilty of something. It wouldn't be enough for the magistrate to sign a warrant, but maybe they'd give up more information during questioning. "I know Andy Morris is on his way, but we need to have a word with the Pickerings. Tashan, come with me. Jay, you're going to interview Andy Morris with DS Wood. This will be excellent experience for you both."

George and Tashan started walking away, with George just about to call Isabella Wood.

"Wait, sir!" said DC Scott. "I've found something else." When George turned back, he saw the young man's face had paled. "The burner you asked me to trace was used to call in about another sighting of Hancock in Cross Flatts Park."

"The one that tipped of Johnathan Duke?"

"That's right, sir."

George walked back towards Jay. The Pickerings had called in one tip on Hancock via their landline. The burner had made the second Hancock tip and was the person responsible for two tips given to Johnathan Duke.

"What if the Pickerings are the owners of the burner phone, sir?" Tashan questioned.

"I was just thinking the same, Tashan." How could they have been so stupid? It was obvious. They had a child killer slash paedophile in Beeston who moved without registering. Hancock's past had blinded him. Whoever had tipped off Johnathan Duke had duped them.

George felt like an idiot and started grinding his teeth; his fists balled tightly. Hancock was a victim. One hundred per cent. And whoever had kidnapped Benjamin had played them like fools, distracting them from the true villains.

"Thanks, Jay. Until Andy Morris gets here, get me every detail you can on the Pickerings. I want phone numbers—land-lines and mobiles—previous addresses, jobs, car registrations and any ANPR hits." George turned to Tashan, his fists still clenched as he nodded for them to leave.

If Thora and Maurice Pickering had orchestrated the entire damn thing, a hoax, putting a little boy at risk of harm to frame Hancock and Morris, then they would feel the full force of the law like a ton of bricks. George would make sure of that!

* * *

George and Tashan pulled up outside Thora and Maurice Pickering's house.

"Someone's watching us from the window", Tashan said quietly. But the twitching net curtains fell back into place, and Thora Pickering appeared in the doorway a moment later, looking forlorn. George and Tashan got out of the car and approached her.

They held up their warrant cards. "If you remember, I'm DI Beaumont, and this is DC Blackburn."

"Detectives," Thora said with a smile, though her eyes remained cold and hard. "To what do I owe this—this pleasure?"

"It would be better if we had a word in private," George said, indicating to the house. "Can we come in?"

Thora frowned but said, "Of course, come in." She glanced up and down the street before escorting them in. "We know about Hancock's death." She smiled. "How terrible."

"That's not why we're here."

"Oh?" A look of fear spread across her face for a brief moment before she said, "Please sit." Thora gestured to the leather sofa that was too big for the living room. "Tea? Coffee?"

"No thanks," George said, his voice firm. "We won't be here long."

"What can we do for you, detectives?" Maurice Pickering said, taking an armchair.

"Yes, what?" Thora asked. "I assume this isn't a social call."

George eyed her carefully. "We need to ask you both some questions."

"Go ahead," Thora said, a smile lighting up her face. But, unfortunately, it was a fake smile, one that he could have spotted from a mile away.

"We need to ask your whereabouts between 10 am and 12 noon on Sunday this week when Benjamin Davidson disappeared.

Thora's smile flickered. "We already told you."

"So tell us again, Mrs Pickering," Tashan said. They'd chatted on the way over about how George wanted to see Tashan's interview skills.

"Where we always are," Maurice Pickering said, jabbing his thumb outside. "Here. We were sorting out this mess of a garden."

"Is that all you did for two hours?" Tashan said.

"We briefly went inside. For a drink. Came out again to finish what we started, but we heard the commotion soon after and got distracted."

George pulled a slip of paper from his pocket, which was eyed very carefully by Mrs Pickering. Maurice had said word for word what he'd said the morning George had spoken to him.

"And what time was that?" Tashan asked.

"About half ten, I should think?" Thora Pickering asked, looking at her husband, who nodded. "Why?"

George nodded. The time frame put them in the picture. It was not unimaginable that they had snatched Benjamin, used a burner phone to report all the sightings, and killed Kevin Hancock, leaving the shoe behind to frame him. They had the motive, the means, and the opportunity. The moment the burner phone came back to them in any way, George had them. But what he didn't have was Benjamin Davidson.

"So you were inside when Benjamin Davidson went missing?" George said, staring at Thora. From the corner of his eye, he could see Maurice writhing. They didn't look like murderers, but then, most murderers didn't. "That means the alibi given by Andy Morris doesn't quite pan out, does it?"

Thora gaped. "What—what are you suggesting?"

"Nothing. Not yet. But you need to give us answers. And fast." Annoyance spiked in George. They were wasting time. "Tell us about Kevin Hancock."

"What about that monster?" Maurice interjected.

Thora said, "We've been through this before, Inspector."

"When I saw you stalking Hancock's flat, you mean? For the Hunters?"

"When we were outside his flat, yes. We haven't done anything wrong," said Thora. "Why are we being questioned in this way? I thought you said this was just a chat? Do we need a solicitor?"

"This isn't a formal interview yet, so no, you do not need legal counsel, though, of course, you can call your solicitor if you wish."

George kept his expression blank as he asked, "How long

have you been members of the West Yorkshire Predator Hunters group?"

"A couple of years." Thora's personality had changed. Before, she was jovial, but now her voice was tainted by darker notes.

"And you participate on Facebook—as group administrators?"

"Yes."

"Are you on any other forums?" Thora hesitated. "Are you?"

She looked at Tashan. "Do we have to answer this, young man?"

"You're not obligated to answer any questions, ma'am, but if we feel like you're not telling us the truth," Tashan said, his tone hardening, "we can take you down to the station and continue formally."

"No, that won't be necessary," she replied sharply. "And to answer your question, yes, we're members on Reddit."

"Please provide your usernames," Tashan said, bringing out his tablet.

"They're private," Maurice protested.

"Not during an abduction case, or a murder investigation, for that matter."

"Abduction. Murder?" Maurice looked at his wife. "You think we took Benjamin and murdered that monster? Us? Really?"

Thora stayed silent, as did George, his hard stare doing the work for him.

"Fine, detectives," Maurice said. He provided both usernames, and Tashan typed them into his tablet.

"Thank you," George said. "You called in the tip, didn't

you? The one suggesting Kevin Hancock was in Cross Flatts Park."

Thora looked at him, horrified. "What? No! Of course, not!"

"I did," Maurice said.

"Why would you do that?" Thora shouted, giving her husband daggers. "And why didn't you tell me?"

"Because I was trying to protect you, my love."

"How many times did you ring in?" Tashan asked.

Maurice frowned. "How many times?"

"Yes, how many?" Tashan pressured.

"Just the once."

"From your landline?" Tashan asked. Maurice nodded. "Did you tell the Hunter group what you'd done?"

"No." Maurice's reaction appeared genuine.

"Do either of you own a mobile phone?" Tashan asked.

Maurice frowned, puzzled. "Yes, we each have one."

"Any other mobiles?"

"No, why?" Maurice asked.

"A pay-as-you-go mobile phone? Or spare SIM cards or anything like that?"

"No," said Maurice adamantly, an annoyance to his tone.

"You're sure?" George asked. Maurice nodded. "Where were you when Kevin Hancock was murdered between 12 midnight and 3 am on Tuesday?"

"Sleeping, of course," said Thora. She scowled at them.

"Can anyone verify that?" Tashan asked.

"What a ridiculous question. We live together and were asleep together, so nobody can verify that!" Thora said.

George stood up. "Mr and Mrs Pickering, I'm arresting you on suspicion of the abduction of Benjamin Davidson and the murder of Kevin Hancock. Maurice Pickering, I'm also arresting you for perverting the course of justice by providing a false tip to the police. You do not have to say anything. But, it may harm your defence if you do not mention, when questioned, something which you later rely on in court. Anything you do say may be given in evidence."

Thora let out a wordless howl.

"Do you understand?" George asked.

There was silence.

"We will take you to the station now," George said. "I can take you by force, or we can go amicably; it's up to you."

For the first time since George had known Thora, she looked weak and defeated. Maurice stood defiantly, arms folded across his chest.

"Before we leave this house, I have a question that needs to be answered honestly," George said. "A little boy's life is at stake. CSI will search your home once we have a warrant. So tell me, is Benjamin Davidson in this house?"

"No, he isn't!" Thora violently shook her head.

"Is that the truth?" Both the Pickerings nodded their heads. "I'm warning you, if he's found dead and your early confession would have prevented his death, I will make sure the full force of the law comes down like a ton of bricks on you both!" George roared. "Remember what Kevin Hancock did to Angelica Peyton. He could have allowed that girl to live, but he didn't. Don't be like him. This is your last chance. If you know where Benjamin Davidson is, tell me now!"

"No." Thora burst into tears, and Maurice stomped across the room and wrapped his arms around her.

"Benjamin isn't here," he said, his balled fists shaking. "We have nothing to do with it except for the false tip."

"Okay, so let us search the house right now."

Thora gaped for a moment before shaking her head. "Absolutely not! We're innocent!"

George glanced at Tashan. "Call DS Mason. Get a magistrate to sign off an emergency warrant. Oh, and speak to Lindsey and get her ready to move in. I'll take Mr and Mrs Pickering to the station, but I need you to stay here."

DC Blackburn gave him a nod, his expression serious. He knew from previous cases that a warrant could be granted within the hour due to the circumstances.

From their behaviour, George didn't think Benjamin was there, but if he were wrong, he would leave no stone unturned. However, with the wild goose chase somebody was leading him on, George wasn't sure whether to trust his instincts any more.

Chapter Thirty-two

By the time George arrived at Elland Road Police Station with the Pickerings and got them processed, the warrant had been granted. The magistrate hadn't hesitated in signing the warrant off, and George was glad they were taking it seriously, considering Benjamin's safety at stake. Though George thought it was most likely because the Pickerings were directly connected to a murder and a missing child, two cases which were growing in interest.

Whilst George waited for the Pickering's solicitors to arrive, he headed upstairs to speak to DC Scott for updates on the Predator Hunters and whatever Jay found out about the Pickering's web activity under the usernames they had provided.

"Any joy, Jay?" George said, cutting straight to the chase.

"Nothing on the two usernames Tashan sent, sir. They're on Reddit and in the subforums like they admitted, and whilst they're active, there's nothing to go on. They aren't part of the trio who admitted to assaulting Hancock."

"Okay, Jay, I need you to double down whilst I interview the Pickerings. We need evidence connecting them with Benjamin's abduction, Kevin Hancock's death, or that burner phone. Anything at all incriminating. Oh, and I know I asked you to interview Andy Morris with DS Wood, but I need you here to work on this. It's more important, and you're going a great job."

"I'm on it, sir. And no problem. I appreciate your kind words."

* * *

DS Yolanda Williams set up an interview room for Maurice Pickering and the family lawyer, Mr Khan, a round, middle-aged Asian man with a dark beard and a sharp suit.

George sat down and looked at his colleague. He hardly interviewed with Yolanda, with Wood being his usual partner, but she was working on Andy Morris, and anyway, he liked how Yolanda could ease or increase the pressure just when it was needed. He also knew she had a keen eye for detail, which would be invaluable during this interview.

DI Beaumont reeled off the details for the tape and stared at Maurice. "I need you to tell me once again where you were between 10 am and 12 noon on Sunday, the morning of Benjamin Davidson's disappearance?"

Maurice recited the exact same answer as he'd said twice already.

"We did not take Benjamin Davidson," Maurice said before his solicitor cleared his throat.

George hoped this wouldn't turn into a 'no comment' interview.

"Maurice, you had the means, the motive, and the opportunity to abduct that little boy to frame Kevin Hancock. Furthermore, you've already confessed to making a false tip to place Kevin Hancock in the area of Benjamin Davidson's disappearance, which led to his potentially unfounded arrest and may have contributed to his death."

"My client has already told you he has nothing to do with Benjamin Davidson's disappearance or Kevin Hancock's death."

"As I said, Mr Pickering, you had the motive, the means and the opportunity." George glared at Maurice. "As we speak, our Crime Scene Investigation team will search every inch of your home."

Maurice flinched. George knew more than ever that Maurice was hiding something. "It is better for you to tell me why you flinched just now."

"Look, we haven't done anything wrong. I know it was wrong to leave the false tip, but we have nothing to do with Benjamin's disappearance. He was a nice lad who we saw a lot. We wouldn't take him. I guess from what you said earlier; you think someone—a Hunter from our group—took Benjamin to frame Kevin?" George said nothing and didn't move. He continued to stare, hoping Maurice would get caught up in his web of lies. "Well, it wasn't us. That's all I can tell you. So stop wasting your time and money searching our house because you won't find anything."

"Why should I believe you, Maurice? Is it because you think you've done a good job getting rid of the evidence?" George leaned forward.

Maurice shook his head, speechless.

"Even hardened criminals leave traces behind. We'll find them."

"No, you won't." Maurice took a moment to gather himself and had a drink of water. "We're innocent. We thought Kevin had taken Benjamin. We knew deep down he'd done it. That's why I rang the tip line, to help the case against him. I knew it would make you consider him a suspect."

"All you achieved by doing that, Maurice, was steer us in the wrong direction." George scowled at him. "You wasted our time, which may have cost Benjamin Davidson his life. If you didn't take him or kill him, and we find him dead, you may as well have killed him with your own hands."

"That's enough, Inspector," Mr Khan said. "Keep this up, and we will revert to a 'no comment' interview."

But George had seen Maurice flinch again. He was hiding something else.

Maurice grinned and said, "We're innocent. Kevin Hancock is dead. That monster suffered at last. I heard on Reddit the murder was gruesome. But, in my eyes, he got what was coming to him, whether he had anything to do with Benjamin's disappearance or not."

"Hancock wasn't involved in Benjamin's disappearance," George said.

"Then you need to find Benjamin, don't you?" Maurice's tone turned serious. "The monster is dead, and he got everything he deserved, but Benjamin doesn't deserve whatever's happening to him, wherever he is. We're innocent."

"You heard about his death on the forum?" Yolanda asked.

"Yeah." Maurice began to nod his head. "Huge news that everyone was talking about."

"Who claimed responsibility?" she asked.

"Nobody."

"Is that because you were scared we'd track you, Mr Pickering?" Yolanda said.

Maurice started shaking erratically when he realised where the interview was heading. "I didn't kill that monster."

"That's what they all say," DS Williams said, her cunning

eyes burning a hole in Mr Pickering. Maurice looked away.

"This is just all speculation," interjected Mr Khan. "Stop wasting my client's time."

"You have no alibi, and we have some excellent forensics evidence from Mr Hancock's remains," Yolanda lied. "Tell us now if you were involved, Mr Pickering. It'll be better in the long run for you." She left the suggestions hanging, observing Maurice Pickering, but he looked down at the ground, not giving much away.

George didn't think the man had killed Kevin Hancock but thought he was possibly involved. Perhaps Thora Pickering had killed him. Out of the two of them, she was the only one with balls enough.

The solicitor's chair creaked as he stood up. "As it stands, Inspector, you have nothing to keep my client here. Yes, he'll likely face the charge of perverting the course of justice—which, given the circumstances, I will fight to be downgraded. However, I'm confident my client will not spend one minute behind bars." Mr Khan scoffed and shook his head. "As for the rest, it's all drivel. Pure speculation. Any court would throw it out, and you both know it. So stop trying to lead my client into confessing something he didn't do."

"I appreciate your words, Mr Khan," George said, his face like stone. "A Crime Scene Co-ordinator and a team of SOCOs are combing Maurice's property right now, and we're checking his Internet history and phone records. We have enough circumstantial evidence to hold him for twenty-four hours, which, by the way, we will be doing."

The solicitor scowled.

"If there's anything to find, we will find it, Maurice, so tell us now." It was a promise as much as a threat.

The two detectives continued the back and forth with Maurice Pickering, but they got little information they could use in searching for both Benjamin Davidson and Kevin Hancock's killer.

* * *

Solicitor Christian Blakely sat with an angry Andrew Morris in a separate interview room. DS Wood had prepared the questions, so George agreed she should take the lead.

"Why the hell am I back here, detectives?" Andy asked. "You've ruined my life enough as it is!"

DS Wood reeled off the details for the tape and stared at Andrew. "Where you were between 12 midnight and 3 am on Tuesday, the morning of Kevin Hancock's death?"

"You what?"

"Answer the question, Mr Morris."

"I can't remember."

"I suggest you try," DS Wood said.

"Sorry. My wife kicked me out Monday night because of you, so I'm struggling to recall what I did on which days."

There was a smirk on Andy's face that George wanted to punch away. "Tell us what you know about Kevin Hancock."

"I know he was a paedophile and that he died—"

"Kevin Hancock was murdered," DS Wood added. "Some of his remains were found in your black bin."

"So what. That doesn't mean I killed him. The murderer dumped the items there. Probably to frame me, just like that little cow Kara Adams!" He turned to Christian. "Are you going to say something about this nonsense?"

"My client categorically denies killing Mr Hancock. Please

provide any evidence."

They hadn't received the report from Lindsey Yardley because she was tied up at the Pickering house.

"You don't have anything, do you? All of this is pure speculation." The solicitor shook his head. "Once we get out of here, we'll make a complaint. Come on, Andy."

Wood slipped a photo across the table, and Andy Morris picked it up. "This is Benjamin's."

"Yes, how did you know." George scratched his beard.

"We're close. We play football all the time. He wears these trainers."

"Did you kidnap Benjamin Davidson?" Wood asked.

"No."

"Did you kill Kevin Hancock?" Wood pushed.

"No."

"Did you leave Benjamin's shoe behind on Hancock's remains to frame him?" Her tone was hard and firm. "Forensics will be back soon, and if you've lied to us, we'll make sure you suffer the full force of the law!"

"No!"

There was a sudden braying on the door, and DS Luke Mason popped his head into the room. "Got an urgent update for you, DI Beaumont."

George rattled off the spiel to close the interview and left Morris with his solicitor, and a Uniform whilst the two detectives sprinted out of the interview room, following Luke upstairs.

"What have you got, Luke?"

"It'd be better if Yolanda explained," Luke said.

"I've just finished talking to Kara Adams and the Lancashire Police. There's something you should know. It doesn't regard

Kevin Hancock, but we can't let him get away with this."

Chapter Thirty-three

DI Beaumont and DS Wood sat there, smiling.

"Care to divulge?" Christian Blakely asked.

"My colleague has just finished up an interview with Kara Adams," George said.

"Oh, not this bullshit again. I'm fucking innocent, all right?"

"Innocent of what exactly, Andy?" George asked.

"Of it all. I didn't sleep with her!"

"We have proof you did," DS Wood said.

Andy was about to protest, but Christian put a hand on his arm and shook his head. Andy turned to his solicitor, a confused look on his face. Then, finally, Christian said, "What evidence?"

"We'll get to that in a minute," DS Wood said. "Meanwhile, if you remember our previous interview, you told us, 'I offered her the sofa to sleep on because she was struggling to get home. When I woke up, she was gone.' Do you still stand by that statement?"

"Yes."

"Did you ever see Kara Adams again after you woke up?"

"No."

"Then can you explain why you continued to have a relationship with a minor after you knew her real age?"

"Excuse me?" Andy asked, losing his grip on his sanity. "What the hell are you talking about?" The blood drained from his face. He was a drowning man being lumbered with stones. "What relationship?"

"Kara has provided emails and text messages going back to the day after Blackpool," DS Wood said. She slid a file across the table. "Every time you messaged or called her, there's a record. This is proof you continued to see her for a year despite knowing she was fourteen."

Andy looked at the phone records, and the room began to spin. The numbers didn't make sense; they meant nothing to him. He shook his head. "This isn't my number," he said, shocked. "And this isn't my email account, either." He looked at Christian. "Look at the profile picture. That's a photograph from over ten years ago. This is a fake profile."

"We wouldn't expect you to use your phone or email address to set up an account to talk to a minor, Mr Morris. We expect you to use a burner phone and a Hotmail address to create a profile. I don't think it's fake; you've just been rattled." DS Wood opened the file. "AMorris69@Hotmail.com. Not very imaginative, granted, and extremely vulgar, but it's you. That's the email address used to set up this profile."

"That's not my email address."

"So are you suggesting Kara Adams was in contact with an entirely different Andy Morris?"

"I've no idea."

"You can see the email address is a variation of your name?"

"And?"

"And the messages are all to Kara, from Andy Morris?"

"So what. It isn't me," Andy muttered. They were trying to

get him to dig a hole he would never be able to get out of. "I'm telling you that is a fake profile."

"If it's fake," DS Wood said, "then where did they get the photograph?"

"Facebook." Andy splayed out his hands in protest. "It's from over ten years ago. Someone has saved it and set up that profile. The kids at school do it all the time. Maybe Kara did it?"

"No. The IP address that sent the emails was different to Kara's. We've traced all of that. Her emails, calls and messages came from a laptop and a mobile phone belonging to Kara," the sergeant said. She brought out the photograph of them kissing. "You remember Kara, the girl you are kissing in this photograph and the girl you invited back to your room."

The massive weight of fake evidence was crushing Andy. "She could have set up a VPN and sent those emails to herself."

George shook his head. "Kara has, again, given a detailed account of having sex with you on the sofa that night. She then claims she went on to have a relationship with you." He paused for the information to sink in. "A year of straight communication right here." She tapped the folder and waited for a response, but Andy couldn't think straight. "Explain this evidence?"

"I can't because this evidence has nothing to do with me. I didn't have sex with her, nor did I ever see or hear from that girl again." Andy muttered. Tears filled his eyes and spilt down his face.

"What about the calls? Where were they made?" Christian asked.

Kara's mobile pinged cell towers in Blackpool, but it looks as if your client is pretty good at spoofing his location. Our tech guys are looking into it."

Christian grinned. "The truth is, you don't know for sure my client sent these do you?" Christian pushed. DS Wood said nothing but held eye contact. "You're trying to get my client to confess. You want him to crack and admit everything because you have nothing but the word of a scorned young girl." Christian's eyes darkened. "You're not getting a confession from my client today, Sergeant."

"That's not all we have," DS Wood added.

"Go on," Christian said. She pushed another piece of paper across the table. Christian read it and closed his eyes. He passed it to his client, who began to weep.

"I don't understand this," Andy said. "I didn't—I didn't—"

"You didn't what?" DS Wood said, a grin on her face.

"I didn't have sex with her, so how could she have gotten pregnant? How could I have forced her to have an abortion?"

"You tell us," Wood said.

"I simply gave her somewhere to sleep for the night."

"Well, looking at the dates, you gave her more than that during her stay at your hotel."

"I didn't sleep with her, so I didn't get her pregnant. Have you spoken with Mike Flanagan?"

"We told you before that Mike Flanagan passed away," George added.

"May I ask why Miss Adams has chosen to make a complaint now? If they were in a relationship, it seems strange."

"Pardon?"

"Why did she come forward now making these wild accusations?'

"When Mr Morris finished the relationship—"

"What fucking relationship?" Andy interrupted. He stood

up again. "I want to leave, Christian. Help me, please."

"Sit down, Andy!" George commanded. "Your innocent little boy act is starting to get on my nerves."

"Answer my question, please, detectives," Christian said.

"She told her parents she didn't know who the father of her child was, protecting your client. When Andy broke off the relationship, it affected her deeply, and whilst her parents took her to see a doctor for medication, she never said a word about your relationship," George explained.

"That still doesn't answer my question, Inspector."

"I'm getting there. Kara's parents were contacted by the Predator Hunting group who outed Andy on Facebook, so they got in touch with us."

"You said it yourself there, Inspector Beaumont; Kara Adams is a liar. She lied to her parents about the pregnancy. She's lying about everything else, too. So either charge him or let him go," Christian said, standing.

The detectives looked at each other. The sergeant nodded her head. The evidence was full of holes.

"We'll find out, Mr Morris, and when we do, we'll come for you."

"I didn't send them, Sergeant Wood," Andy said, shaking his head.

"You don't have to say anything else, Andy. They have nothing." He turned to George. "Ask the custody sergeant to discharge my client ASAP," Christian said, opening the door. "Come on, Andy, let's go."

"Look, detectives. Ask Chantelle to confirm my alibi. I haven't killed anybody. I haven't kidnapped anybody. And I certainly haven't groomed anybody!"

* * *

"What do you think?" George said.

"I don't think he's involved in Benjamin's disappearance, to be honest, nor do I think he killed Hancock. As for Kara Adams, guilty as sin."

"I think we need to go and speak to Chantelle. She's the only one who can alibi him. If he was there with her, and the relationship is real, then he can't have killed Hancock."

"You want to go and see Chantelle now?"

George checked his watch. It was nearly 6 pm. "Yeah, it's getting late."

Chapter Thirty-four

Chantelle was lying on the sofa in a thick haze of smoke, her eyes fixed on the television screen.

"Sorry to call on you again," George said, "but we have a few questions."

"Oh great." Chantelle hit the mute on the control. "What else could you possibly want from me?"

"We need you to talk to us about Andrew Morris," Wood said.

"Andy from next door? What about him?"

"Chantelle, we have reason to believe you are in a romantic relationship with him." George sat down in an armchair. "Is this true?"

"Romantic?" Chantelle started nibbling her nails. "No. It's purely sexual. His wife doesn't know."

"How long has this been going on for?" Wood asked.

"Since I moved in here," Chantelle huffed. "He's a nice guy. Fit, good-looking. Rich. I don't know why he likes me. I asked him to leave his wife years ago, but he wouldn't. So we fuck now and then."

"Does Mitchell know?"

"Yeah. Mitchell and Andy are bisexual, so we often have sex together. There's nothing wrong with that, is there?"

"Other than sleeping with a married man?" Wood asked.

Chantelle glared at Wood. "Oh, come on. He's the one cheating, not me!"

"Andy told us he was here with you on Monday night slash Tuesday morning. Is that right?" Wood asked.

"Yeah, his wife kicked him out. He stayed here. He arrived after Cathy left."

"What time was that?" George asked.

"11 pm. No, half ten. Cathy left at ten."

"What time did he leave?"

"In the morning?" George nodded. "About half seven. Cathy gets here at eight, and he wanted to be gone by then. I didn't want Cathy to know about him, either. So he set an alarm and stuff." She shrugged.

"Anything else?" George asked.

She shook her head. "What do you mean?"

"Is he the one filming you?"

Her face turned scarlet. "Sometimes Andy does, yes. Other times he joins us. Is that a crime?"

"No," George said, "but lying to us is. And it's all you've done, Chantelle. So stop lying, and tell us the truth. We're trying to find your son, and all you're doing is hindering the investigation!"

Chantelle shrugged.

"You don't seem concerned about Benjamin," Wood said.

"Don't!" she screamed, getting up from the sofa and pointing her finger at DS Wood. "I love Benjamin. You don't know how I feel, so shut up!"

"Sit down, Chantelle!" George ordered.

After realising what she'd done, Chantelle looked at George and sat down. "I'm sorry, but you're accusing me of not loving my son. I love Benjamin more than anything."

"So help us," Wood said.

Chantelle frowned. "I am. I can't tell you anything else."

"Do you think Andy Morris would take Benjamin?" George could feel his patience slipping.

Chantelle hesitated and George noticed. "No, why would he? He has his wife and kids; why would he want to throw that away and go to jail over Benjamin?" Chantelle snapped. "No, definitely not. Fucking ridiculous..."

"Do you know about Andy's history with Kara Adams?" Wood asked, not meeting George's eyes. Bringing Kara up was always their last resort, but George understood. There was no judgement.

"That little bitch who made up all those lies. I swear I'd punch her lights out if I ever saw her. Silly little tart!"

"So you're aware of the abortion he forced her to have?" George said.

Chantelle shrugged. "Where's your proof?"

"There's a record on her medical file. There's your proof," Wood said.

Chantelle shook her head and laughed. "Bullshit. That's not proof. That's proof she had an abortion, not that Andy forced her to have one. He said he didn't sleep with her, and I believe him. She probably wanted him, and because he said no, she decided to fuck his life up. Happens all the time. He'll be cleared."

"You're right; I will be cleared," a male voice said.

George and DS Wood turned to where the voice had come from to see Andy Morris standing in the kitchen.

"I brought you these, Chantelle." He passed her a carton of cigarettes and then slumped down on the sofa next to her.

"We're interviewing Chantelle right now, Mr Morris, so please leave," Wood said.

"No, it's fine, detectives," Chantelle said. "I want him here. He's my rock."

George shook his head in disbelief. "Your wife and kids are literally next door."

"She threw me out, and the kids won't talk to me. So I'm guilty until I can prove I'm innocent in their eyes, which is bullshit." He turned to Chantelle and planted a kiss on her cheek. "At least Chantelle believes me."

"Could Mitchell have taken Benjamin?" Wood asked. She didn't think he was involved any more, but they were desperate.

"No, he didn't like Benjamin all that much, so why would he take him. He always said he'd prefer if I didn't have a kid."

"Maybe that's his motive?" George said.

"Nah. You showed me Benjamin's shoe. Cathy told me you found it on the dead body of that paedophile. So it's him, right? Kevin Hancock. He did it. And now he's dead."

"Maybe two people kidnapped Benjamin?" George said. "Maybe Mitchell's accomplice killed Hancock and planted the shoe?"

"You could be right, Inspector, but I don't think so. Mitchell doesn't play well."

"Oh, I don't know," Andy said. "He plays very well with us."

When Cathy came downstairs, George stood up and was about to bollock the pair for messing about. "Hello, sir. DS Wood."

The two detectives said hello, and then George asked, "What's wrong? You look pale."

Cathy picked up the remote from the sofa and changed the

channel to ITV. The 6:30 pm Evening News was on.

"Henry's being interviewed about Benjamin."

"What?" Wood said. "He never told us."

"He didn't tell me, either," Chantelle added.

Cathy explained, "Henry didn't tell anybody."

DS Wood sat down in the remaining armchair, and Cathy stood whilst they watched Henry Davidson being interviewed.

After the interview was finished, Andrew Morris stormed off without a word. They heard an engine fire up outside before the car screeched off.

"What the hell is his problem?" George said.

"I don't know, but I think you'd better leave, detectives. I'm tired, and it's nearly 7 pm."

The two detectives gave Chantelle their thanks and left Chantelle's, buckling themselves in the Honda. Before George could fire up the engine, Isabella put her hand on his.

"Stop."

"What's wrong?"

"Henry Davidson... that interview wasn't genuine."

"What do you mean?" he asked.

"I did body language training at Uni and when I first became a DS. I was getting red flags from Henry."

"Such as?" George wanted to wind the window down, but they couldn't be too careful. Spies existed everywhere.

"Okay, so his emotions at losing a child were inconsistent. Whenever he stated a fact, he shrugged his shoulders. Why would he do that?"

"If they weren't facts, I guess?"

"Exactly," Wood said, a smile on her face. "He was animated, too. But, of course, if you lost your son, you wouldn't be that animated."

"True." He thought about Jack. There was no way he'd have been able to speak to the press like that if he'd lost Jack.

"Also, he took ages answering each question as if he had prepared himself. That, or he was thinking about what he'd told other people. We could do with somebody looking for inconsistencies with his statements and the interview tonight."

"Good idea," George said. "Anything else?"

"Yes, he kept on giving out superfluous information. People do that to pad out stories to sound truthful. He told the events in chronological order. This is unusual."

"Maybe he did write a statement and memorised it?"

"True, George, but I was watching him blink."

"Watching him blink?"

"Yeah. The average person blinks twenty times per minute. I counted him blinking forty to forty-five times per minute. This suggests he was nervous."

"He probably was, Isabella. The interview was being shown live on ITV."

"It's a different kind of nerves, though, George." He nodded his head at her but allowed her to continue. "Whenever he answered a question, he looked away and up to the right as if he was constructing a memory."

George sat forward in his seat. "So he was making it all up." She nodded. "How accurate is this, Isabella?"

"The memory construction on its own, not so much. But George, the man was definitely lying."

"How do you know?"

"It was the insincere way he appealed for information like he was trying too hard. Henry kept breaking down a lot, which is very different from the appeal at the station where he was stone-faced and unfazed."

"It's been over three days since his son went missing; I don't blame him for breaking down," George added.

"Look, George, I know you think this is all nonsense, but it's not. I think we need to go see him, and now. It can't wait. If I'm wrong, then I've wasted three or four hours. But if I'm right, then we can crack this case wide open."

"Okay, fine," George said with a smile. Isabella had never let him down before, and if they got in trouble for wasting time, then George would take it on the chin. But, on the other hand, they'd barely explored Henry as a suspect, so maybe it was time. "I'll call the station."

* * *

"Okay, Yolanda, whilst DS Wood and I are on our way to Hull to interview Henry Davidson, you lot may as well make yourselves useful. Go over everything we have so far on Benjamin. Sightings, statements, DNA results, Chantelle's, Claire's, Andy's and Mitchell's finances. I want to make sure we haven't missed anything. These four are our main suspects, but DS Wood thinks there was something dodgy about how Henry Davidson acted in the interview."

He hung up before Yolanda could confirm the orders and headed east out of Beeston towards the M621, where he could get onto the M62 to Hull.

His phone rang as they passed Escape at Castleford. "DI Beaumont."

Yolanda's voice echoed around the Honda from the speaker. "Sir, DS Fry was looking through Claire's bank statements when he came across a payment to Golden Beaches dated a week before Benjamin's disappearance. He googled the name to find it was a holiday park in Withernsea."

"Right."

"I called them, and after explaining who I was, the owner confirmed that he had received payment from a Claire Murray for booking one of his caravans. After seeing the appeal, his wife also called the incident line to report this. This caravan was booked over the weekend that Benjamin went missing and is paid up to next weekend. The owner's wife handed over the keys to a woman and a child."

"How the hell was this missed?" George said.

"It's my fault," DC Scott's voice boomed out of the speakers.

"Explain, Jay!" George demanded.

"Yolanda mentioned one person claimed that Chantelle was renting her caravan in Withernsea over the weekend. I laughed, and we dismissed it because we thought it was too far away."

"I'm sorry, sir," Yolanda said, "Jay's right. Do you remember we got distracted by the Paige McGuiness article on Kevin Hancock? I forgot all about Withernsea."

"Me too," Jay said. "But why Withernsea?"

"That's what I need you guys to find out. It could be a meeting point if they were offered a large sum for illegal adoption. Find which suspects have a connection to Withernsea. Ask Holly about their phone records, and check for landline numbers based in Withernsea. Cross-reference the lists against numbers we know about."

"Will do, sir."

"Yolanda, get hold of Humberside police and ask them to check it out. Is Josh in the office?"

"Yes, sir."

"Good, get him and DS Mason to find Claire and bring her

in. Ask them to interview her straight away and call me with the details. Yolanda, did you get the ANPR information I asked for?"

"I did, sir. Nothing."

Shit! If Benjamin was in Withernsea, how did Claire and her accomplice get him there? "They must have gone by car, surely."

"I agree, sir," Yolanda said.

"Ask Josh to check for any bus or train tickets in the accounts," George said.

"Yolanda, It's DS Wood. Get Josh to check for any money being paid for car rental. I'll speak to DSU Smith now and ask for a warrant to access Henry Davidson's accounts. I'll call you back because if he's a suspect, he may have taken Benjamin himself. We only checked his vehicle."

"Okay, Wood."

George hung up the phone and called DSU Smith's mobile.

"Beaumont, where the hell are you?" Smith said, his baritone Geordie voice making George wince.

"On the way to Hull to speak to Henry Davidson," George said. "We've just seen him on the evening news being interviewed. There's something not quite right about his body language, sir. So we're going to bring him in for questioning."

"Sir," DS Wood interrupted. "We need you to speak to a magistrate and ask for a warrant to access Davidson's bank accounts. Mark it as a threat to life. We need to know if he hired a car or whether he purchased bus or train tickets to get Benjamin to Withernsea."

"Withernsea?" Smith asked. "Why Withernsea? Do any of the suspects have a connection to the place?"

"The team are working on that, sir," George said. "We know

that Claire Murray paid for a caravan rental in Withernsea but hasn't been. She made no mention of a holiday. We believe it's where Benjamin is being held. Yolanda is speaking with the Humberside Police as we speak. Once we get to Hull, we will liaise with them. Yolanda also asked Josh and Luke to bring her in for questioning."

"Great job, Beaumont. Wood. Keep me updated."

"Thanks, sir," Wood said. "We will do."

The call disconnected, and DS Wood turned to George. "Henry was the one who found Hancock's body. Do you think Henry killed him?"

"It's possible. Jay and Tashan are still working on the IP addresses. Hopefully, they'll find something to tie Henry to the crime."

Chapter Thirty-five

Phone calls came through with updates from his team as George raced down the motorway.

First, Holly called to say she'd tracked calls made by Chantelle, Mitchell, Henry, and Claire but found nothing connected to Withernsea. Next, Yolanda called to tell them Luke and Josh had brought Claire in for questioning, and she would update them soon.

As they passed the Humber Bridge, Yolanda called again to tell them what Claire had said.

"We didn't even need to pressure her, sir," Yolanda said. "The first words out of her mouth were, 'He's safe.' We got her to clarify she meant Benjamin on the tape."

"Good. What else did you get?" George asked. He indicated left at a large roundabout, north on the A164.

"Claire said whilst she understands she may have wasted our time, she's not a criminal. She insisted she didn't have a choice because social services wouldn't listen to her, and she was fed up with seeing reports on the news of neglected children, children beaten, starved, or killed at the hands of their parents or the parents' partners."

"So she took Benjamin because of Mitchell."

"That was part of her reasoning, yes. But not all."

"Go on," George said.

"Because Chantelle was an unfit mother. They wanted to take Benjamin away from her to protect him. She even told us how they did it."

"They?" DS Wood asked. "Was her husband involved?"

"No, Claire's husband knew nothing. It's Henry. They've been having an affair since Chantelle and Henry broke up."

"I knew Henry was involved," Wood said. "Did she confess to killing Kevin Hancock?"

"No," Yolanda said. "She said she had nothing to do with that, and she doesn't believe Henry had anything to do with it, either."

"Right, so how did they do it?" George asked.

"Henry was waiting for Benjamin, hiding in the bushes. When the young Archie Morris turned his back, he simply walked Benjamin away, up through the park, and out one of the east entrances. Henry then took Benjamin to Withernsea, where Henry has been looking after him."

"How?" DS Wood asked. "We checked every camera."

"They hired a car in Hull. We'll get confirmation of that from Henry's bank statements."

"What about when he was here for the appeal? Both Claire and Henry were there. Where was Benjamin?" Wood asked.

"Claire says they gave him sleeping tablets when they needed him to stay in the caravan alone."

"Bastards!" George shouted.

"Indeed, sir. Claire admitted to planting the footprints in the woods, too. She wore both pairs, which is why the cast from the trainers was deeper at the front."

"Makes sense," George said. "Get Lindsey Yardley to test Mitchell's trainers for Claire's DNA. We'll need it later on."

"Of course, sir." He heard her asking DS Mason to ring Lindsey. "Claire was at the house the morning Benjamin went missing. She dressed in Chantelle's clothes and left the door open for Benjamin to walk out into the back garden. I guess that's who Andy Morris saw that morning. Henry dropped her off at home so it wouldn't look suspicious."

"Yeah. It's probably why Henry came late to pick Benjamin up that Sunday."

"My thoughts exactly, sir."

"Did you ask her why they buried the clothes in the woods?" Wood asked.

"She said it was to implicate Chantelle and Mitchell. They wanted you to think something bad had happened in that area, so they had time to settle Benjamin in Withernsea. They buried the clothes and left the prints in the early hours of Sunday morning. Claire returned the trainers when she dressed up in Chantelle's clothes. Mitchell and Chantelle were out of it."

"What was their endgame?" George asked.

"They knew Mitchell was in custody and would likely be given a sentence, so at least he would be off the scene. Once that happened, they'd release Benjamin, and one of them would go to the police and say they'd received an anonymous call saying they could have Benjamin back but was warned not to call the police or Benjamin would be gone forever."

"Sounds like a terrible plan. Once Benjamin was back, he could easily have told us who had him," George said.

"I think they panicked, so their plan wasn't perfect. They had a backup plan to leave the country with Benjamin, but they struggled to get him a new identity."

"So Hancock and Morris weren't involved?" Wood asked.

"Doesn't look like it. Claire said they tried to implicate

Chantelle and Mitchell so that once they released Benjamin, Chantelle would have Benjamin taken from her. Then Henry would swoop in and get custody."

"Right, thanks, Yolanda. Let me know if you get anything else?"

George hung up and indicated right to go around the roundabout and down Riplingham Road.

They were driving past a golf course when George's phone rang again. "DI Beaumont."

"Sir, it's Jay. Tashan and I have got something—something big."

"What is it?" George demanded.

"We've managed to find out who owns the burner phone and who posted the information regarding Hancock's death."

"Go on!" George said, his tone oozing impatience.

"If you remember, sir, we were waiting for the provider to give us the details from the IP address we tracked," Tashan added.

"Yes, I remember. Who the hell is it, lads? Come on!"

"Henry Davidson, sir," Jay said. "Benjamin's father. He pays for the broadband connection at his parents' house."

Icy fingers gripped George's guts.

Finally, it all made sense. Henry Davidson deviated from the plan and killed Kevin Hancock. What didn't make sense was why.

* * *

The pair pulled up outside Henry Davidson's parents' house, one of a pair of semi-detached houses running the length of the road, with trees dotted along the pavement. Each house had a long front garden with low, wooden fencing separating the properties.

George's phone rang. "Sir, it's Yolanda. We've found him."

"What?" Beaumont said as he opened the gate and stepped through. George's heart began to hammer in his chest.

"We've found Benjamin. He was at the caravan park like Claire said he would be. Perfectly healthy and happy."

"Brilliant. We're outside Henry's now. Hopefully, she didn't get time to tip him off." With Wood on his tail, George continued walking down the garden path, taking in the wide borders filled with rose bushes.

George battered the door with his fist.

An older man answered with a look of shock when George held up his warrant card. "Where's Henry?"

"He's just left. A man came to the door for him."

"A man?" Wood asked. "Who?"

"Andy?" The man shook his head. "I don't know. They seemed to know each other, and they went up there." The older man pointed to the left just as George heard a scream.

George and Wood sprinted back along the garden path and saw a man lying on his back in the middle of the footpath. "Wood, we have a man down," George said as they closed the distance. "Call it in. Get Humberside police to cordon the scene off." Unfortunately, a rapidly spreading pool of blood beneath the man suggested they may have been too late. He attempted to pull out his mobile to call an ambulance but realised he'd left it in the car. "Wood, call an ambulance, too. I'm going to try and find Henry."

"George, I think this is Andy Morris."

"Shit!" Of course, it was. Why the hell had Andy Morris raced off to Hull? "Is he alive?"

"Barely."

"Put pressure on the wound. I'll be back in five."

"Be careful, George," Isabella said.

With a thin smile, George said, "I always am, my love."

But George didn't need to because Henry Davidson's Audi flashed by, and the two men met eyes. Henry's were full of fear.

Sprinting to his Honda, George unlocked the door and got in. He forced the seatbelt into the buckle and turned the key in the ignition, the Honda roaring into life. The tyres screeched in protest with his foot to the floor as the Honda raced away from the scene. George needed to tell DS Wood what he was doing, so he pressed the button to call Isabella from his Bluetooth car kit.

Fucking thing didn't work. George tried again.

Nothing.

George looked around the car to try and find his phone, his arm knocking the steering wheel, causing him to narrowly avoid a parked car he hadn't seen. The shock made him forget about his phone, and focus on making up the ground on the Audi, roughly two hundred metres ahead.

Chapter Thirty-six

The traffic built as he sped through the outskirts of Hull. George understood he was partaking in an ill-advised pursuit, one that may see him being reprimanded by his superior, especially considering the speeds that they were achieving. George saw his speedometer approaching sixty miles per hour in the built-up areas, which he knew could become lethal at any moment. He blasted his horn at almost every junction, his attempt to alert other road users and pedestrians to his approach. The Honda strained to keep pace with Henry's newer car. The engine whined as he shifted up the gears, and, much to his frustration, the gap between them increased every minute.

In complete contrast, Henry Davidson accelerated through every hazard and often used the oncoming lanes and pavements to assist in his escape. The man was driving like a man possessed and was reckless beyond measure. Nevertheless, George continued after him.

As the signs flashed by, George realised they were heading south towards the Humber estuary. He figured Henry's escape route was more than likely improvised than by design, which made Davidson even more dangerous. What would Henry do if backed into a corner? George knew despair often led to severe reactions and appeared strongly in George's thoughts as he gave chase.

Up ahead, the Audi swerved out into oncoming traffic to pass a slower Renault Clio, the startled occupants veering towards the kerbs as Henry accelerated between the two before pulling back into the correct lane sharply, the rear left of the Audi delivering a glancing blow to the front end of the slower Renault Clio. After the impact, the driver of the Clio struggled to maintain control and mounted the kerb for a brief moment before the car snaked from right to left before finally hitting a bus stop and coming to a standstill. George eased off the accelerator but flew passed the Clio, its driver staring blankly ahead, trying to comprehend what had happened.

Henry Davidson was nearly out of sight as George crested the next hill, bringing the Humber and its suspension bridge into view. The road before him swooped down and away before widening into a dual carriageway, and George pressed the accelerator to the floor as he encouraged his car to find extra speed as he tried in vain to reduce the gap. Looking up, George saw a helicopter in the sky with a dark blue and yellow livery, identifying it as belonging to the Humberside Police. Now that he was no longer alone, George focused on the road, navigating past vehicles, his horn blaring.

George passed signs that indicated Henry was heading for the Humber Bridge, which restored George's confidence. If Henry maintained that course, George knew there would be an opportunity to contain Henry there. He cursed himself for dropping his phone and hoped the Humberside Police reached the same conclusion.

George soon reached a roundabout where several busy roads converged, and George saw Henry's Audi for the first time in ten minutes. Henry raced past the carvery, down the A15 towards the suspension bridge far too quickly, putting the car into an uncontrollable skid, only correcting the Audi at the last moment, undertaking a vehicle that had stopped on the outside lane. Other drivers around them came to a halt, and George had to weave his way through the stationary cars to an accompanying symphony of blaring horns. Pleased to see his target was still headed towards the bridge, George looked skyward to look for the helicopter, but he could no longer see it.

Taking a deep breath and pushing the fear from his mind, George accelerated hard, willing the Honda to hold on. But, unfortunately, he was nearly out of fuel, and as he burst down the dual carriageway, the distinct smell of burning permeated through to the interior. A warning light came on, telling him to stop the car, but he ignored it, and he raced on after Henry, the traffic building as the giant suspension cables, rising far above them into the harsh brightness of the summer sun, became ever more present.

Henry weaved his way between the slowing vehicles, which were fighting for position to access the toll booths and central express lanes. George watched Henry misjudge the space, his Audi clipping a Jeep as he raced towards the centre express lanes usually reserved for people with a HumberTag. The Jeep driver careered off to the left and collided with a Vauxhall. The resulting impact pushed the Vauxhall into the path of Henry's Audi, who swerved to the right, clipping the central reservation and blowing out a tyre on the impact. Henry battled to keep the car under control as it snaked from left to right, him wrestling with the steering wheel.

George picked his way through the stationary vehicles whose

passengers were already getting out to inspect the damage Henry had caused. George, sensing victory, careered towards the toll booths as the barrier descended. He accelerated through the red and white pole, following Henry's Audi, and shouted "Close the bridge!" at the attendant. He hoped she'd heard him but was much closer to Henry now to care. Sparks showered from the Audi's rim as it bounced along the carriageway at a significantly reduced speed.

Several vehicles had driven onto the bridge via the remaining booths and express lanes, three of which had slowed after witnessing Henry's flight, unsure whether they should stop or continue. Two proceeded across the bridge whilst the third stopped, and George had to undertake him, getting closer to Henry, whose Audi was struggling up the slope.

As George closed the gap, he watched as the Audi stopped in the nearside lane, nearly half the way over. Henry Davidson jumped out onto the carriageway and attempted to flag down one of the two vehicles that had continued their journey across. Neither stopped, despite the frantic gesturing of the lone, desperate figure.

George saw Henry go back to his Audi and open the boot. He turned as George approached, recognising the Honda, before turning back to the boot and pulling out something silver. Instinctively, George lifted off the accelerator and thought about stopping before quickly realising that he was unarmed. What could he do to Henry in this situation, especially as Henry had a weapon?

It took a second for Henry to launch the silver object towards George, striking the windscreen of his Honda. That second where his concentration had lapsed meant he braced his hands on the steering wheel, expecting to run Henry down. But, at the last moment, he hit the brake pedal and pulled the wheel to the right. The car swerved violently and clipped the back end of the Audi, throwing the Honda into a roll where it rolled several times before colliding with the central reservation. The sense of weightlessness and being out of control dominated his mind as he was flung around inside the car before his head struck something. What it was, he didn't know, but it meant the car had finally come to a stop, and relief washed over him before dissipating to be replaced by a pain that rushed throughout his body.

The Honda was parked in the middle of the dual carriageway, his engine facing the central reservation. To his right was an information board flashing to signify that the bridge was closed to traffic in both directions. People on both sides of the bridge were getting out of their cars, some rushing towards George. A large knife was embedded in his windscreen, which had begun to crack in different directions.

All George could hear was pounding, and a damp patch was spreading down the side of his face. Blinking his way through a horrendous dizzy spell, he inspected the wet patch with his hand and found blood on it.

After a moment of confusion, George remembered where he was and why. His heart hammered in his chest as he opened the door, the grating metal protesting with every push. After easing his way out and placing his feet on the tarmac, George heard crunching glass. He cast an eye over the Honda, seeing steam, or smoke, escaping from under the bonnet. That same smell of burning filled his nostrils. A glance reassured him that the car itself wasn't on fire, at least for now, and he looked over towards the Audi some ten metres away, but there was no one there.

George searched for Henry, even walking around the car, hoping to see Henry on the ground, but there was still no sign of him. Had I hit him after all? He even dropped to his knees and looked underneath, half expecting to see the flattened body of the kidnapper lodged under there, but he didn't. Instead, the whirring of rotor blades, accompanied by the distinctive roar, made him look up at the helicopter, hovering approximately fifty metres above the bridge. George saw flashing blue lights coming from the south side of the bridge.

Wherever Henry was, he wasn't getting away. Then, suddenly, George saw Henry, who had made off along the pedestrian walkway. His progress was laboured, and George figured Henry was injured. Henry glanced up, down, left and right, acknowledging the significant police presence. Then, turning back towards George, away from the flashing lights, he rested his hands on his thighs to catch his breath, a crowbar in his hand.

George stepped over the barrier and onto the footpath, feeling victorious. He knew it'd be easier to let Humberside Police make the arrest, so he sat down, resting his back against the railing, and used the sleeve of his shirt to wipe the blood from the side of his face. It had already clotted and was stuck to his skin, indicating the wound was superficial and not much to worry about. Looking toward the helicopter, he took a deep breath and appreciated the warmth of the blistering sun on his skin. Henry was walking away from him, stumbling every metre. Sirens and flashing lights were now coming from the north side of the bridge. Henry had nowhere to go. George smiled.

But that smile didn't last for long.

Chapter Thirty-seven

Henry Davidson climbed up the railing and sat, looking down into the estuary.

The wind whipped across the bridge, howling as the water crashed against the supports below. The weather was changing rapidly, the sky above going from a cornflower blue to a steel grey as the clouds drifted in ominously.

George got up and staggered towards him, not daring to take his eyes off Henry.

"Henry?" George called.

"Stay away, Detective!" came the answer. "I'll jump, so stay back!"

George edged closer, and his stomach churned as he glanced down and the roiling waves far below. Henry was still too far away; a lone figure in the centre of the two-thousand-two-hundred metre suspension bridge sat atop the waist-high railing. There'd been talk of banning pedestrians for years—and doing nothing about it, even as each fresh death was splashed over social media and the newspapers.

"I'm only here to talk, Henry."

"I don't want to talk to you! Leave me alone, or I'll jump!" the man screamed back; his voice was raw. He was in agony. As a father himself, George understood.

"Okay, Henry," George said but kept approaching, slow and steady. He was soon only thirty metres away... then twenty... then ten... then Henry screamed, and George stopped.

"I said leave me alone, Detective! Don't come any closer! I'll jump; I'm not joking!" Davidson's hands were shaking, losing grip on the railing. George worried a slight gust would force him off the top.

This close, George could see defeat and weariness in Henry's eyes. Henry looked old, far older than George remembered, but committing crimes did that to people.

"It's all right, Henry. We know everything. Come down so we can talk. Everything's going to be all right." George's voice was deep and low.

"Everything's not going to be all right! You've no idea about—about any of it!" Henry spat, his words riddled with pain.

"I understand enough. Claire told us everything," George said.

"Claire told you?"

George nodded. "I know about the affair. I know you only took Benjamin because you wanted to protect him, Henry; that's right, isn't it? He's your son, and you never meant him any harm, did you?"

"My son?"

George simply nodded.

"No, of course, I didn't want to harm him. I love my boy."

"I don't understand why you killed Kevin Hancock and Andrew Morris."

"I—I had to! I couldn't let him hurt anyone else. I couldn't let him live when I heard Hancock was living in Beeston and what he did to Angelica." Henry crumpled. "I had no choice."

"You thought Hancock hadn't been punished enough?"

"I believe in an eye for an eye, Detective. That sick paedophile could never endure enough for what he did to Angelica." Henry said as an ugliness contorted his face. He twisted his head to the side and met George's eyes, his own burning with hatred. "And as for Andy Morris, well..." Henry's eyes darkened before he looked down at the waves below him.

"That sick bastard was living next to my boy. He was playing with my boy. I had to take him away from Andy. Did Claire tell you he was having an affair with Chantelle? That they were going to run off together with Benjamin? Yeah, over my dead body."

Henry breathed heavily, his eyes red and wild. "It's why I joined the Facebook group to get back at scum like Morris and Hancock. I got justice for their families where you got none. I ended Hancock's disgusting, sick excuse for a life in as much pain as I could. All you officers are a waste of space!"

George stood firm, but he wanted to crumble too. He understood where Henry was coming from, not wanting to think about the horror that anyone could inflict that upon a child, but he believed in the law. "I agree those men were monsters, Henry," George said in a low voice. "But it wasn't your justice to provide." He thought about Jack and wondered whether, in the same position, would he have done the same? After all, he'd killed a man to protect somebody he loved. Is that not what Henry had done?

Henry laughed. "The justice you provided was a fucking joke. Those monsters tore families apart. Andrew Morris tore my life apart."

George heard a sharp edge in Henry's voice but risked another step forward.

"What did Andrew do?"

"You don't know?" Henry asked. George shook his head. "He was shagging Chantelle when we were together. Still is. She moved into that flat when she was sixteen, and that filthy bastard groomed her from day one. He's always had money, being a teacher and that. Chantelle told me once when we were stoned. She used to give him blow jobs for money."

"So your ex-girlfriend cheated on you? That's your motive?"

"No, Detective. Benjamin—Benjamin's not my son. Not biologically. He's Andy's. I found out a couple of months ago. Andy knew. Or he had an inkling. He'd make comments about how much Benjamin looked like Archie. Fucking bastard! Claire and I ordered a DNA test online, giving me the much-needed proof. That's when we made the plan to frame Morris and take Benjamin."

George now understood precisely why Henry had done what he'd done. What choice did he have? He'd believed for five years that Benjamin was his son. George thought about Jack, Mia, and Adam Harris. "I understand, Henry. More than you'll ever know." He risked another step forward.

"When I found out that Andy and Chantelle were back in a relationship," Henry said, ignoring George, "I just knew I couldn't live without my boy. So do you blame me for trying to take him away from an unfit mother and his paedophile biological father? That's why I had to kill Andy. If I'd have gone for custody, he'd have stepped in. So I had to get rid of him."

Henry looked to George again, the fight in his eyes gone. They were simply pleading now. "Don't let Chantelle have him. Please. He's not safe. She's not fit."

"I'll do what I can, Henry."

"But that might not be enough. Father to father, please. Promise me you won't let her near him. And let Claire go. None of this was her fault. She loves Ben. Please, George. Detective Beaumont let Ben live with Claire. Please."

"I can't make promises, Henry. It would be unfair to do that, but I will do what I can to keep Benjamin safe. But Claire is a part of this, too. She confessed willingly." George edged closer, now only a few metres away.

"I just wanted to change Benjamin's life. Claire would have been such a wonderful mother to him." Henry looked at George. "Why couldn't you just leave it? My plan to pin it on Morris was nearly perfect."

"It was a brilliant plan, Henry. But you made a mistake by using the Hunters."

"No, it's your fault I'll never see my son again, Detective. I used the Hunters perfectly to get what I wanted. Our ideals aligned, and their quest was mine. It was the same for Kevin. I needed Benjamin to be safe. They wanted Kevin to pay for what he'd done, too. We watched him for years, you know. We gave him that scar on the inside. Yet the tenacious bastard recovered, and then he walked free." Henry paused and swallowed hard, his hands still shaking.

"Come down, and we can talk somewhere safe."

"There isn't a safe place for me any more, just as there wasn't a safe place for Kevin Hancock. I thought God smiled at me when he showed up in Beeston. I saw him one day after dropping my son off. I could take Ben and blame it all on him whilst dishing the dirt on Morris, hoping to take out two birds with one stone! My original plan was to frame Andy Morris, as I said, but Hancock seemed an easier target. My patience had rewarded me. Or I thought it had until you arrived."

George kept his mouth shut. The man despised George for doing his job.

Henry shivered, the wind biting into him. Above, the clouds were getting darker. "You nearly stopped me from getting Morris, too. Nearly." He wagged his finger and grinned. "What he did to Kara was disgusting. Fancy getting a fourteen-year-old girl pregnant, then forcing her to have an abortion?"

"I agree, that's disgusting behaviour. But you should have let us deal with it."

"I'm glad I didn't, Detective. I gave the Adams and the Peyton families justice."

"You did, yeah. But at what cost? You hurt an innocent boy, your son, and tore apart his family—they didn't deserve that."

"The only person I hurt was Chantelle. I admit I wasn't thinking straight and that I reacted to Hancock being in the area. But I needed to take him away from his abusive mother."

"I don't believe it was just a reaction, Henry. You must have thought it through; you even hired a car to avoid our ANPR cameras."

Henry looked away, down at the water below. "I knew you'd catch me in a lie if I used my car. When I meant reacted, I meant the day before. We'd played football with Andy and his son, and how he touched Benjamin whenever he scored made me so angry! I still hadn't decided who to frame at that point, but taking Ben away from the situation was for the best."

"What was your end game, Henry? You may as well tell me."

Henry looked at him once more, his face creasing in anguish. "Claire and I were going to release Benjamin once you charged Morris and Hancock. We told him it was a secret holiday and not to tell anybody." Henry wept. "Then I was going to get custody, and we would leave the UK and live together as a family. If Morris were behind bars, he wouldn't have been able to contest."

"Come down so we can talk some more? Come on, Henry."

"No!" Henry said sharply and then, realising how close George was, pitched his body forward, holding on tight. "My hands are slipping, so stay the fuck away! I'm not rotting in prison for giving two paedophiles the punishment they deserved. And because of you, my son will know it was I who snatched him. There's nothing left for me here."

"Of course, there is. Have you heard of a man named Adam Harris? The press called him the Miss Murderer."

"Yeah, the stalker guy who was killing teachers? Didn't you kill him?" An intriguing look stretched across Henry's face.

"I did, but it was in self-defence. Harris had kidnapped my partner, a teacher. I rescued her but killed Harris."

"What the fuck has this got to do with anything, Beaumont?"

"Because Mia, my partner, was cheating on me with Adam." The intrigued look turned into a broad smile. "Mia told me she was pregnant the day I saved her."

"Was the kid yours?" Henry asked.

George shrugged. "We've never checked. I don't think I want to. It doesn't matter because I am his father, whether biologically or not. You were brave in taking that DNA test, Henry. Very brave. But the result didn't matter. He was your son. He is your son. And if you get down from there and come with me, your son can visit you. That way, you can explain your side of the story. Maybe Benjamin can live with your parents? Do your time and come out a free man."

"No, George. I'll rot in prison until the day I die. Benjamin would never forgive me. I wouldn't want him to." Henry looked down at the water for a moment, then back at George, his eyes filled with fear. "I don't know how much longer I can hold on for."

"Come on, Henry," George said, holding out his hand. "Plead mitigation. Do what you can for your son. But don't do this. Please." It felt like he and Davidson were balancing on a knife's edge.

Henry's hands shook, his fingers white from holding on. "No, Detective," Henry whispered. "I have nothing left. Because of you, my son will hate me for the rest of his life. And after what I've done, I probably deserve it."

Henry let his fingers go.

"No!" shouted George, surging forward. Time slowed as George lunged, his snatching fingers grazing Henry's forearm. George's action stopped Henry's fall, but now he was dangling precariously over the edge, the railing digging into George's ribs.

George had his left arm wrapped around a stanchion and, through gritted teeth, he held on tight. The wind buffeted them whilst they were locked in a timeless embrace, the roaring of the wind drowning out George's gasps of exertion. He hoped reinforcements would arrive soon, and as if to reinforce that point, George's grip faltered, and his hand slipped down towards Henry's wrist.

"Let me go, Inspector," Henry said.

George didn't reply, grimacing at the pain he now felt, tearing throughout every muscle.

"I mean it, George. Dangling here, I realise this is the only way out."

Henry tried to twist his wrist to free himself from George's grasp. "Keep a hold of me, you idiot. Reinforcements should be here any minute! We'll get the best outcome for you and Benjamin. I can promise you that!"

"That's your problem, George. You do everything by the book. You had me on the bridge, a child snatcher and a murderer, yet you pulled the car to the side, injuring yourself." Henry gave him a wry smile. "Even after everything I've done, you still think I'm worth saving." Henry laughed. "I'm beyond saving."

"That's not why I did it," George whispered.

"Then why did you save me before?" Henry coughed. "Why are you trying to save me now?"

"For your son. Benjamin. And because I understand why you did what you did. You were brave where I was a coward. Be Benjamin's father. Please."

Henry grinned, and tears fell from his eyes.

They met eyes, but neither man spoke. Henry nodded instead.

And then Henry Davidson was gone, swallowed up by the water.

The pounding of boots on the tarmac behind him announced his Humberside colleagues.

But they were too late. The police always were.

Chapter Thirty-eight

George sat in the accident and emergency department of Hull Royal Infirmary, waiting. When he eventually was summoned into a consultation room, the doctor smiled genuinely and said, "You have a mild concussion, nothing more."

"Good. So, what do I need to do? Take it easy in the office for a few days?" George asked.

"I'd advise you to take a few days off. Rest. But when you get home, don't go to sleep until your usual time." George raised his brow, so the doctor continued explaining. "If there's a change in your condition, George, such as blurring of your vision, nausea, any symptoms like that, then you should go to A&E immediately."

George nodded and said thanks before leaving.

Whilst he appreciated the doctor's words, there was no way he could take a few days off. There was a ton of paperwork still to do.

Whilst they'd found Benjamin—and Kevin Hancock and Andrew Morris's killer—they hadn't yet recovered Henry Davidson's body from the Humber or the North Sea, despite the Humber Coastguard calling out the Humber Rescue crew immediately.

On his way to the hospital, the paramedics had told George the Humber Bridge was ranked number one in the UK as a suicide location and that the Humber Rescue, based out of Hessle, has attended more than two hundred incidents since the bridge opened in 1981. The crew would search for Davidson, assuming he was still alive, but George doubted that, considering only five people had survived the freezing water of the estuary.

As he left the hospital, DS Isabella Wood pulled up. She wound her window down and blew him a kiss.

"You're a sight for sore eyes," George said, wincing as he sat down and buckled up.

"Everything okay?" she asked.

"Mild concussion. Sore ribs. Not too bad."

"Good."

"How's Benjamin?"

"He's well. Henry and Claire took excellent care of him at the caravan in Withernsea. He's currently in the children's ward, and Chantelle's on her way." She pointed in a vague direction, but George only looked at her. She looked mad.

"You're mad with me, and I know why. Go on, give it to me."

"You're a fucking idiot, George Beaumont. You could have died. You could have killed somebody while racing through the streets."

George said nothing, knowing Isabella was right.

She squeezed his hand before saying, "DSU Smith says there will be an investigation." Isabella put the car in gear and pulled away from the hospital.

"I expected nothing less considering it was an officer-involved death," George said. Professional Standards and the Independent Police Complaints Commission had investigated him during the Miss Murderer case, so George knew what to expect.

"I don't think you need to worry, George. The bridge has cameras, and from what I've heard, you swerved your Honda out of the way and tried to stop him from jumping."

George stared straight ahead at the evening traffic as they headed towards the M62. The bridge being shut was causing chaos on the roads, but George didn't mind how late it was when they got back. The longer, the better. It meant he and Isabella could chat for hours without worrying about being caught.

But Isabella didn't take George home. They arrived at the back of Elland Road station instead, attempting to avoid the media circus camped at the entrance.

Whilst flying down the M62, Isabella had told George about the social media videos of George chasing after Henry Davidson through Hull and across the Humber Bridge. So naturally, the press wanted a piece of the action.

George would let DSU Jim Smith and their press officer, Juliette Thompson, deal with it. He didn't like being the centre of attention, nor did he want to give any interviews.

They entered the CID floor to enthusiastic applause, and George felt somewhat self-conscious and rather embarrassed. Nevertheless, he smiled and thanked his colleagues.

DSU Smith approached George, his hand outstretched. George took it, and Smith clapped George's shoulder simultaneously, sending a shooting pain down his ribs. "Good job, Beaumont. Well done."

"Thank you, sir."

"How are you feeling?"

George shrugged, "I've felt better."

Smith smiled as he said, "I'm pleased you found the boy alive."

"Me too, but what I did after was reckless, and I know it was, sir."

"I'm sure you know then there'll be an investigation?"

"With the IPCC?" Smith nodded. "Yeah, DS Wood told me."

"It's just routine, George. But, considering the circumstances, I'm obligated to refer it to them. It's no reflection on you."

George nodded. He knew his boss was being reasonable. "I understand, and I've nothing to hide."

"The helicopter has it all on camera. The bridge has plenty of cameras, so it will be tied off quickly enough."

George looked around at the smiling faces of his team before he said, "I know."

"Now, Juliette and I have been talking, and we think it's appropriate that you address the press."

George started to protest before Smith cut him off. "DS Wood is on her way to yours as we speak to get you some clean clothes. The press wants to hear from you, and you alone. You're the talk of social media, news bulletins and the papers. You don't normally shy away from this, George."

"Fine, sir," he said, not meaning it. If he could get out of going to a press conference, then he would. Maybe he could use the concussion to his advantage. "What's going to happen to Benjamin now, sir?"

"Social services will decide, son, not us."

"And Claire?"

Smith's face darkened. "That's up to the CPS."

* * *

Despite his attempts, George did not get out of the press conference. He spent two excruciating hours dealing with camera flashes and questions he could only answer with, "I'm unable to comment due to ongoing investigations." Fortunately, as deputy SIO, DS Wood was allowed to attend and picked up the slack. She was brilliant in front of the cameras, a calm, composed beauty with the confidence to match.

The press lauded the case as a success, but George wasn't so sure. Andrew Morris had died from his injuries. Henry Davidson had stabbed him twelve times, and despite all Wood's efforts and the efforts of the paramedics, he bled out. Kara Adams would now never receive justice.

And then there was Kevin Hancock, an 'innocent' man. He hadn't been involved in the kidnapping, and while some would say he got what he deserved, George believed in the law. The CPS would almost certainly charge Claire despite reaffirming that she took Benjamin for his own safety. She had also told Yolanda she had nothing to do with Hancock's murder, which they all believed was true.

George, not wanting to face the inevitable congratulations and concerned questions from his colleagues at CID, headed downstairs to seek solace in the car park as he was required to stay at the station until the IPCC could debrief him.

The weather had turned sunny again, and despite the late hour, the heat was still blistering. George undid his tie, unbuttoned the top three buttons of his shirt, and sat down on the step.

He was annoyed at himself for his compassion towards Henry Davidson and his apathy for closing the case. What Henry had done was wrong, but George understood why. As a father, George understood why Henry wanted to take

Benjamin away from the dangers that lurked in Beeston. He understood wanting to take him away from an unfit mother and Benjamin's paedophile biological father. Henry had been Benjamin's father for five years. George had been Jack's for eighteen months. He couldn't even come to terms with the heartbreak and anguish he would feel if Mia tried to take Jack away from him or deny him his rights as a father. Yet, George didn't even know for sure whether he was Jack's biological father or not. They certainly looked alike; he was on the birth certificate and had George's last name. But then that was the same for Benjamin and Henry.

George wondered how long the doubts would last. Would he ever get over not knowing whether Jack was biologically his? Did it matter? Should it matter? George wasn't sure, but he knew he loved the kid more than anything, with only Isabella being a close second.

Glancing up at the sky, he thought not. No. It didn't matter. Jack was his son, whether they had the same DNA or not. He would always be Jack's father, no matter what.

George stood up from the step and walked back into Elland Road Police Station, his head held high and feeling happier within himself and more content. He had Isabella and Jack, and he didn't think he'd ever felt happier.

Afterword

Thank you all for following DI Beaumont and his team on another case! If you enjoyed it, I would be grateful for a positive review on Amazon and any recommendations to your crime fiction-loving friends and family.

As a self-published author, word-of-mouth recommendations in person and on social media are hugely important to help the series find new readers. Please could you do that for me? Thank you.

I'd also like to thank you for purchasing, or reading via Kindle Unlimited, book 4 in the DI Beaumont series.

The Humber Bridge, the setting for the climax of this novel, is a Yorkshire landmark, and it is very accurate that the bridge is famous for the many people who have taken their lives there over the years.

The bridge is a single-span road suspension bridge that, when it first opened in 1981, was the longest of its type in the world. One of my favourite weekend trips is travelling to Hessle and walking across the bridge into Barton-upon-Humber. It makes you aware of what an incredible feat of engineering the bridge is.

Again, thank you for reading, and take care,

Lee

Also by Lee Brook

The Detective George Beaumont West Yorkshire Crime Thriller series in order:

The Miss Murderer

The Bone Saw Ripper

The Blonde Delilah

The Cross Flatts Snatcher

The Middleton Woods Stalker

The Naughty List

More titles coming soon.

Printed in Great Britain
by Amazon

23084209R00185